# HELPLESS

*Also by Jessica Knoll*

Luckiest Girl Alive
The Favourite Sister
Bright Young Women

JESSICA KNOLL

# HELPLESS

SIMON &
SCHUSTER

London · New York · Amsterdam/Antwerp · Sydney/Melbourne · Toronto · New Delhi

First published in the United States by Scribner, an imprint of Simon & Schuster, LLC, 2026

First published in Great Britain by Simon & Schuster UK Ltd, 2026



1 3 5 7 9 10 8 6 4 2

Simon & Schuster UK Ltd, 7th Floor,
199 Bishopsgate, London, EC2M 3TY



Simon & Schuster Australia, Sydney
Simon & Schuster India, New Delhi

www.simonandschuster.co.uk
www.simonandschuster.com.au
www.simonandschuster.co.in

The authorised representative in the EEA is Simon & Schuster Netherlands BV, Herculesplein 96, 3584 AA Utrecht, Netherlands. info@simonandschuster.nl



A CIP catalogue record for this book is available from the British Library

Hardback ISBN: 978-1-3985-5872-4
Trade Paperback ISBN: 978-1-3985-5873-1
eBook ISBN: 978-1-3985-5874-8
Audio ISBN: 978-1-3985-5875-5



Printed and Bound in the UK using 100% Renewable Electricity at CPI Group (UK) Ltd

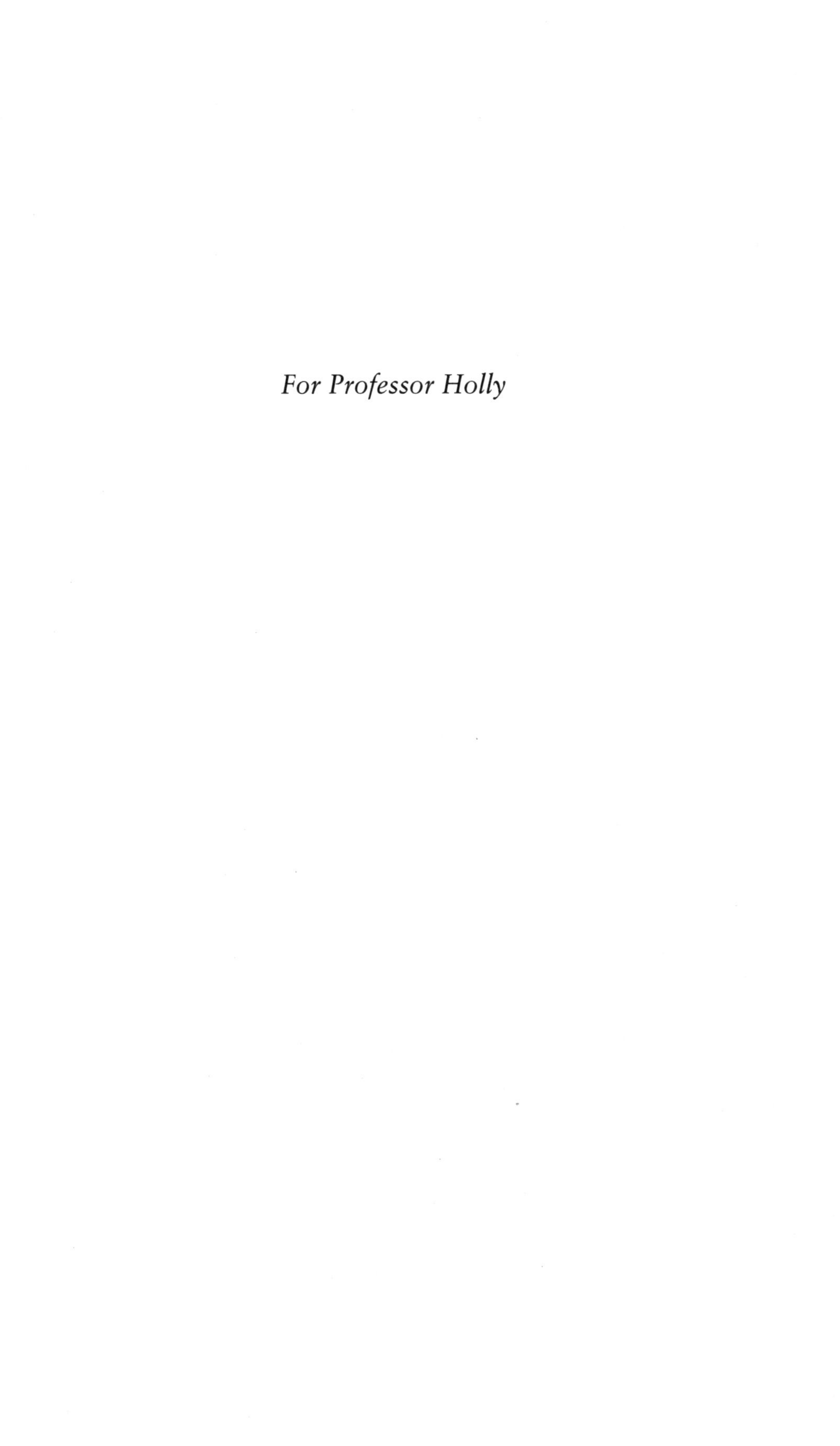

*For Professor Holly*

# Chapter 1

I arrive late to the funeral, wearing black linen and the ugliest ballet flats money can buy. Fellow stragglers crowd the vestibule, heads bowed, listening to a muffled version of the service behind chapel doors. I slip sideways between polyester shoulders, mouthing *Sorry*, and press close to the rose window above a bench dedicated to a student who died in the Civil War. Inside are disguised figures, washed violet by the Gothic glass, but I know it is him up there delivering the eulogy. The sound of his voice still makes me feel like I've sat on a stick of dynamite.

I go out into the courtyard with my hair gathered in my fist, fanning the back of my neck. It's the third week of April and eighty-seven delirious degrees in the Finger Lakes region of New York state, two hundred miles closer to Toronto than Manhattan. There are no direct flights from Los Angeles to the town where I attended college twelve years ago, and the hypervigilance required for this day is now mazed with jet lag. I am digging through my bag for sunglasses, debating whether to walk or drive to the repast, when someone grabs me from behind. I do not scream. I'm told there is no such thing as normal, but how else to describe myself other than not?

"Hey, asshole." I turn and shove Campbell in the chest. A boy with red hair stands solemnly by his side. Four years old? Six? I can never tell the ages of children.

"Tookie," Campbell says. "This is Daddy's friend Faye, and she's on TV, so she's allowed to use bad words."

"I'm in the movies too, Tookie."

Tookie gives me a tentative smile. He has small teeth that don't touch, and he's wearing linen pants that are too long and too tight, creased around the crotch from sweat. Silently, he slips his hand into his father's and crosses his legs at the ankles like he needs a bathroom.

Overhead, the chapel bell tolls like a rebuke. "I missed most of the service," I admit. "I got delayed for two hours in Detroit."

Campbell grimaces. "Brutal, Faye." He reaches out and relieves me of my shoulder bag, slinging it over his own. Campbell was assembled in a factory that trademarked 1950s male Americana—block jaw, dimpled chin, a shiny pat of blond hair parted neatly on the side. The manufacturers chipped him with chivalry too, right before they shipped him off for some lucky little girl to unwrap on Christmas morning.

"How did that go?" I tip my head toward the chapel.

"Oh, " Campbell answers with a sigh, "it was definitely a funeral." He bends his head, scuffs his shoe on the pavement, loosening a pebble caught in the treads. When he looks at me again I am startled to find him gray-faced and unguarded.

"It's really good to see you," I say, staring riveted at the replacement grief has made of of my oldest friend.

"Kind of can't believe you came." Campbell knocks my shoulder gently with his own.

"Not many people I'd take a multi-leg commercial flight for." I say this with a straight face and a spike of panic. It is Campbell's uncle who passed away. He does not need a reason to be here, but I occupy a nebulous realm. If only I could say I came all this way to honor the profound impact that my former film professor had on my life and leave it at that.

"The studio couldn't spring for a PJ?" Campbell grins, squints up one eye handsomely in the sun.

"Doing my part to minimize carbon emissions."

A breeze off the lake parts the flowering dogwoods, dusting us with pollen, and Tookie sneezes twice into the crook of his elbow.

"Bless you," I say to him.

"Thank you," he whispers back with red eyes.

"We snuck out early to meet the caterers at the house," Campbell says. He tugs Tookie's hand and turns to go. "I'll walk you to your car."

Behind me the doors to Saint Thomas the Apostle open. People begin to file out of the limestone tower, to tighten around us like a public stoning. "That's okay," I say, trying to keep my voice bright. He could be anywhere. "I'm down the street in the opposite direction."

"You sure?" Campbell reluctantly returns my bag to me.

I can tell it goes against every well-bred bone in his body to allow a woman to walk to her car alone, even on a street lined with hydrangeas.

"I'll see you in a few." I find my small black sunglasses and walk briskly to the rental car before anyone else can grab me.

I drive through campus with the air-conditioning blasting, trying to get my skin to stop buzzing. On the lawn of the last standing fraternity house, two shirtless guys toss a lacrosse ball back and forth, feet sliding around in battered brown leather flip-flops. I slow in front of the small yellow house where I lived my senior year with a group of girls who always felt more like colleagues than friends, then come to a complete stop when I see the front door open. One brunette, one blonde, their hair in matching high ponytails, come bounding down the stairs with tennis rackets strapped to their backs, laughing and bumping hips in a way that more or less foretells their future. They'll be roommates in a moldy prewar building in Back Bay, maids of honor three or four Septembers after, then, by the time I'm forty, they'll be gifting each other the most expensive item off their baby registries, the white oak crib or the NASCAR stroller, whatever the in-laws didn't snap up first. It's not longing with which I watch them. I would not be who I am now if I were able to trade affection so easily, and I happen to like who I am.

I turn right at the President's House, a stereotypical white stately thing, and coast alongside the deepest and largest of the Finger Lakes, the water so clean you can open your eyes four feet deep and see the kelp swaying like worshippers. A single sailboat ruffles the gray-blue surface, and on the dock a couple of girls are sunbathing with their shirts thrown over their faces. Aside from the sign posted at the water's edge that provides the number for a suicide and crisis hotline, everything is as I remembered it when Campbell called me last week with the news.

I was finishing a late lunch with another writer (I write and direct the movies too, Tookie) when I glanced at my phone to see two missed calls from Campbell and a text. **Call me when you can**. Few things more ominous than that.

I excused myself and went into the bar garden, where phone calls are permitted, but both couches with the green botanical print were claimed, and in the smoking garden, people were smoking, so I went outside on the street by the valet and called Campbell back from there. The whole time I was running through the possible scenarios of what could have happened. Campbell is one of the few people I've stayed in touch with from the colleges, and we do not speak that often. Technically my alma mater is a women's college that merged with the men's campus down the hill around the time the Nineteenth Amendment was ratified, and so everyone refers to it as *the colleges*, though doing so makes me feel like an awful poseur. I wondered if Campbell was calling about the scholarship student whose script I had agreed to read in what can only be described as a full-circle moment, because I attended the colleges on the same writing scholarship. My former professor had emailed me about it last week, and because the former professor is also Campbell's uncle, and because Campbell is still involved in the happenings at the colleges, it seemed conceivable it could have something to do with that, until Campbell picked up the phone and I heard the worn-out quality of his voice, like I was the fifth or maybe tenth person he'd had to terrible-text today to get them to call him back.

"Sorry," he said. "I hate to send a message like that."

"What's going on?"

Campbell cleared his throat, started to speak, and had to clear it again. "PT passed away two nights ago."

"Campbell," I gasped. I was pacing the street, and I had just pivoted and was facing the valet, where Melanie Griffith was getting out of her car. It struck me as fitting, that I would hear about PT's death while watching a Hollywood legend fish through her bag for her car keys. Professor Toner, or PT as I would come to know him, was the reason I was a member of this members-only club in West Hollywood that requires guests to cover the camera lens on their phones with branded stickers so that people like Melanie Griffith can eat their chop salad without fear of being photographed with their mouths open and one eye closed. People like me too, I suppose.

"What happened?" I asked in a high, nasal voice.

"It looks like he had a heart attack at some point Sunday evening. The house cleaner found him Monday morning."

Vaguely, I recalled that PT had some sort of inherited heart condition, and this is why he walked everywhere and avoided red meat and, though it took great effort, eventually kicked the Pall Malls. He was tall and trim, and he looked like he belonged in Los Angeles, which he tried out for a few years before his prodigal return to the East Coast to inaugurate the film department at the colleges. When I made it here myself, I found tons of other industry people, just like him, who were fastidious about their health but would never turn down a light.

"I'm so sorry, Campbell." I was trying to picture PT lying dead on a bathroom floor. In what, a robe? Pajamas? Death seemed beneath him somehow. I don't think I ever saw the man wearing anything but a slim-fitting black T-shirt, even at his cabin on the lake during the summer. I used to see PT all the time in the summer, because Campbell's family has a cabin on the same lake and so does his cousin, Henry Spalding, who is the one with the voice that makes me feel like I've sat on a stick of dynamite.

"I'm sorry too," Campbell said back. "I know what he meant to you."

My nose felt peppery. "Yeah" was all I said.

"You two were in touch about the scholarship student, right?"

I groaned. "He sent me her script a week ago, and I never even wrote him back. In my defense, she turned it in a week late."

"Don't beat yourself up, Faye. You've got a lot going on." I could picture the kindness in Campbell's face as he said this. Though it goes against every rule in Central Casting, Campbell is as decent a human being as he is handsome. In college, he remembered that orange was my favorite flavor of Gatorade, and he got a husband pillow because I had one, and we would fester on the floor together watching marathons of *Project Runway*. When I broke up with Henry—not just Campbell's cousin but his constant companion since they were in diapers—he sent me a text: **I love him but I get it.**

"Have you made any of the funeral arrangements yet?"

"This weekend. At the chapel on campus. I was wondering . . . if you might be willing to speak?"

A warm, buttery feeling enveloped me. I was always on the periphery at a place like the colleges. Even after I became a frequent guest in PT's home, I would suffer lashes of self-consciousness, wondering if I was only included because I was dating Henry. Fame has done an all right job of soothing my fears that I don't matter to the people who matter to me, but having your name listed on the funeral program of a person who loved you the way your parents should is more of the elixir I'm after. "You want me to do the eulogy?" I said, touched.

"Sorry," Campbell said, because I'd misunderstood. "Not the eulogy. Henry and I are doing that."

"Oh." Melanie Griffith had found her car keys, and she was laughing with the valet, something about how she'd lose her head if it weren't attached to her body, probably.

"I think we are going to do some sort of ceremony on the dock the day after the funeral. He wanted to be cremated and have his ashes spread in the lake where Sarah is."

I had dipped my head, swallowed hard, the totality of the tragedy summed up neatly in one sentence. PT had a wife who drowned herself in the lake just before I graduated. She had wanted children, noise, mess, chaos, and instead her life became too quiet to tolerate.

"I was thinking you could speak at that," Campbell said, and when I didn't respond right away, he spoke to the thing that we both knew was giving me pause. "I know it's awkward with Henry being there, but he's coming with his wife and kids, and honestly he's, like, a totally different person now."

A pleasant electricity lifted the soft blond hairs on my forearms, thinking about seeing Henry again. Besides my head, my eyebrows, and my lashes, grown thick and dark with one of those serums that is probably also making me blind, my forearms are the only place left on me with hair. This was the year I got everything lasered, vanquished. You could slip me on like a cashmere glove and my husband has no idea.

"But . . . ," I said. "The show." I played a small but zeitgeisty role on the first season of a show created by a thirty-year-old sitcom star who had enough of reading canned lines set to a laugh track. People liked me enough that my role went from recurring to regular. In the third season, I wrote and directed an episode based on my breakup with Henry that made a viral, career-making splash.

"Faye, he didn't watch it."

I didn't think he would have, but put so bluntly I was instantly reminded that there was a whole world out there that did not give a shit about me, that I could disappear into thin air and it would be news for about a week. "But he must know what it was all about."

"He has two under four. He's underwater."

In theory, I understand that children are a cover for

everything. It's just that I do not aspire to understand in practice. I had looked down at my nails, realized I needed a manicure. Did I have enough time to get my eyebrows done before I left? It didn't matter that Henry and I were both married to other people now. We had shattered each other. We would be checking, inspecting, merciless in our appraisal. "Okay," I agreed.

We spoke for another minute or two and said goodbye. Inside, at reception, Melanie Griffith was spelling the last name of her guest for a staff member in a green-piped blazer. She put her hand on my elbow as I walked by and told me in her sweet, seductive voice that she was a fan.

# Chapter 2

I drive around in circles for too long, and by the time I feel ready to face Henry, there is no space left on PT's street, or the street before that, or the one before that. I park in the lot for the science building, an almost-too-long walk from PT's waterfront painted Victorian at the edge of campus. For a while, when PT talked about his lake house, I assumed the Victorian was the house he meant. But when Henry and I became a couple toward the end of sophomore year, he explained that when PT said he was going to the lake house, he meant the one located on the shores of Lake Wanika, a private community in the Adirondacks, about four hours west of the colleges, to which Henry's and Campbell's families also belong. I was envisioning a cushy chalet with snow-covered eaves until Henry brought me there and introduced me to the curious nuances of East Coast generational wealth. The cabins were only accessible by boat, and they were humble, sure, but not without antique Turkish rugs on the floors and thoughtful finishes in the kitchen. There was limited electricity by design. Just enough to power some interior lights and the fridge, and even that they could only run a few hours a day. That was the first time I realized that not only will wealthy people pay to live like they're poor, but they'll call it a vacation too.

The front door to PT's home-home is propped open to welcome mourners, and at the threshold time collapses in on itself. I can see straight back to the patio doors that open to a private dock where PT's wife used to keep their sailboat shrink-wrapped in winter. Sarah was the coach of the girls' crew team, and the foyer was usually jammed with rowing shoes that clipped into racing shells. During the pandemic, when my husband and I acquired a Peloton along with every other intially optimistic workaholic in the country, I would look down at my feet in my red-and-black cycling shoes and think of all the evenings I stepped out of my snow boots in this foyer. PT and Sarah used to host movie nights, usually between Thanksgiving and Christmas when PT would receive DVD copies of either movies that had been in theaters but weren't available to rent yet or, even more exotic, movies that had not yet come to theaters. Now that I'm a member of all the guilds—actor, director, writer—I get them every year between Thanksgiving and Christmas too, though now instead of DVDs they send you QR codes to scan.

PT's dog, a tubular, squat thing already memorialized in the brass doorstop next to my foot, throws back his head and howls as an ambulance races north on Main. The house is packed with people, but for a moment the grim revelry wanes as everyone listens to the dog lose his mind with small, sad smiles. The irony that the tragedy is already here.

The president of the colleges notices me, comes over, and embraces me with open arms. We exchange condolences for the various ways we get to call this our loss.

"Professor Toner was our longest-serving member of the faculty," the president tells me. For a moment we stare silently at a photograph of PT and Sarah on their wedding day at the courthouse down the street. Sarah was fifteen years younger than PT, and normally that sort of thing irks me, but there was something about the pair of them that looked right together. Sarah was a stout woman with muscular legs and a big, booming voice, messy topknot, and chewed-off nails. Even on her wedding day she did not have a manicure.

"They were happy," the president says now. The grief on his face is acute, and I look around the room at all the people gathered here, and it soothes me to see that you don't need to have children to matter deeply to people.

I am introduced to a trustee in a sweat-wicking golf vest whose daughter is a fan, and on our way to the bar, we collect the director of financial aid, and then at the bar another trustee in a baseball hat. I still remember the first time I was the only woman in a standing conversation with all men in a professional setting. It was the moment I realized I'd gone from being someone recognizable to someone who had financial influence, and that those two things were decidedly not the same and I'd been an amateur to think they were. I had swayed on my feet, dizzied like I'd woken up in a different body, Freaky Friday style. I don't dare look around, but my private hope is that Henry is watching me float through the room like a lightning bug, invisible until my sudden flare attracts yet another board member holding a mason jar. My captors deposit me in the dining room, where Corrine Holland is sedating herself with a clear, deadly drink.

"Faye, wow," she says with bland surprise, though she must have known I was coming. "It's good to see you." Corrine is the lucky little girl who married Campbell straight out of college, an aloof blonde who eschews makeup in favor of a tan, a real one that has prematurely crinkled the skin beneath her eyes. She is tall and triangle-shaped, like an Olympic swimmer, and nowhere near as good-looking as Campbell. I might ascribe this to Campbell's decency—the sort of guy who falls for what's on the inside—only that Corrine is a rarefied bitch.

"You too," I say, and then we stall out, wondering if we should hug, and whatever we decide we wait too long and miss the moment. We stand there, smiling unpleasantly at each other, until Tookie comes bounding through the room to save us.

"Mom," Tookie pants. He looks like he's been running around outside, screaming in that way children do that could mean they're having fun or someone needs to dial 911. "Where's Dad?"

"I don't know, Tooks."

"But he has my wand."

Corrine stares at Tookie's grass-stained knees, chewing hard on a piece of ice. "Have you seen Uncle Henry?"

*Uncle Henry.* My pelvis throbs like an open wound.

"He's in the kitchen."

"He's probably with him."

Tookie dashes off. "His wand?" I say. "Is he into magic?"

"It's his lacrosse stick," Corrine says with a snort. "He's not very good. He used to have blond hair," she adds, apropos of nothing. Here she takes out her phone and begins to show me images of Tookie from when he was first born. "He was the most stunning baby."

"Beautiful," I agree, and then I ask her to show me more, but what I'm really doing is studying the wistfulness in her face as she gazes at her child before he entered his awkward stage, and I'm trying to commit the moment to memory because, of all the things I do, I consider myself a writer first and the steal never stops.

"Anyway." Corrine puts her phone away and rolls her eyes at herself. *Enough of my mom shit.* "I haven't seen you in forever. Congratulations on, well," she laughs, uncharitably, "everything."

"Thank you," I say in the same half-assed tone that she used to congratulate me.

"I keep meaning to go back and watch your show," she says. "It came out right when Tookie was born, and I could barely keep my eyes open. Nothing personal—I missed like three seasons of *The Bachelorette.* It's still streaming, right?"

It is. On the big one. But I wave her off. "It won't be your cup of tea." The show is about a group of young women trying to make their way in Los Angeles. They live in seedy first apartments and date unkind men and work soul-crushing assistant hours that leave them with vitamin D deficiencies. It was a full-scale cultural phenomenon because it touched on something true, though not for everyone, and certainly not for someone like Corrine, who arrived at the colleges more or less betrothed to Campbell, her boyfriend since freshman year of boarding school. Not that long ago, my interior designer dragged me to some art show—I have a staircase landing with a blank wall begging for a statement piece that can be seen from the front door—and I got to talking with the artist and discovered she had grown up with Corrine. *Does she still write?* the artist had asked me, and for a moment I was sure there had to be a mix-up, something to do with Corrine's maiden name, that we were not in fact speaking about the same person, but the artist had been resolute. Corrine Holland was the editor in chief of their boarding-school literary magazine, and not only that, but her father published the *Newport Daily*, Rhode Island's oldest newspaper, and her mother was their art critic. *That's a shame*, the artist said when I told her that I never knew Corrine to be a writer. *I think she met Campbell and decided she wanted a different kind of life.* Really, it's less that my show isn't Corrine's cup of tea and more that she does not want it to be.

"You might be right," Corrine agrees, no offense taken. "But you know who loved it?"

I stare at her indifferently.

"My brother. Who is demanding we bring you to Sig Phi after this."

"Oh God," I say with a shudder. "How can he live at Sig Phi when he's only twelve years old?"

Corrine nods in a commiserating way. "We got old, Faye."

It must be something children do to you, make you feel like your time is over and theirs has just begun. Because I don't feel old at all. I'm in it, this is *my* time, and what floors me is the people—the person, really—who is watching time bleed me dry like that is his kink. To waste me. Maybe, partly, that's why I came.

I feel light fingers on my elbow, turn to find a woman with her gray hair held back in a satin headband, introducing herself as Marjorie, the head of student outreach whom I have emailed but never met. "May I borrow you?" she asks with whispered reverence. "I'd like you to meet Emma King." When I give her a blank look, she elaborates with just a touch of reproach. "She's the scholarship student who submitted her script to you."

"Yes, of course," I say quickly.

Corrine raises her glass in a Gatsby-like send-off. "We'll grab you later," she promises.

At every turn, I brace myself to come face-to-face with Henry, but neither he nor Emma are anywhere to be found.

"I just don't know where she could have gone," says Marjorie. "I know she was over the moon to meet you."

"Will she be at the lake tomorrow?"

"I can't imagine she'd miss it," Marjorie says. A corollary of the scholarship is access to PT in a way that breeds an almost paternal bond, particularly during your senior year, when you work closely with him on a feature-length script to be submitted to his other former star student, Jonathan Granger. Jonathan graduated seventeen years before me and has gone on to produce a canon of award-winning content as well as fund the scholarship that allowed someone like me, and presumably someone like Emma, the opportunity to attend the colleges to begin with.

Marjorie says we will try again tomorrow. Dinner is being served buffet style, and I must escape, must not see Henry for the first time since I left him in a near-catatonic state on the side of a country road while we are ladling balsamic vinaigrette onto our mixed-greens salads. The downstairs bathroom is occupied, so I sneak upstairs and into the guest bedroom that Sarah had briefly set up as a nursery and where Henry put his hand down my pants for the first time.

I use the en suite bathroom. Wash my hands. In the mirror, I adjust the drape of my asymmetrical blouse and smooth my hair. It's fuller and bouncier at the ends than it is at the roots, a unidimensional light brown that has suddenly become trendy. I stare for a moment at my face. I have oval, alien eyes; a heart-shaped upper lip; high, plump cheeks. Some days it feels flat-out greedy to wear makeup.

A women's magazine once described me as "superlatively beautiful" and now every time I ask my husband how I look, that's his hokey answer.

Back in the dark bedroom, I stand at the window and take in the scene down below. The caterers have erected a large white tent in the backyard, installed those temporary interlocking tiles that function as a dance floor at outdoor weddings, and I watch people file out from the house and disappear under the covered space, balancing dinner plates and drinks in their hands. My eye trails the border garden that runs along the side of the house and lands on two figures, gesturing animatedly. It is Henry, I realize with a shot of adrenaline to the heart, and his wife. She is a monochromatic towhead with inoffensive features. I do not know her name and I've tried here and there to find out, but neither of them appear to be on social media, at least not any account I can find, and I'd rather a root canal than ask Campbell. In my mind the wife is a genuinely nice person who initially found Henry's idiosyncrasies charming, then annoying, then exhausting, an impediment to a good marriage that she would gladly trade away. I can't live in a world where he ended up with someone who knows what to do with him.

The wife is wearing a clingy, shirred-jersey black dress and unbranded black flats. She carries an overpacked tote bag with a short canvas strap that keeps sliding off the slippery material. I can tell by the way she keeps hitching the bag up her shoulder, the tight shapes of their mouths, that they are fighting. I am in thrall. They do not at all fight the way we used to fight, that tense and terrifying two-step that always ended with my back against some wall, Henry goading me in soft tones—*Keep crying, Faye. Keep fucking crying*—as he undid his belt and slipped inside of me like we had already spent hours on the kind of foreplay I have always begrudged. I don't need someone's tongue drawing endless figure eights between my legs, just someone who knows what to do with me too.

The room is suddenly flooded with overhead light. I whip around to find a guy with his fingers on the switch, one foot in the room and one out, unsure of what to do next. Down in the garden, Henry is staring up at his spotlit audience. He rubs the arch of an eyebrow with a knuckle, exasperated but tender too. *What do I do with you?* That's what the gesture means. He used to make it when I was bent over the back of the couch and sometimes just with my hands on the wall, welted and whinnying for more. I step back, mortified.

"Didn't realize anyone else was in here," the guy says, and maybe I'm imagining it, but I swear there's a droll edge to his words. He's student-aged, with dark eyebrows and unruly blond hair, wearing that peculiar uniform I'd forgotten about—blue khaki shorts and dark blazer, loafers with no socks, his longish hair tucked wet behind his ears after his shower so that the ends have dried flipping out. He has not moved from the doorway and I need to get by.

"Excuse me," I say, and he turns sideways so that our bodies brush as I squeeze by him. My linen blouse crackles with static electricity, and he smiles down at me in a lascivious way. I swish my hips for him on my way down the stairs.

I am seated at a table with Campbell, Corrine, their formerly blond child, two trustees, and their wives. My presence at the table, once I'm seated, has an effect that I once relished but is now so commonplace the novelty has worn off. The conversation about schools peters out. I am asked about a scandal with the mayor of Los Angeles that briefly united the nation, if I am planning on renting out my house three years from now when the city hosts the Summer Olympics. Even for a week, I could make a killing.

"Now is the show done?" the trustee in the sweat-wicking golf vest wants to know.

"Yes. That's been done for a while now."

"To be honest," this trustee says, "I didn't watch it. I think it would have gone over my head." He sails a hand hence and we all laugh.

"That's okay," I say. "I think what makes something great is when it's not for everyone." This is a platitude exchanged by fellow creatives to buffer us against future bad reviews.

"Don't sell yourself short." Campbell pats the man's arm the way you would a dog's flank: hard and with affection. "We loved it."

*We.* No way. I glance at Corrine, who is using her thumb and index finger to coax a bone from her piece of salmon. She wipes fishy pink foam from her fingers with a curled upper lip. If she's embarrassed to be caught in such a juvenile lie, she's a better actress than some of the scene partners I've been paired with over the years.

"What are you working on next?" the trustee's wife asks. I am so glad she asked, because it is behind her that Henry sits with his family, and she has provided me the opportunity to observe them through zoo glass while I answer her question.

"I'm directing my first feature," I say. Henry is cutting his daughter's food into small pieces. She is in a high chair and eating straight off the table. I did not know children needed high chairs once they could walk. What I know about children is limited to the certainty that I could not handle having any.

"How exciting. And you wrote it?"

"I'm still writing it, actually." I tell her how, after this, I'm headed to an Airbnb in Ithaca, where my goal is to hunker down and finish, alone and without distraction.

"Will you act in it too?"

I shake my head. "The acting thing was kind of a one-off for me. We'll go out to someone else for the role once it's ready." Henry is leaning toward his daughter, with his hands clasped between his knees and his head turned so that she can speak into his ear, and she is telling him something with a protruding lower lip. He frowns and encourages her to say more. Henry knows how to console. That is his singular talent. Sometimes I'd let him whip me up just to bring me down. Not only because I liked it but because I sensed it was the only way Henry knew how to connect with people, that he was desperate for it, actually. I can't believe it didn't occur to me before that Henry would make a great father. Kids are so upset so much of the time.

"Sorry to interrupt." Marjorie is standing tableside, and by the looks of the eager young woman next to her, she's found my protégé.

"This is Emma King," Marjorie says, "our senior Granger Scholar."

Emma is brunette and very tan. She flashes a crisp white smile. "It is such an honor to meet you," she says to me with a demure dip of her knees.

"I'm looking forward to reading your script."

There is a flash of disappointment on Emma's face that I did not immediately devour her magnum opus the moment it landed in my inbox, despite the fact that she turned it in late. "I know you must be very busy," she says in a sullen tone. The kids are always like this. Champing at the bit to be read, to be discovered. I was out of my mind with impatience at Emma's age.

"I promise I'll get to it soon," I assure her. I glance at her dull shoes. The uneven stitching in the pockets of her pants. *I was not one of them either*, I want to tell her, *and it turned out all right.*

"When the torch passed to you," Campbell says with a grin, "were you like, 'Now I've made it'?" He has his hand on the back of Corrine's neck, and he's pulsing the points beneath her ears. She twists her head like she's trying to direct him toward a sore spot, but there is something like anger in her eyes.

"When they start calling it the Faye Heron Scholarship," I say, "then I'll know." This is the first year anyone but Jonathan Granger will read a student's script. It's his scholarship, in name and in funding, but he's been shamelessly checked out for a while now. Twelve years ago, when I sat down for my feedback session with him, I could not shake the nagging suspicion that he had only read the CliffsNotes version of my script that one of his assistants had typed up for him. I found out I was right when I eventually became Jonathan's assistant myself and learned all about the time-honored tradition known as script coverage.

"Well," Marjorie says. "We should take our seats. Looks like the slideshow is about to start."

"Nice to meet you," I say to Emma, who dips again at the knees.

I turn my attention to the front of the tent, where the president stands patiently while someone adjusts the gain and dinner conversation dies down. He begins the solemn task of welcoming everyone for a weekend to celebrate the life and impact of his dear friend colloquially known as PT. "The film students wanted to put together the following tribute for their professor," the president says. "And if I may be so bold—Faye Heron, you have yourself some competition."

I laugh with everyone else, but my body is tense enough to snap in two. I had not stopped to consider what it might feel like to hear my name spoken in the same room as Henry in a way that acknowledges my ascent. I feel like we are images on one of those infrared cameras, everyone else in blue, us in red. The only two in the room burning with the truth about who I really am when it is just the two of us.

The president steps away as the projection screen fills with an image of Professor Toner as a young man with a beard and gold aviators, a Bob Dylan track playing, though the picture looks to be from the eighties. A voiceover begins, and the camera cuts to a self-tape from Jonathan Granger, talking about the premiere of the first show he ever made, how he brought PT as his date and he wound up on the worst dressed list and PT on the best. The film students managed to dig up a twenty-year-old issue of *US Weekly*, and a cheer goes up from the crowd, seeing PT in his suspenders and dapper velvet slippers. When everyone settles again I realize that there is a scene unfolding behind me, a child demon-growling the word *no* over and over. I only dare to glance back when the screaming starts in earnest and only then because a few others do too. Henry unbuckles his youngest from the high chair, her legs swinging and kicking, and carries her into the house without expression. But there is some sort of amplification that occurs once he's inside with her. It's like listening to your neighbors fight, wondering if you should call the cops, if that would be overkill, if it will make it awkward next time you run into one of them taking out the garbage. The tribute is going, but everyone is stiff with these kinds of thoughts, and after a moment Henry's inoffensive-looking wife whispers something to her older daughter, and she scoots off her chair and follows her mother into the house, dragging her rapidly blinking doll by one arm. And with that, Henry leaves without ever saying hello.

# Chapter 3

This is where it starts, really, with my decision to head back to the hotel. Corrine and Campbell try to convince me to come to Sig Phi with them, but I am far too injured to drink tepid beer while bleary-eyed barely legals assure me I'm much smaller in person than I appear in photographs. I slip out the side door, but innocuous little Emma King spots me and asks if I'd mind company. Though I tell her not to leave on my account, she insists in a way that will come to matter later. We tango around the line of cars in the driveway and fall into step. It's tenish, muggy but mild, and the air is stuffed with the scent of some perennial so sweet it smells rotten.

"I love LA," Emma declares. She says it on an exhale, and I am in no mood for this brand of youthful whimsy. I want to be alone, to lick my wounds, to think my strange thoughts.

"It's a great place to live," I say in a lackluster tone.

"I mean. I've only been there once. PT took us to visit Jonathan on set."

I nod. I remember the year they came. The show was

still going, but we were on a hiatus, and my husband and I had taken a trip to Hawaii that went poorly for us.

"It's not easy to get there," Emma remarks. "From here."

There is some suspicion in how she says this. It is complete conjecture on my part, but my brain instantly leaps to a scenario where Emma knows that while of course I went to the trouble of returning to campus to honor PT, I was also hoping for a run-in with the ex who ruined me exactly the way I told him to. Paranoia is also an option here.

"I have a writing retreat planned for myself right after this." I feel ridiculous, explaining myself to Emma, like I am a teenager whose parent has detected alcohol on my breath.

"Professor Toner canceled all his classes the day before he died. Did you know that?"

This is a very abrupt thing to say, and I don't know how to react, so I only shake my head. *No*. I did not know that.

"Do you think that's weird?"

I frown. Consider it. "Did he say why?"

"He didn't give a reason. Just sent out an email letting us know and gave us some reading to do."

"Okay," I say slowly, fitting this information in with what I know to be true. "He had a massive heart attack. From what I understand, people don't feel very well in the days leading up to that."

"He had Band-Aids. All over his hands." Emma demonstrates, turning her hands front to back.

I stop walking. "How do you know that?"

"I'm the one who found the body."

I stare at Emma, gobsmacked. She's lying. To my face. About finding the body of our professor. "I thought it was the house cleaner."

"I mean, technically, yes. But he had emailed me the night before and asked me to come over first thing in the morning. She was already there when I got there. She told me he was upstairs in the bathroom, and so I ran up to check on him. And he was lying there and he had at least, like, ten Band-Aids, all over his hands, and I mean, clearly he had something to tell me. And then he died before he could." Emma is wringing her hands, like she's nervous, but her eyes are also sheened with excitement. Maybe what she is saying is true, but from my vantage point, there is something unbelievable about her story.

"Did you tell the police this?"

"No. I left before they got there."

"Emma," I say, firmly, "if this is true, you need to be talking to the police, not me."

"Come *on*," Emma says with sudden, snotty force. And then she has the gall to roll her eyes at me.

"Come on what?" I repeat in a new, icy tone. Emma is displaying that overfamiliarity that I loathe in young people with dreams of becoming somebody. Fear is underrated. It's okay to show it, to certain people, in certain situations. Fear has taken me far.

"I guess it's not so much that they don't care," Emma relents, "as they're out of their depth."

*Their depth.* Emma no doubt cribbed that from whatever true-crime podcast she listens to on her incline treadmill walks while she tries to burn brown fat. "You're going to need to talk to someone else about this," I tell her, and start down the street again.

"Did PT say anything to you? About my script? Because I think that's why he wanted to talk to me that morning."

Gross. Is this Emma's misguided way of trying to pique my interest in her work? "He apologized on your behalf," I say out of the side of my mouth, "for turning it in a week late."

"I know, I know," Emma groans, hurrying to keep pace with me. "I'd been working on something else all semester, and I just knew it wasn't right, and then it was, like, the deadline was coming up and I switched gears in a panic."

"I'd carved out time to read it the week it was due. So now I'll get to it when I get to it."

"Wait," Emma says. "There's something else."

Emma puts her hand on my arm, trying to stop me so we can have this conversation standing still. She shouldn't touch me. I give her a look that communicates as much, and she removes her hand, looking startled and a little bit hurt. I don't feel bad. Would I have touched Jonathan Granger without his permission when I was twenty-two years old? Not even with.

"I'm parked here," I say, but where the curb slopes for the entrance to the parking lot of the science building, I can see that I'm blocked in by another car. One of those dark gas-guzzlers with three rows of seating. Connecticut license plate. Rangers sticker on the bumper. I cup my hands around my eyes and peer through the passenger-side window. Tookie's wand is wedged between the driver's seat and the center console. This is Campbell's car.

*

Someone is sitting between the peeling columns of the old Sig Phi house, holding a vape box to his lips in an overhand grip, bare legs dangling off the side of the porch. I don't immediately recognize him, but then he hops onto the grass, turning his newly acquired baseball hat backward as he approaches me. It is the kid who turned on the light in the upstairs guest bedroom and blocked the door when I was trying to leave, still wearing his shorts and his blazer. Leather flip-flops stained with oily toe marks have replaced the loafers.

"We've been waiting for you," he says to me in a witchy way.

"Good," I reply without smiling. I know the way the light is hitting me right now. I know all my angles. I know exactly what he's looking at when he sees me.

"Come inside for a cocktail," he says. From the fraternity house thumps an old Jason Derulo bop. I remember how we used to listen exclusively to Talking Heads and David Bowie, a little Chaka Khan, because we thought it was proper drug music from another, cooler era. We wouldn't have been caught dead listening to anything current like Jason Derulo. That theory hasn't changed, evidently. What's considered throwback has.

"Faye doesn't want your plastic tequila," Emma says in an uppity way. I had hoped she would go home when I told her I had to swing by the Sig Phi house to find Campbell and ask him to move his car, but to my dismay, she has remained dutifully glued to my side.

The kid fists his shirt, twisting the fabric like he's been shot. "It's not shitty, Emma. It's Casamigos."

"Casamigos *is* full of additives," I counter.

"It's good enough for my brother-in-law and Henry," he says.

I stare at him in astonishment. This is Corrine's brother? "You're Corrine's brother?"

He rocks back on his heels with a triumphant smirk.

"Oh my God," I say with a laugh. "You know I met you once at the lake. You were sitting backward in a chair, crying because you were bored."

The smirk doesn't disappear, but I no longer buy it.

"Remind me your name."

"Winthrop. But everyone calls me Win."

*Of course*, I think, *they do.*

The first time some fat junior appraised me at this very door and deemed me hot enough to step inside, I remember thinking that the house didn't feel like a house, though I couldn't say why. But if my androgynous interior designer has taught me anything besides to submit to terrazzo flooring, it's that too much space and not enough furniture are what conspire to create a general atmosphere of ennui. It's why I can feel the playlist in my central nervous system, why it seems as though there are fewer people inside than a census would show, like a marathon-set nightclub before 1 a.m. Miami, not Los Angeles. No one stays out past ten in California.

There is a smattering of students around the pool table, pretending not to stare, and two guys spazzing with laughter in the corner. I have no doubt I am what's so funny. I do need a cocktail, actually, but saying so would be unbearably corny.

"Everyone is upstairs," Win says.

To my relief, he starts toward the great room. We pass the small second kitchen on our left, where a kid with skinny legs and a square torso beats a bag of ice on the ground; to our right a couple of girls huddle together on a futon, taking a selfie before their mascara melts off their faces. Then we are climbing the coffin-wide stairwell and turning down a long, lopsided hallway, stopping before the door to the room where Campbell and Henry used to live. "Ain't Nobody" synthesizes softly from the other side.

"It's me," Win says, rattling the pretty old crystal door-knob I am noticing for the first time.

We wait for close to a minute for the pushpin lock to pop, and then it is Corrine standing there with an impatient set to her mouth, as though we have been the ones to keep her waiting. I can tell by the way she's swallowing over and over—like she's nervous, which she is never—that she's coked to the gills.

"You changed your mind," she says with a welcoming smile I almost believe.

"I think your car is blocking mine," I tell her. "I just need someone to move it."

Corrine opens the door wider and steps back like a gracious host. "Have a drink with us first."

The room is massive, ceilings slanted like an attic, two twin beds pushed into an L shape against one side and the rest a considered living space. There is a television too big for the wall between the windows, a bad leather couch and matching bad leather chairs. Campbell has taken one, Henry the other, and he is watching me with the same controlled dispassion with which he used to tell me to arch my back.

I feel like I've waded into a cold spot in turquoise bathwater, the currents bringing in something dangerous from the deep. I'm petrified, but I force myself to face him. Henry has the darkest blue eyes you've ever seen. He is all warm undertones, rosy cheeks and lips, sandy brown hair, but his eyes are like two inkblots from a psychological exam administered to someone who may or may not be a psychopath. I feel crazed looking at him this close after all this time, to see that while he still has the healthy flush of a kid who's been playing outside in the fresh air, the bow-shaped, girlish pink mouth, that in other places his features have hollowed and sharpened. It is him, but it is not him, like buying a vintage designer bag. Even in great condition, nicks and scratches have accumulated from a lifetime with another woman.

"Ladies," Win says to Emma and me with a performative kind of gallantry, "meet our great friend Henry Spalding."

Henry rises from his chair in his languid, predaceous way. He hunches as he offers Emma his hand, like a dog pinning back its ears to let you know he's not a threat. Henry is so tall he has to duck through doorways; he used to have to bend at the knees to hear me when I was upset about something and explaining it in a quiet, hurt voice. Emma's hand disappears into Henry's and her tanned chest burns scarlet. I am instantly flooded with a possessiveness I usually only experience around work, which bitch got which gig that was meant for *me*. I wanted

Henry when everyone else thought he was Campbell's scary friend with the sweet and boyish face, before he grew into himself and became objectively hot to a tight little twenty-two-year-old.

I go and sit at the far end of the couch, catty-corner to Campbell's chair, before Henry can be the one to snub me. My hands are numb. I shake them out, wonder if I am having a stroke, if Henry would call 911 for me if I were.

"What is Faye, chopped liver?" Win says.

"Behave," Corrine says to Win with a small, fond smile that only eggs him on more.

"Ohhhh," Win says, glancing between Henry and me with mock concern. "Is this the first time you two are seeing each other? You know, since *the episode*?"

Emma blinks innocently at Henry. "That was about you?"

Often in my new life, I have to think about what to do with my face. Right now, I decide it's okay for it to reflect the heinousness of the situation. Yes, this is the first time I'm sharing oxygen with the person who inspired a character of mine who the public unanimously reviled.

"Win?" Campbell addresses his brother-in-law in a sharp voice. "Relax, please."

Win plops down next to me, putting his feet up on a coffee table that I just know used to anchor some palatial Connecticut mansion in the early aughts. "Tell Emma to stop playing dumb while you're using your dad voice."

"What's that supposed to mean?" Emma shrills, her shiny lips parted in outrage. At some point between outside and in here, she has applied a fresh coat of lip gloss.

"You're, like, the president of the Faye Heron fan club. You know that episode was based on real life."

"But how would I know it was about a person I just met?"

My discomfort has grown hair and teeth at this point, like one of those monster tumors that lives undetected in the alleyways between your organs. Win glances over at me, his head cocked in concern. "You're making my girl uncomfortable, Emma." He drapes an arm around my shoulder, loosely, like we've been dating for years. From Henry's corner of the room, a pulse, a raptorial focusing of those cold eyes.

"You should really ask first," Henry says in a quiet voice I feel to the quick.

"That's not what I heard," Win returns in taunting singsong. His fingers type a gentle code on my upper arm. Too gentle. I'll need a bleach bath later. I pick up Win's hand by his thumb, nose wrinkled like it is an animal carcass I am carrying to the edge of the canyon in my backyard, and unwind his arm from around my shoulders.

"Look." Campbell raises his hand, litigation style. "We are talking about something that happened a long time ago, and everyone has grown up—"

Corrine seal-barks a laugh.

"Sorry, sorry," she says, patting her cheeks with cool palms, trying to compose herself.

"I just know," Campbell tries again, "that Henry has something he's been wanting to say to Faye for a long time now." And he shifts his knees in Henry's direction, as if to say, *The floor is yours*, and I am on the edge of my seat but turned around in every which direction as well. What could Henry possibly have to say to me?

"Quite the segue," Henry says with polite contempt. He stares at the floor a moment. "I'm sorry, Faye." He looks at me then, in that way he has, his eyes searching and searching for my tenderest pressure point. When he finds it, pins me down, I can't get a good breath. "I should have said that a long time ago."

The room goes still awaiting my response. I feel like I've been proposed to in a public setting, that I cannot say anything other than yes, though I have a long list of reservations. I suppose, if you only watched *the episode*, you would believe that Henry is the one who owes me an apology. It's not that he doesn't; it's just that I am nowhere near blameless.

"Thank you," I say.

Henry twists the gold wedding band on his finger because he can. I stopped wearing mine a few months ago. It was giving me a rash—make of that what you will—and so I left it home one day, and then again a few days later, and then it became as routine as it had been to put it on in the first place.

"I'm going to—" I stand, indicate the makeshift bar station on top of the mini fridge. I peel off a Solo cup and uncap the bottle of tequila with the intent to give myself a healthy pour. I have never understood people who drink to dull the pain. Alcohol goes down easiest when I am ripped through with adrenaline.

"Taking off," I hear Henry say from behind me. I right the bottle as quickly as one can when they've been mortally wounded.

There are the sounds of hands clapping backs as I stir my plain tequila with a plastic knife and give myself a quick talking to. I am starved for attention for various reasons and just because Henry looked me in the eye with that old look, told another guy to ask before putting his hands on me in that old voice, does not mean there is something unfinished between us.

"Good to see you, Faye," Henry says.

"You too," I say with my megawatt Hollywood smile, like I am not bleeding out right in front of him.

# Chapter 4

Back at the hotel, I take off my clothes and zip the pieces preciously into my garment bag. I get under the covers in my lacy silk set and thumb the papyrus roll of messages on my phone. Casting has sent me some audition reels for a supporting character in another series I'm producing, but earlier, as I waited for my phone to pair with the rental car, I was prompted to reenter my email password because my carrier did not believe I would voluntarily choose the Finger Lakes as a destination. I had guessed at it, then again and again, until I got myself locked out. Now when I go to check my email, I am informed that the server has detected too many authentication attempts and I need to wait a moment to sign in again. I Google how long until I can sign in to my email after getting locked out, and the responses range from one day to a week. I screenshot a summary of the problem and text my assistant: **Help.** And then I open the message from the person I should not be speaking to. **I enjoyed our meeting**, she has written. **Let's chat again when you're back in town.**

Guiltily, I navigate to a message from my husband,

asking how things are going. It's the middle of the night where he is—London, on set for one of our joint productions—but I need to unload, and so I tell him about my conversation with Emma. **Isn't that weird?** That's how I end the text that details her claim that she found PT's body, her intimation that there is more to the story than I've been led to believe. Then I put my phone screen-down on the bed and lie there, thinking about the parts of the night that were also weird but that I cannot tell anyone about, least of all my husband. Henry's coerced apology. Him telling Win not to touch me in that voice that did not just imply *or else* but all kinds of creative consequences. I play that voice over and over again in my head, roll onto my stomach, and slip my hand into my silk shorts.

The fall of my sophomore year, PT was teaching a semester abroad in Los Angeles. Sarah went with him because crew is a spring sport. Henry and Campbell were always given a key to the house when they went away. PT relied on his nephews to water the plants, secure lines on the boats, bring in the patio cushions when it started to sleet in October, and to clean up after themselves when they inevitably threw a party.

It's hard to recall now how I put together that Henry liked me. But he was always watching me, giving up a prime seat on the couch for movie night, or offering me a ride home in his school-bus-yellow Defender that he ordered off eBay drunk, where I would find myself crammed into the back seat with his girlfriend, an anxious girl with a perfectly patrician profile known by variations of her last name, Barrington: Bear, Berry, Blubs. Bear was Corrine's best friend, and when Henry broke up with her at the start of sophomore year, she took it personally. That was when I started hearing the rumors about Henry that made me like him back.

It was just before Thanksgiving. Campus had thinned out, and Henry and Campbell decided it was a sensible time to have a party at PT's house because they could keep it small. I got ready by taking a scalding-hot shower where I shaved everything and conditioned my hair for ten minutes straight. I could not stop thinking about the rumors I'd heard about Henry and Bear and hoping they were true. I wore a bra that matched my underwear and very little makeup because I did not want it to come off on the sheets if that was where I ended up.

When I arrived at PT's house, I located Henry but I did not go over and say hi to him immediately. I mixed a drink. I chatted with a girl from one of my writing classes. I went upstairs with her for a little and came down sniffling with courage. I found Henry and asked if he had a cigarette. *What will you give me for it?* That's what he said, in an earnest and thrilling way that told me it better be good. I had the sensation that my blood was humming as it traveled through my veins, on the way to somewhere good.

We sat on the naked wood slats of the patio furniture and lit our Pall Malls. Henry made everyone who came into the house smoke the same brand of cigarettes as PT so that if he missed an errant butt in the cleanup process, PT would not immediately suspect that he had thrown a party at the house. Henry was wearing a nubby navy fleece with the collar turned up to the cold, and I remember thinking how compellingly it framed his face. We talked about what we were doing for Thanksgiving. Henry always spent the holiday at Lake Wanika. The three brothers—his father, Campbell's father, and PT, technically not a blood brother, but the son of their father's second wife, whom he married later in life—had kept this tradition alive for years. He told me that they had to cook everything at the clubhouse because it was the only structure on the property that was connected to the main power grid. There were nine other cabins on the island, and no one really went during the offseason because the cold was too extreme. The staff started opening the place right before Memorial Day and closed it down after Labor Day. *Sort of like camp*, I said, and Henry told me that's literally what upstate people call their lake houses. *Camp.*

I had gestured out at Seneca Lake before us then and said it's so funny to me that PT refers to that place as his lake house when isn't this technically a lake house too? And Henry had shaken his head and said it was different. Seneca Lake was public. Anyone could swim or apply for a permit to boat and fish, and right down the street was a town center with restaurants and bars and dollar shops. The colleges are located in a municipality with its own hospital and public school system, chain hotels and boutique ones too. Four hours northeast of here in the Adirondack Mountains—a region larger than Yellowstone, the Everglades, Glacier, and the Grand Canyon National Parks *combined*—more than half of the six million acreage is privately owned and unconnected to public utilities on purpose. The cabins are only accessible by boat. Henry showed me pictures on his phone of what Lake Wanika looked like in 1929, the year a collective of writers, critics, actors, and wits pooled their resources to purchase 250 acres of the Adirondacks and build a clubhouse and hire staff so they could spend the summers drinking, skinny-dipping, supposedly writing. Dorothy Parker engraved a tree with lines of poetry. *"Scratch a lover, find a foe."*

By the 1950s, Henry said, the writers had died young of alcohol-related complications and the actors moved back to the Midwest to teach theater at their old high schools. That's when the land was purchased by PT's grandfather, an investment banker from Albany with a passion for the arts who had been a guest at Lake Wanika when he was a young man dabbling in a bohemian lifestyle. He kept everything to the west side of the lake and sold off the remaining cabins to the east. He created a small board and established membership rules and monthly dues. It's a tight-knit, exclusive community that prides itself on a spartan existence, outdoor recreation, and wildlife conservation.

After all that Henry asked me what my family did for Thanksgiving, and I laughed. Our lives were poles apart. I told him that I had three brothers and everyone sat around rooting for the Patriots even when they weren't playing while my mother had a meltdown in the kitchen. Henry wanted to know why, if I was from Massachusetts, I didn't have a warmer winter coat. I looked down at my anorak without lining. It was the first time I realized Henry noticed everything. I liked that about him. Even at nineteen years old, I knew this was a rare quality for a man to have. I explained how my mother got me a winter coat for my last birthday, something huge and hideous. I returned it to the Marshalls where she got it from and used the cash to purchase a subscription to Final Draft, the software program that Professor Toner said professional screenwriters use. I was writing in Microsoft Word. Clunking my keyboard at a glacial pace. Space. Left alignment for action. Space. Center. Bolded font for character's name. Space. Center. Unbold for dialogue, which I could no longer recall exactly as I'd heard it in my head before all this maneuvering, when it was undoubtedly perfect. Final Draft did all the formatting work for you, but it was expensive and the school wouldn't cover it, and even the kids who could afford it didn't care enough to go through the trouble. I cared, even though PT assured me that when the time came to submit my senior script to Jonathan Granger, he would not be put off by an amateur document. But every time I read what I wrote in Word, I did not believe it. No one would say this. No one would act like this. And I became convinced it was the page that was the problem. A serious painter would not work on a piece of construction paper, I told myself as I forked over $179 for the same software used by Aaron Sorkin, and then I curled up into a ball and did not move for a very long time after I discovered that the new version could not be downloaded onto my ancient Dell laptop, handed down to me from my oldest brother. Of course it couldn't. It had one of those fans that never stopped running.

The patio door opened and Corrine walked out. She

stared at us a moment, breath steaming from her nostrils like a medieval beast, and then she made a flicking gesture to Henry, and when he didn't move, she groaned with impatience that he didn't understand. "Your lighter," she said. "Can I borrow it?"

"Say please," Henry told her.

Corrine laughed. "I'm not Bear." She turned to me. "You know he tells her she's not allowed to eat."

That was one of the things I had heard, yes.

"That's weird," Corrine told me, with an ugly widening of her eyes.

Even if I did think it was weird, which wasn't what I was thinking, wasn't the tight feeling wrapping itself around my rib cage, I wouldn't give Corrine the satisfaction of an alignment. She was in and out of this house a lot too, on account of dating Campbell, and we'd sat together on the couch for movie night at least ten times since the fall of our freshman year. This was the most she'd ever spoken to me.

"It's none of my business," I said.

"He would handcuff her to things and leave her there. You've got to think *that's* weird," Corrine emphasized, like she was giving me one last chance to distinguish myself from the freaks.

I shrugged. Not really. Not at all, actually.

"Okay, then," Corrine said with one of her more terrifying smiles. "Don't want to be near this." She turned and walked back into the house.

"Your teeth are chattering," Henry said to me.

*

We went upstairs and into the guest bedroom, where twelve years later I would watch Henry argue with his wife in the garden at dusk. In the en suite bathroom I shimmied out of my stretch jeans, sat down, and peed in front of him like we'd been married for thirty years.

I flushed the toilet and washed my hands in hot water. Henry was using his thumb and index finger to flick the rocks in whatever substance the local Canandaigua dealer had filched from his laundry room and passed off as a sixty-dollar stimulant. He came up behind me and floated a small pile under one of my nostrils. I plugged the other and sniffed, threw my head back the way they do in the movies. It was an overperformance and I wobbled a little. Henry caught me around the waist, and for a few moments we stood like a couple at a concert, swaying sweetly to the overtly sexual rap song playing downstairs. I put my hand on his wrist and stared at the two of us center frame in the glass. I could see that Henry was nervous, that we were moments away from an escalation, and normally I did not like vulnerability in the men I was with. I liked to be railroaded, dominated, to feel like I was in brutal and capable hands. But Henry refined all that. Taught me that nothing made me feel more alive than being degraded by someone who also happened to worship me.

I pushed down on his wrist, squirmed my hips needily. Henry had dipped his head, smelled my hair, pressed his erection into my lower vertebrae. *Is that what you like?* he asked, and I knew he was referring to the conversation downstairs, to all the things I'd heard he'd done to Bear.

I nodded and Henry looked at me in the mirror and said,

*Okay*, with a quiet kind of resignation I still think about. He hooked a finger in the strap just barely holding up my little going-out top and removed it from my shoulder, put his lips on my skin. I had that look on my face, the one that embarrasses me—sleepy, sexed—and I'd closed my eyes so I wouldn't have to see. Henry gave my cheek one hard pat. Some girls might have called it a slap.

"*Watch,*" he said in a new, formidable tone, and then he pressed his thumb into my chin so that I had to see the change come over my face the moment he slipped his hand into my underwear and covered me whole. He squeezed me, and in the mirror I looked melted, like my eyes and ears might slip off my skin. I sank down into his fingers, settled in like a cat on the warm engine of a car. We exhaled, hard and in unison.

"Put your hands on the mirror for me?" he said, somewhat politely, and it is the care with which he asked me to humiliate myself that remains one of my most precious souvenirs from our time together.

For him, for Henry, I braced myself on the mirror at the same angle as a strip search, and, less politely, Henry told me to fuck his hand so he could see what I liked, hear what kinds of sounds I made. He stood behind me, motionless, the palm of his hand curled warmly around my pussy, watching me grunt and rub on him with a manic focus on my face. It was ugly, desperate work I would lick a public toilet seat to do again.

When I came I bent deeply at the waist, like I was sinking into a curtsy before the queen. After a while I became aware that I was no longer supporting myself. Henry was holding me upright, balancing the entirety of my body weight with his fingers still inside of me. I was making a pitiful noise and he shushed me then. He told me I was okay. He said he knew what to do to me now and I would never have to do anything like that again. It was a lie. I made sure of it.

# Chapter 5

In the morning, I stare at a yellowed patch of water damage on the ceiling, running through my speech. I'm planning on sharing something about my family, a topic I generally avoid, and I have to be prepared for the outside chance that someone in attendance could tip off the media, that it will become a headline. With each whip of the ceiling fan, I imagine what they might say. *Faye Heron recalls feeling unloved*, or something that will piss off both my parents and the people in the comments who do not like to be reminded that famous people have feelings. *Your fans freak out about everything you say*, my best friend said to me before I left, and this was her way of saying that I should share and if it gets out there, so be it. My best friend also happens to be one of my agents, so her advice is always framed through the lens of my career. My husband is always cautioning me about making friends with members of my team, but I find those relationships less fraught with competition and risk than those I've had with my fellow creatives. I no longer speak to the woman who created my show, a woman who was once like a big sister to me and who now certainly has my number blocked.

I pat down the sheets, feeling for my phone, and when I find it, I see that my husband has responded to the story I told him about Emma, her dubious claim that she was the one who found PT's body. **Weird,** he said. Then, **I think I have to extend this trip. Jack is really unhappy with Susie's work so far.**

My husband does not have the appropriate reactions to things. Either he is not that interested or he is neurologically incapable. I used to wonder which it was, I used to try to express with nonjudgment how invisible it made me feel, until one day the single most explosive thought occurred to me. Who cares? Who cares why he does it? What if what matters is that *I don't like it*?

I heart the message and ask him to keep me posted. Then I get up and open the blinds, silence the alarm I've set to remind me to take my pills, the ones that stop my brain from sucking up all the serotonin I've got.

I button a pair of billowy linen pants, disappear into a cloud of cashmere a moment, and slip my feet into the unassuming pair of loafers that cost as much as a loose diamond. I made sure to pack things I already own. I did not shop. I knew Henry would be able to tell if I'd gone shopping for him.

I pack my purse and try one last time to convince my computer that I am me to no avail. I remove the chair from underneath the door handle, fit the feet neurotically into the carpet grooves. I would hate for the cleaning staff to come in here and think I don't trust them with my life. But last night, when I got home, I noticed some scuff marks along the baseboard of the door, like someone had been kicking at it from the outside. Had that been there all along and I was only noticing now, at night, alone? Between that and Henry treating me like we were settling an HR dispute, I slept like shit.

I park next to the lake, the current moving west in soft gray ribbons. It's like clouds outside the window on a plane, the way it tricks you into thinking they're going slower than you are. They say Sarah drowned quickly, that she suffered, though not for long. She was only three or four years older than I am now when she did it, and I thought I would come closer to understanding as I approached her in age, but if anything, I feel more baffled by it all.

She lost a pregnancy during my junior year. I remember being so stricken by this that I called my mother and told her about it, and I rarely go to my mother about things that devastate me. My mother had four kids; I thought she would have some insight into the matter, wisdom to share. I thought she might be able to articulate for me why I was so shaken up. Even though I was only twenty years old, I could tell I would do my life differently than other girls my age, who cooed and melted at the sight of a tiny human in socks. And while I cared about Sarah, my relationship with her was always secondary to the one I had with PT.

*It happens all the time*, my mother had said. She was not saying this in a dismissive way. Her voice was strained with a kind of emotion I rarely heard from her. *It doesn't mean she can't try again. It's part of the process, Faye.*

I would later learn that my mother was not wrong. It would indeed become a part of the process for others around me as I got older, but the difference was that the same emotion I heard in my mother's voice was not limited to pat sentiments. My generation was the generation that finally spoke about it, sobbed about it, went on medication for it, exorcised the anguish around fires in Arizona with a heaping dosage of psilocybin bound to the brain. I had been right to suspect that losing a baby was a pernicious blow, and Sarah was walloped over and over again until she couldn't take it anymore. That was the part that was baffling to me—not that Sarah had done what she did, but why anyone was surprised.

I suppose it's rage too that I feel about it. People should pay attention to the ones they love. They should feel shame, not surprise, when the inevitable happens.

The dock has expanded since I was a student, from a lone, unbarricaded strip into a mazey walkway with bucolic white fencing and a shingled boathouse. Neat rows of Chiavari chairs flank the dock, the same chairs I bet Henry had at his wedding. I'm early enough to grab a coffee at the campus café that opened when I was a sophomore. I remember swanning to class with a skinny latte in hand, feeling like I was at long last a grown-up.

I slip between two parked cars and get a streak of grime on my cream-colored sweater. I'm cursing, slapping at it, when a dusty SUV comes roaring up the hill. I am not in the middle of the street, but I am in the street, and I am almost positive the driver presses harder on the gas pedal, whizzing past mere inches from my nose.

The SUV stops a few feet ahead of me. Henry climbs out of the driver's seat, and his wife out of the passenger side. She is crying, I realize, and she calls out to me in a shaky voice. "Sorry."

"It's okay," I tell her. These are the only words we will ever speak to one another.

Henry drops the keys in her hand and leans down to kiss her. Betrayal seizes my stomach. But she brushes past him, gets behind the wheel, and drives off without so much as saying goodbye. Henry stands in the street, watching until the car disappears. He's wearing slim khakis and a sage-green blazer. He is tan. He always liked being tan, and I'm surprised it hasn't weathered him more.

Henry turns back to me, looks me over as I brush aggressively at the stains on my sweater. "You need dish soap for that," he says. Henry has always liked clothes too, and he knows how to take care of his things.

We are close enough to speak without raising our voices but not close enough to spread disease. "Does your wife often apologize on your behalf?"

"You got an apology from me last night."

I cannot believe we are joking like this. "She's not coming today?"

"My youngest came down with something," Henry explains, becoming Henry and not-Henry to me. The Henry who used to tell me he loved me with his hand around my throat, and the Henry whose vernacular has expanded to include *my youngest.*

"How will you get home?"

"My car is back at the hotel."

"Which hotel?"

He says the name of the one I'm staying at, the *inn* the rich parents used to book years in advance for graduation. This weekend is my first time inside, and it's not as nice as I'd imagined all those years mine were staying at the Marriott "downtown." The town where the colleges are located can only be described as incohesive. It was a summer retreat for wealthy city families back in the forties and fifties, and the beautiful old Victorian homes bordering the lake are still occupied and mostly well maintained. But there is little local business to speak of anymore, one good restaurant a mile outside of town, plenty of fast-food chains, and a Walmart the size of a small planet.

"That's where I'm staying too," I say.

Henry slips one hand in his pocket, thumb out. Looks at me with an indiscernible squint. His hair has been neatly combed back from his face, but a lock the shape of a Nike swoosh keeps slipping free, curtaining one eye in an absurdly dashing way. It is making me crazy, thinking about how he is out in the world, looking like that, capable of what he is capable of, and he is no longer mine. I might as well say it: I miss fucking Henry.

"Are you leaving right after the service?" he asks.

"Tomorrow." I twist my finger in my long pendant necklace. Something to do with myself while I remember what it's like to clench Henry's cock from the inside. "You?"

"Same," he says. "Then I'm headed to the lake. Some things to take care of there."

It is still April, and despite the oppressive, out-of-office-for-the-month quality to the humidity, it's too early to begin summerizing the cabin. In the Adirondacks it will snow into May. I stare at Henry, wondering what things he needs to take care of, and then I realize I'm staring and I need to stop.

I check the time on my watch, a thirtieth birthday gift to myself. "I was going to grab a coffee before everything starts," I say. When I look up, I catch Henry scowling at my wrist, and for a moment I allow myself to imagine that he is looking at me as I am looking at him, furious that I am no longer his to control.

"Is it weird if I join you?"

My heart palpitates irregularly. "Yes."

He gives me a rare, real smile, and we step closer, check both ways to make sure the street is clear before crossing. A small, juvenile part of me feels precious and protected knowing I don't need to worry, that Henry will signal when it is safe for us to cross. Walking alongside him is a stupidly erotic experience. I have become accustomed to short Hollywood men, and something in my gut ignites, remembering that when Henry gets in my face, takes me down to my studs, he has to bend at the knees.

"How was the rest of last night?" he wants to know.

"I left not long after you. Campbell tried to get me to stay out. Corrine too. She must be hurting right now." I laugh for Henry's sake. We could talk for hours about Corrine. *Yeah*, he once said, *she does not like you*. It wasn't to be mean. Henry is curious about interpersonal relationships. He was good at letting me vent, even better at analyzing the smallest of interactions. Some might call that gossip; with Henry it felt like intelligence gathering.

"I can't wreck myself like that anymore," he says.

A year ago, I might have agreed. But something about my last birthday has set me off, turned me feral again at the advanced age of thirty-four years old.

"Hey," I say. "Can I tell you something?"

Henry pauses at the top of the short stone staircase that leads down to the quad, his chin touching his chest and his brow furrowed, ready to hear it.

"That girl, Emma. She told me she found PT."

Henry raises his eyebrows. "You're serious."

I nod.

"But you know the house cleaner did."

"Yeah. And I said that to her, and she quickly corrected herself and said technically yes, but then she arrived at the house before the police got there and she ran upstairs and found him in the bathroom. She said she left and didn't tell the police, which just doesn't seem like something a person would do. She also went into this whole thing about how PT canceled all his classes the day before he died and his hands were covered in Band-Aids—"

*"Band-Aids?"*

"Yeah. It was like she was trying to imply he had defensive wounds or something, but then why—"

"Would he have Band-Aids?" Henry finishes for me.

I sweep my hand in his direction. "Exactly. Like, what,

PT's killer stopped and took care of his boo-boos before he slunk out into the night?"

"And what is she doing showing up to PT's house at eight in the morning anyway?" Henry asks, his lip curled with distaste.

"She said he asked her to come over. To discuss her script. She was like, 'Did he say anything to you about it?'"

Henry laughs at that, affects the voice of someone reading an email. "'Dear Faye, the script I'm presenting you is from the most singular talent I've ever come across in all my decades of doing this.'"

That's exactly what I thought Emma was hoping to hear. I stare at Henry in amazement. It wasn't just a rose-colored memory that Henry's operating system runs complementarily to my own. "Meanwhile all he did was apologize for the fact that it was late. I don't think he'd even read it yet."

"I don't feel old," Henry says, "but then I spend ten minutes with someone like that and think, thank God I'm not young anymore."

That's a great line. I repeat it back to myself so I will remember to put it in my Notes app later. "I meant to tell you," I say. "You did a really nice job with the eulogy."

"And here I'm supposed to say that means a lot coming from you." But there is no malice in his tone.

"I'm sorry this happened, Henry."

Henry nods with a hard expression. Men always look so angry when they're sad. "If we're going to stand here and be saps like this, then I may as well tell you thank you for coming, that it would have meant a lot to him to know you were here."

Henry and I are standing close. His eyes, this morning posing as true blue, scan me back and forth like a line of text. He is so tall he eclipses the sun. It bursts from behind him, a magical shot I wish I could bottle and uncap on set of my next production. Henry turns and begins to descend the stairs.

"I have some of your things," he tosses casually over his shoulder. "I brought them in case you came."

I follow Henry down the stairs, thinking about his careful hands, folding my things, placing them carefully into a little shopping bag. I'm thinking about Henry thinking about me, wearing whatever skimpy fast fashion time capsule I left behind. I did not know I was leaving Lake Wanika for the last time when it was the last time.

"I could make some money on eBay," I joke. "It's vintage now."

"Want me to swing by your hotel room after the ceremony?" Henry offers. We are walking alongside each other again. He does not look at me as he says this, but I glance over and catch him drumming his fingers against the outside of his thigh. He's nervous about what I'll say to that. My head is hot and full of noise.

"That works," I say, matching his neutral tone.

We cross the trimmed green of the quad in an old silence, like now that an arrangement has been made, there is nothing left to discuss. I know what it feels like to make an arrangement with Henry, because we made all sorts of demented ones when we were together. From the opposite side of campus, I see Corrine and Campbell approach the café doors, their nanny bustling Tookie along behind them. Henry calls out and they stop, visor their eyes with hands, wave when they realize it is us. Corrine turns to brush something off Campbell's shoulder, and as she does this she whispers something to him. I am surprised to see the deep groove between her ghost-blond brows relax the closer we get to her. She looks relieved, happy even, to see Henry and me getting along. Another woman might have thought about this moment a little harder, but I did not come all this way to think.

# Chapter 6

I had never heard of the colleges until my guidance counselor turned to its page in that guidebook they all carried around like men of the cloth with their Bibles. *Why would you show me this?* I had asked when I saw the sizable tuition number inside the small bubble graphic. *They offer a writing scholarship*, she replied. She asked if I had heard of a show that of course I had heard of. The guy who made that show, she said, went to this college, and he created the scholarship in his name, and sometimes he even helped students attain jobs writing on his show after they graduated. It was not a full ride but close, and if I got it, I would be permitted—obligated, actually—to focus on the thing I was good at for the next four years. No more math or science swirling before my eyes. *Is this for real?* I had asked then too.

To apply, I was to pick my favorite film and come up with an idea for a sequel, write the first five pages of the script, and then outline the rest of the story in what was called a beat sheet. I had never done that kind of writing before, but I was the star of my English class, a show-off summer reader, and my theater teacher supplied me with a volume of David Mamet classics to help me get a feel for formatting and stylistic f-bombing. I pretended to be sick for two days so I could sit at home alone and perfect my application, to read my dialogue out loud without my meathead brothers around to harass me. It sounded good. It *felt* good. Two months later, when I was invited to campus as a finalist, I can't say I was surprised. Call me obnoxious; it keeps me in business.

Campus was stupid beautiful: handsome Jacobean buildings knit tightly around plots of manicured green and an October sun that made a mirror of the lake and doubled the perimeter of fiery trees. In PT's creaky and enchanting office, I clocked pictures of him on various red carpets and even some kind of award for cowriting a short film in the nineties. But it was the methodical way in which he assessed and then managed my parents that I tend to revisit in my mind.

Sometimes I marvel at my luck, to have been born into a family that simultaneously did not know how to love me and found a way, eventually, to find the value in my imagination. The gash of that gives me something to nurse on the page, and without their sudden and supportive turnabout, I might have been too scared to try to make a go of it. My mother was an accountant, my father did something with computers. Neither of them were creative types. Later PT would tell me that when he met them and asked what they did for a living, he saw a kind of alchemy between their lines of work—my mother identifying places for financial opportunity, my father securing sensitive databases—and he spoke to that to get them to see that while my potential was foreign to them, it was a potential that should be safeguarded against superfluous drains on my energy nonetheless. My parents couldn't argue with a scholarship that subsidized nearly everything, but they were concerned I would miss out on a well-rounded education. Did I not need, say, linear algebra and Introduction to Financial Accounting, and how about some Spanish if I wanted to graduate with any hope of finding a real job?

"Here's the part no student likes to hear," PT said, rather jovially for someone who was about to tell me something I was not going to want to hear. We were sitting on one of the cracked leather couches in his office, and I was between my mother and father, like I was in trouble, which I often was with them. "I cannot guarantee that a career as a writer will work out for Faye. For *anyone*. It has to do with talent, but it also has to do with an innate understanding of how to position oneself, as well as all the lightning-in-the-bottle stuff like right time, right place, et cetera, et cetera." PT crossed his legs and clasped his hands around one knee. It was an effeminate gesture, and his black T-shirt was snug, but PT was tall and built well, and I knew later my father wouldn't stoop to the level of making a twinkle-toes joke. "That being said," he continued, "Hollywood is a big industry, filled with successful people behind the scenes who are still engaged creatively and are very much working real jobs. She could move into the development space at one of the studios, she could be a literary agent, a film editor, a publicist."

"A publicist?" my father repeated as though it were the first time he'd ever heard the word.

"What is the trajectory of something like that?" my mother asked in a pleasant voice a decibel louder than usual. At this volume I knew she was annoyed with my father. *Yes, a publicist, you fucking idiot.* That was what she would have said were PT not there. I might have cleared my throat, shifted my position on the couch, breathed differently than usual, I really can't say, but PT's eyes were suddenly at attention, on me, and in them I saw not just curiosity but hope. In a couple of months he would issue me a writing assignment for the first time and it would be to compose this scene in the office. I didn't need a bad guy with a gun to create tension and stakes and drama. It was all right there, between my mother, father, and me: an interior world with intricate and messy human dynamics. Characters he didn't necessarily like but did want to spend more time with and understand.

"Here is a great place to start," PT said.

PT had us over for dinner, where my parents actually drank wine and got a little tipsy, and then we sat down and watched the first episode of Jonathan Granger's new show. There was a fuckton of cursing and simulated oral sex, and though my father promptly fell asleep, my mother took off her shoes, curled up, and got comfortable. I sat on my side of the couch, stiff with terror the entire fifty-three minutes. My parents were Catholics who never went to church. They used religion to justify their discomfort around anything that stank of hot, hedonistic garbage but couldn't quote a line of scripture to save their lives. When the episode ended, my mother turned to me with saucer eyes and declared, *I loved it.* To this day absolutely nothing has shocked me more. My father roused himself as the credits rolled, in time to see PT point to the names of an associate producer and a marketing executive and explain that they were former Granger Scholars too, that Jonathan was known to take on recent graduates as assistants or to recommend them to others in the industry. There were real careers to be had in Hollywood, with health insurance and not enough vacation days and communal kitchens where people labeled their food in the fridge and shamed you on mass email if you poured their almond milk in your coffee. It wouldn't be some fanciful indulgence, to sit in front of a computer and transcribe the imaginary world in my head for the next four years. I had neon.

Neon. That was PT's word for it, a kind of naturally occurring talent. But neon doesn't glow on its own. It needs an electrical current, and that's what the scholarship was—a charge. Without that, without PT, I would not be standing here today, burning like a bar sign for a drunk.

While I've told this story, heavy granite clouds have banded together overhead. Behind me, I can hear the agitation of the lake, smacking the underside of the dock. A gentleman in the crowd suddenly caps his head with his hand and glances up at the sky warily. I hurry to bring it to a close before we all get drenched.

"The strangest thing happened the last time I saw PT in person," I say to the crowd, smaller today than it was yesterday, even some empty chairs. The party atmosphere is gone, and it's all so much sadder and so much more urgent that I leave them with this. "It was three years ago and he was in Los Angeles and I invited him over for a drink. We had just bought our house and he wanted to see it. But when I opened the door, he walked right past me without so much as even saying hello. He went immediately into the living room and stood staring at this jagged crack in the brickwork of our fireplace. 'You won't believe this,' he said." A few people are holding programs over their heads, the paper wilting with rain, and I'm reminded of the music they play at awards ceremonies to signal to the winner that their time is up. I tightly time all my potential acceptance speeches so that I am never *that* person shouting into a cut microphone, but for some reason right now I keep going, I can't stop until I finish this story, until everyone is as staggered by the synchronicity as I am. "Our house was built in the fifties, and my husband and I had assumed the brickwork had cracked from age, but PT told me that during the time that he lived in Los Angeles in his twenties, he had been a PA on a film that was shot here, in our house, and that they were shooting the day of the Northridge earthquake and that was what caused this crack. He said that, during the editing process, they had problems with continuity because in some of the shots the fireplace wasn't cracked and in others it was, and we stood staring at each other in disbelief because I knew this story, he always used it as an example in class when we covered elements of narrative, and then I had gone and unwittingly bought the earthquake house."

I continue, rain pricking my skin so lightly I keep looking down thinking there are gnats crawling on me. "Sometimes, you meet people in life who offer a kind of cohesion." I pick out Henry in the crowd. He's squinting at me as hard as if the sun were out. "I don't know why it came together like this for PT, but I do believe that somehow in the end it did come together for him. His story made sense in a way none of us can imagine. And I can't explain this either, but I am certain I will somehow bump into him again."

The minister passes out individual plastic baggies containing a couple tablespoons each of remains. Bone is the color of the thin sweater I am wearing, that's what it said on the website. The cashmere Kelly cardigan in *winter's bone*. But bone has a yellow cast, like a molar closer to the gums. I wander the dock, find a place away from everyone, sink down onto my knees. I'm peeling apart the seal when Henry's large form materializes by my side. He stares down at me, his exquisite face tormented and tender.

"You want to do it downwind," he says.

"Which way is that?"

Henry tips his head. "Other side of the dock." He offers me his hand, pulls me to my feet so fast my head clouds with blood. It's a thing, isn't it? That people fuck after funerals, hoping to forget that they will one day die too. Henry's fingertips are soft, but his palms are calloused and rough, and he uses both, I remember now. Occasionally, and never often enough that it lost its impact, he called me sweetheart. *Spread your legs for me, sweetheart.* I feel stabbed through with want, reprehensibly giddy as I stand next to Henry downwind, peppering the surface of the lake with ash that looks more like sand than bone.

"Faye," Henry says alongside me, and there is a hushed, secretive quality to how he says my name. But when I turn, I find him looking over my shoulder, and then he brings his hand up and holds it in a stagnant wave. I follow his gaze to see Campbell and Corrine approaching us from the shoreline.

"God damn it, Faye." Campbell draws a hand down his face, agonized. "That fucked me up." He clears his throat, frowns hard at the shallow puddles collecting on the dock.

"We have to take off," Corrine says, and this time she moves in to embrace me before either of us can think about it too long. Her blond hair is beaded with rain, so wispy and fine I could count the number of droplets if she gave me one more minute. Campbell and Henry exchange a few final words, clap each other on their backs. Campbell moves in to give me a hug that lifts my feet off the ground.

"Jesus, you're light," he says, and I sense something familiar waft off Corrine. Her irresistible distaste for me. I imagine she finds my smallness and aversion to the sun prissy and high-maintenance, and that she is glad for the reminder that we have little in common.

And yet I never feel thin-thin until I hug someone outside of my strange endemic world, though I know exactly what Campbell feels when he touches me, that impossible birdlike lightness that unnerved me when I first started booking meetings with iconic Hollywood women, as though they had not just lost weight but eliminated their insides too. The hollowing happened to me gradually but with such minimal effort that sometimes I picture the type of high-powered studio executives you think don't exist anymore but absolutely do dispensing henchmen to creep into my room in the middle of the night and empty me out, organ by organ, bone by bone. Would I even tell them to stop if my suspicions proved true?

Then, somehow, Henry and I are riding in a car together, only this time I am the one at the wheel. I don't think I ever drove when Henry and I were together. I had nowhere to take him. I had no *car.*

I park in the small hotel lot, and we make a run in the rain, slipping on wet dogwood petals and huddling together under the first window awning, startling the manager with teased hair who sits in front of her blocky desktop. We flee to the cover of the next awning, this one long and thin, shielding the red carpeted walkway into the bar and restaurant. The garden doors are open on the other side, and beyond the hedges trimmed to match a *Bridgerton* set, the lake is gray and pockmarked with rain.

"You head back to LA tomorrow?" Henry checks. He removes his blazer and brushes it dry with the flat of his hand.

"Actually, no. Not for another week."

Henry frowns, confused. "Another week?"

"I rented an Airbnb on the other side of the lake. Sort of like a solo writing retreat. I get more done alone."

Henry digs his hands into his armpits and squeezes himself against the damp. "Let me swing by with your stuff. What's your room number?"

We really are doing this, then. This dangerous, combustible thing. I am suddenly so nervous I could cry. The rain against the lake is like a setting on a sound machine. I let it soothe me. I think, *This is Henry. It will be what you want.*

"Three F," I tell him, and I'm startled by the sound of my own voice, its ultrafeminine and frightened tenor.

Henry swings his blazer over my head and settles the shoulders on my shoulders, a cape to keep me dry. He gives me a quick, reassuring smile. *It's me. It's okay.* That's the meaning I assign it as he turns and strides under the scalloped awning with his head bowed to the rain, disappearing into the secondary guest tower, which is not a tower so much as a long, low dormitory-looking structure with sliding glass doors lining the back. I'm staying in the original building, the older but prettier one with the higher rate to match.

I raise Henry's coat over my head and set off for my room at an unhurried pace, in case anyone is watching, in case Henry can still see me. But my heart is pounding like I'm running uphill.

Last night, when I got home and noticed the marks at the foot of the door, I briefly imagined that I might find Henry sitting on the fusty floral couch. I would tell him that he shouldn't be here. He's married, and so am I. I imagined him standing, approaching me, ignoring my continued pleas to leave me alone, knowing the way only Henry knows when my no means yes.

Now my hand shakes as I turn the key to the door,

knowing he will be inside soon. I brush my teeth, apply an extra coat of deodorant. Henry is sensitive to smells, and he always smells good. I used to joke he had his sweat glands removed, his tongue professionally bleached, and he would smile in this soft way, as though touched someone finally understood him. I kick off my shoes and wash my feet in the tub. Thank God I got a pedicure before I came. I'm standing in an inch of soapy water when my phone rattles on the countertop. It's my best friend who is also my agent, calling on a Saturday. I answer on speaker.

"Hello?" I say, the question evident in my voice. *What's happened?*

"I have news," she says without preamble. "It's good but it comes with a catch." She wants to loop in my husband, but first she wanted to check to make sure that would be okay with me.

"Go right ahead," I say benevolently. "We're acting like everything is fine, as usual."

"Are you ever going to tell me what happened?" The most I've told her, acting in best friend capacity, is that something *has* happened and I'm thinking of leaving. My husband has a secret. Not the one you're thinking, the normal one that normal husbands sometimes have.

"Try him now," I say. "It's, like, nine or ten at night there."

"Okay," she says, uncertainly, and for a moment I think the line has dropped, but then she comes back on and says, "Everyone still with me?"

"Here," says my husband. He must have popped out of whatever exclusive supper club he's been invited to for the evening. I can hear someone in the background ask to borrow a lighter, the wet spray of the cars rushing by on a rainy London night.

"Here," I echo.

My agent, who I alternately refer to as my agent and best friend, depending on which role she occupies in the moment, says the name of the actress who is asking for someone to slip her a not-quite-ready copy of my script. The name of this actress is cause to scream, and so I do.

"Hold up, hold up," my husband says. "I thought she was doing that Apple show and then right into the Marvel movie and unavailable until 2029?"

"She has to drop the show," my agent is delighted to report. "They pushed the start date, and now it's a scheduling conflict with Marvel. She's essentially free this whole next year and looking for a film, something with a short production window."

"Faye," my husband says, a kind of awe in his voice, "you were right. Holy fuck, you were right." I can tell that he's smiling, which means he's had a few drinks. In the eleven years we've been together, he's smiled infrequently, even though we've produced three television shows and two indie films, all of which have been well received critically but did not quite manage to dent the culture in a way that matters to the studios. Still, they will always hear a pitch from us. Not all of them will make an offer on that pitch, but enough that occasionally a project of ours gets competitive. We've been photographed for the cover of *The Hollywood Reporter* and given a tour of our production offices to *Architectural Digest*. We are usually invited to the *Vanity Fair* after-party. Objectively, we are doing well, but one thing my husband and I agree on is that the term *objectively well* can kick rocks. We want our white whale, something unapologetically commercial and occasionally brilliant. One thing we cannot agree on is what that looks like. My husband is after me to pitch something dark and female-driven and, most important, franchise friendly; I sat down and wrote this script instead. He read it, asked why I wanted to waste two years of my life on another quiet indie thing. The caliber of the actress who has requested a copy of the script makes mincemeat of that question. She will get us money. She will make us noise.

"We love a man who can admit when he's wrong," my agent jokes, and I am glad we are not on a FaceTime so I am free to roll my eyes. I know what she's doing—selling my husband back to me. She thinks it will be professionally disastrous for the two of us to split. My husband's older brother runs the venture capitalist arm of the agency that represents us; I could triple my writing and directing quote and I still wouldn't be considered an earner, not when my brother-in-law is bringing in Mint Mobile partnership money. If my husband and I do separate, if things do get ugly, if it ever does come down to a choice between the two of us, it's me who will be shown the door. My best friend and agent has not explicitly said so to me, nor does she have to.

"Tell her it will be ready to read next Monday," I say. "But that means no one can bother me for the next week. No check-ins. No updates about set drama. Nothing. If I need something, I'll reach out, but otherwise treat me like I don't exist."

"Will not disturb," my agent solemnly vows.

"Do your thing," my husband says, and I can hear in his voice that he's grinning ear to ear. "I love you, baby."

I am saved from saying it back by the knock on my door.

Henry is standing in the hallway, the handle of a small shopping bag hooked around his pinkie. His hair is spiked with rain and his eyes are a bit wild. "Did you scream?"

"It was good news."

"I was worried, Faye," Henry says in soft admonishment. He puts his hand on the door above my head and pushes it open all the way. There is a moment as he steps past, him looking down at me, me looking up at him, that is eddied with turbulence. I want him to toss the bag with my cheap old clothes and pin me against the wall with his pelvis. No. Scratch that. This is Henry. We can do better; we have done much. I want him to keep the bag. I want him to pull out one of the slutty sundresses I used to wear without a bra, tell me to go into the bedroom and put it on, don't even think about coming back out unless I'm crawling on my hands and knees. I want him to be sitting on the couch with his feet propped up on the coffee table and his arms crossed behind his head, watching me with all his furious control. *Stop*, I want him to say. *Get down on your elbows*. I want him to take his time standing, coming over to me, I want him to circle me a few times, tilting his head this way and that while I hang my head in remorse. The sundress is psychotically short. Bent over, the wet slash in my underwear is on display until Henry decides it isn't. *Look at me, Faye*, he'll say in that aristocratic voice, and

I'll have to twist my head over my shoulder because he will be standing behind me, and he will want me to see that he is looking at me too but not in my eyes. *Reach around. Take it off.* When I do, I want him to kneel behind me, adjust my nice underwear so that it's sitting just right in the crooks of my knees. *Jesus, Faye*, I want him to sigh, sounding brokenhearted and heartless in the same breath. *I could pick your pretty pussy out of a lineup.*

"Want to make us drinks?" I say, feeling woozy. I am swollen like a tick. "I need to make one quick call." I lead him through the sitting room and point him toward the small kitchenette, where a bottle of bourbon sits on the counter. I am not a bourbon drinker, but it seemed a safer bet than the selection of wine at the liquor store that shares space with the tanning salon that still charges a dollar a minute. Henry picks up the bottle, stares at the label a long moment.

"How do you take it?"

"Little bit of water."

"Look at you," he says quietly.

I slip into the bedroom and close the door so that I can change into the black underwear that sits low on my hips and high on my ass. I call my assistant on speaker as I do this, and when she doesn't answer, I leave her a message telling her to cancel the few Zooms I'd kept on my calendar this week. I stare at the damp prints I've left on the screen. I'm scared. How long has it been since I was scared? I use the top sheet to wipe away evidence of my nerves. This cannot be happening, and yet it is.

I go out into the faux formal sitting room and catch Henry staring out the window in a moment of deep thought. He has taken the grand Louis IV chair in the corner, next to the modern media center. He turns to me, his face grim, and then topples me with a sorrowful half smile. "Bourbon?" he says, and the word is the sun around which so many unasked questions revolve. *When did you start with this? When did you become not-Faye, the way I've become not-Henry to you?*

"It was that or Cupcake chardonnay." I tuck myself into the corner of the grandmotherly couch. It's late afternoon and the light is gray and forgiving, the rain lazily streaking the windows. We have all day, I realize. We can do it mean. We can do it nice. We can do it mean again and again. I reach for my glass, sip amber, wondering which one of us will make a move first and how we will even get there.

With his cold blue eyes, Henry tracks the motion of my hand to my mouth and back to my lap. "You don't wear a wedding ring," he remarks.

I feel cool and clean under my clothes, ready for his hands, the rough way he will want to do it after all these years. He must be so angry with me. It's a little bit about the episode, I'm sure, but mostly it's because I've surpassed him. That was not how things worked when we were together.

"It gave me a rash," I say.

Henry brushes his lips with a knuckle. "At first I thought you said it gave you a rush."

"Oh." A light laugh at the misunderstanding. "No. Just a red, itchy rash."

"Kind of a metaphor, no?" He's doing this thing, parting his lips while he waits for me to speak, his eyes narrowed, brow heavy and furrowed, like he must turn over everything I say before deciding if he believes it.

"Putting that English minor to good use, I see."

Henry rolls his glass around in his hands, frowning down at his lap. He locates a wrinkle in his pants, sweeps it away with the heel of his hand. "Are you getting a divorce?"

"Why would you ask me that?"

"You're not acting married."

"And you are right now?" We stare at each other, standoff style. His tongue is behind his front teeth, pushing forward in frustration.

"There are a few things I need to understand first." First. That word is interesting to me, for some reason. I watch as Henry sets his drink down on the small desk where I've been attempting to polish a scene in my second act but mostly watching porn.

"What things?"

Henry uncrosses his legs, leans back, and reclines luxuriously, like the bored heir to an empire of rustic cabin furniture, which is exactly what he is. His family invented the Adirondack chair, if you can believe it. "How far this goes."

I can feel my drink, that all-over surge of chatty, confessional courage. "I want a divorce," I say out loud for the first time. "But I'm scared it would ruin me."

There is a sudden flash of fury on Henry's angelic face. With slow menace, he gathers himself and stands, making his way over to me. My heart rams my ribs. So this is how it happens. I track his movements in a sleepy kind of awe, watching as he sits on the other end of the short couch, drapes his arm over the back, taps an index finger on the padded frame, inches from my shoulder. I do not know where to look—into his malignant, concord-blue eyes? Or at his hands, fingers twitching like he is trying to restrain himself from hurting me? I'm worried I will explode before he can touch me, that he'll be staring at my brain matter in his lap like Jackie Kennedy in the back seat of that convertible.

"Is he waiting for you? Your husband, I mean."

"He's in London."

"What about friends? Your family?"

A small wave of sadness, realizing how few people I needed to alert to my sudden sabbatical, but also confusion too. Why would that matter to Henry? "I pretty much told everyone to leave me alone this week."

Henry's fingers relax, then still altogether. He goes to reach for a piece of my hair that has come untucked from behind my ear; then, to my immense disappointment, he seems to lose his nerve. Is this one of those dreams, those nightmares I have about him? Where we get so close to being together again, and then we are thwarted, somehow, by some impropable dream turn.

"So you thought you would, what?" Henry is smiling now, but there is a kind of venom in it. "Come here and flaunt your shit?"

I blink at him, dumbfounded. "My shit?"

He draws his eyes up and down my body. "Your

fancy clothes. Your tacky watch. Your fucking face and whatever you're doing to it to still look like that." He looks away from me when he says that part, swallows hard, like he regrets giving me anything even bordering a compliment. Then he turns back, leans in closer, staring at me with unmitigated hatred. My pulse should be pounding with panic. This is wrong. All wrong. But I feel nothing.

"You couldn't wait to come here and try it out from my side," he says, alarmingly calm.

"From your side?" I repeat, feeling dimmer than I'd like.

"You think you're the one with the power now."

Though I am excessively tired, I can't help but antagonize him with a smile. "Didn't I always have it?"

"Because I was in love with you."

I don't say anything. I don't need to. Henry's eyes redden with rage.

"I do not love you anymore," he informs me callously.

"I should hope not," I say, doing my best to mask my disappointment.

Henry looks past my shoulder, trancelike. "I did, though. And then you just ... massacred me in front of the world. How *you* said it went down between us—that is not what fucking happened, Faye."

A flare of fear, somewhere deep within the wilderness of me, barely seen, barely felt. I am aware enough still to know I should be afraid, even if I cannot access the feeling. I expected Henry to be angry. I expected that to convert into something tawdry and memorable between us. But Henry is not angry, I'm realizing. Henry is humiliated. A humiliated man is sometimes the last thing a woman sees. How had I failed to discern the difference before I let him in here, before I allowed him to mix me a drink? There is so much I could say to defend myself, if only Henry hadn't so obviously drugged me.

"That is what happened," I manage. But when I try to remember the details of it all, I find I cannot.

"You have no idea what you're talking about," Henry says, and for some inexplicable reason, his voice is choked with emotion.

It is an effort to focus on him. My left eyelid feels heavier than my right. There are surgeries to fix that, I think. "Why apologize to me, then?"

Henry purses his perfect lips in victory. "How else was I going to get you to let me in here?"

A warm, hazy feeling overtakes me. I could fall asleep, right here, listening to Henry tell me what a terrible person I am. The delicious dreams I would have. I'd never want to wake up. "You put something in my drink," I say, but it comes out rearranged and all wrong. *Put my drink in your something*. Or something. Something . . .

"I didn't think it would be this easy." Henry exhales, almost disappointed. "I didn't think you would make it this easy for me."

I put my lips together and try very hard to produce a word, any word. Henry props his elbow on the back of the couch, and with his thumb he strokes his rosy bottom lip, watching me begin to nod off with clinical fascination. My phone is balanced in the seam of the couch cushions, tipped up slightly, so that when it begins to rattle, I can see it's my assistant, texting that she got my message and she will cancel my week for me, no problem.

"Are you going to write her back?" Henry asks. He's sincerely asking. He does not do anything to impede my efforts, but the problem is I am not making any. Just before the screen darkens, Henry taps the message. And then he's in my phone, my world, my *life* that he so flagrantly despises.

"Let's see," Henry says to himself, trampling through my beautiful digital gardens with his big bully thumbs. At last I muster up the strength to make a grab for what's mine, but Henry catches my hand and places it in my lap and gives the top of it a kindly little pat. *Valiant effort, Faye*. My left eyelid seals completely shut.

"That's not very pretty," Henry says. He uses his thumb to drag my other eyelid down to match. I think of what I must look like, sitting there with my eyes closed and fish lips smacking, and I realize that must not look very pretty either, and despite what's happening—what *is* happening?—I still want to look pretty for Henry. I rest my cheek on the back of the couch, and my body sinks, expands, forgets its own solidness.

"I've waited a long time for this," Henry says from somewhere in the dark. His hand moves to cover my mouth, like I am screaming. But why would I be screaming? I've been waiting a long time for this too.

A minute or maybe the rest of my life passes, and then a prick of consciousness. There is knocking at the door, and Henry has gone to answer it. He is speaking to someone in an easy way, telling them that everything is fine and, no, we don't need anything and, yes, have a nice evening too. I'm picturing the manager with the teased hair, maybe the young guy in the cargo pants who carried my bags up the stairs when I first arrived.

*Help*, I cannot say.

# PART 2

# Chapter 7

The summer I turned twenty-seven, I was nominated for an Emmy for the episode I'd written about Henry. The category was Outstanding Dramatic Writing for a Comedy Series, and I was the only woman in it. Right away, the studio sicced their director of publicity on me, and we began shaping my responses to questions like why I thought women were overlooked for writing and directing nominations and what did I think needed to happen for this to change. My responses had to satisfy the discontent of feminist bloggers with hundreds of thousands of foamy-mouthed Twitter followers (it was still Twitter back then) without alienating the mostly male voting body of an awards organization that rarely elevated women but had chosen to honor me. This was not the only land mine I had to sidestep in strappy heels at all the luncheons and dinners and benefits and Q&As and special screenings in the months leading up to the ceremony.

The series was a comedy series, but the nominated episode fell into the Dramatic Writing category, tackling an issue the director of PR referred to as coercive control in intimate-partner relationships, all words I'd heard before but never together like that. We partnered with an anti-sexual-violence organization, and I filmed a conversation with an expert in this field and someone from the leadership team who had survived an emotionally abusive relationship. Everyone was big on using that word. Survive. We spoke in soft, careful tones, and when the woman from the leadership team told her story, I cried for real, and I said things myself that were true but platitudinal. Still, when I watch that interview now, I inwardly coil. I only know how to write about what happened with Henry and me. When I try to talk about it, it sounds one-note, earnest, and, frankly, revolting.

In the episode, my character lands an interview for a big job in a city across the country. Her boyfriend is brooding, handsome, controlling, disapproving. He finds all kinds of ways to poke holes in the opportunity. Her friends have been gently trying to get her to see the truth about this guy all season, but it comes to a head when he offers to drive her to the airport. The boyfriend starts complaining about chest pain. They were partiers, the two of them, and he'd gone out the night before and put all kinds of things up his nostrils. *No, really*, he's panting, clutching the steering wheel with bone-white knuckles, *I think I'm having a heart attack*.

My character is staring at the time on the car's dashboard, panic-stricken, torn in two perfect pieces. She is worried sick about her boyfriend. He could be having a heart attack. They put substances in their bodies that cause those. But her flight. Her interview. *I have to pull over*, he says, and he abruptly takes an exit, and she looks at the clock and realizes she's going to miss her flight, and all at once, she's angry. She sees what's going on. She screams at him that he's deliberately trying to sabotage her and she wants to break up.

The boyfriend doesn't seem to hear. He's driving until there are no other cars or homes, and then he finds a dirt path to pull onto. I got some pushback on this. The characters lived in Silver Lake. Which airport was he taking her to where he could pull off the highway and find a rural murder passageway? They were right, but I fought to keep it anyway. Because when Henry did this to me, he was driving me to the airport from the Adirondacks, and he pulled into one of many rural murder passageways where he could have taken his time ending my life and gotten away with it.

The boyfriend character shuts off the engine and at this point becomes somewhat catatonic. He's staring straight ahead, and he's reciting a sort of mental to-do list out loud. Things that have to do with the logistics of a breakup. That he will have to end their lease. That he would like to keep the Le Creuset pan they bought together at HomeGoods. That she can't do this to him. That he's dying. My character takes out her phone, and he snatches it away from her, and she thinks on her feet and says, *We have to call 911. You're having a heart attack*. She holds out her hand, and she screws her face up into one of concern and compassion, and he returns her phone to her. And she calls her best friend, and she pretends like she's on the phone with 911, and she's giving the operator their location. And she tells her boyfriend she is going to get out of the car and walk back to the road so she can wave down the ambulance, and he permits it. She staggers to the street and begs her best friend to come and get her as fast as she can. In real life, it was PT I was begging. He came and got me. He made sure someone came and got Henry too. I made my flight. I got the job. I met the woman who put me on her show and let me write the episode I was sitting there talking about with an expert in coercive control in intimate-partner relationships.

By the time I climbed the six steps to the stage on the second Sunday of September and accepted my award for Outstanding Dramatic Writing for a Comedy Series, I was positively seething. The red carpet had been a hoot for my male fellow nominees but for me a gang rape of breathless questions about the plight of women in entertainment and heterosexual romantic relationships, and then I won, and I had to get up in front of hundreds of my colleagues and the world and talk about how women's stories mattered even though I still had not told mine. I did not lie; I was very careful about how I phrased everything. The episode was inspired by something that happened to me. Henry was controlling and he frightened me at times, but there was more to it than that. There were things I wanted from him too, things I wrote into the episode that no one wanted to touch down on. Seven years later I think people might be ready, might understand that even though some pieces of the story don't seem to fit with the others, they indeed come from the same puzzle box. And if they're not, oh well. I think I'm in danger of imploding if I don't finally tell the story of what really happened with Henry.

# Chapter 8

I have remembered this room often, and now I see all the places I have remembered wrong. Where are my cathedral arches? The oppressive dark wood? The bed faces three adjoining windows, and between my feet Lake Wanika is as blue as the ocean, shimmering with resentment that memory had cast its waters gray-brown. *This is why you cannot convict someone on eyewitness testimony alone*, I think with outrageous clarity before my brain goes back to feeling like it's in one of those jars in a laboratory, submerged in blue liquid. Or is that the stuff hairdressers use to disinfect their combs? Certainly not my hairdresser.

I reach for my phone on the nightstand out of habit, finding instead a Nature Valley granola bar and a Dasani water. He hates both items with a fiery passion. I did not know granola bars could make you fat or that water had a taste before I met him. I feel infirm, trying to twist the cap off the water bottle. When my Pilates instructor guides me through a sequence to improve my grip strength, I stop trying. I want to reserve my energy for my core and glutes.

But if I get out of here alive, I will hire a fucking personal trainer for my thumbs.

I finally get the cap off and gulp until the plastic craters, wipe my mouth, then wolf down the granola bar in four bites. I collapse back on the bed, lie there covered in crumbs. Wait for the shaking to stop.

Eventually, I drag myself into an upright position and set my feet on the ground. Wait again for the spots to clear from my eyes. The rug I got right, at least. Red, rough plaid that used to burn my knees.

I walk hunched and hurting to the door and find it locked from the outside. On Henry's lot there are two structures—the main house with the kitchen and rustic, gnarled log furniture arranged around the fireplace where we used to gather with wine and dark chocolate after dinner, and then this studio apartment–like cabin. It's where Henry's mother used to put him before he learned to swim and, worried he might wander into the lake in the middle of the night, she had the door outfitted with a lock from the outside, like Henry was a valuable in a safe. There's nothing in here but a bed and a minuscule airplane bathroom and a closet containing a pair of slippers the size of boats, I find when I peer inside. Someone must have finally recycled the endemic collection of wire hangers from the dry cleaners. I go to the windows, and though I see they are double paned and possibly soundproof—there is an insulated silence to the room that feels manufactured—I give them a shove so I can say I covered all my bases. I look around the room. The dresser is without drawers and there are two circular stains on a console table at the foot of the bed, telling on the pair of table lamps that used to frame the space. Anything I could use to break the windows, to cast the walls with the demented splatter of Henry's brain, has been removed from the room. It is just me and the granola crumbs and my roofie juice. I stumble haphazardly toward the bed, land like a chalk outline of a dead body.

It is night when I wake again, and Henry is sitting on the edge of the bed with his face turned away from me. I lie still awhile, wits thawing, eyes adjusting to the dark. I count to three, sit up with a gasp. Henry's head whips in my direction, and I catch it, the flash of relief on his face, in the way of someone sitting bedside to a loved one in a coma. *Nurse. Nurse. She's not a vegetable after all.*

"Henry," I whisper cautiously. "What . . . what is this?"

He says nothing for a long time. Then, "It's just for a few days."

I stare at his potent silhouette in the dark, my heart inching up my throat. "A few days for what?"

He ignores me, reaching for something on the nightstand. Water, in a Yeti. He offers it to me and I do not take it.

"I'm not drinking that."

"There's nothing in it this time."

This time. His medal is in the mail. "Can I . . . Could I just go home?"

"I'm trying to make that happen for you."

Something about the way he says this, like it's out of his control, infuriates me. "You're trying? What the fuck?

Unlock the door, then. Give me my phone. My phone. Where is my—"

My head slams into the pillow. Henry is on top of me, his hand around my throat. "If you try to tell me what to do again, you will regret it."

Henry has had his hand around my throat before, he's even squeezed as hard as he's squeezing now, but it is how he is looking at me that is new and incomprehensible. He is afraid. *Afraid.* Why would *Henry* be the one who is afraid?

Like he is telling me a secret, Henry leans in closer. "Say you understand, Faye." Gracefully and with deep benevolence, he lifts the index finger at the base of my windpipe, permitting me to suck in a wheezy breath. He smells the same. Like he's been fixing something outside. Fresh air and good, clean sweat.

"I understand." My voice is sandpaper. My hands, I realize, are pressed against Henry's chest. I'm holding on to him like he's saving me from a burning building.

Henry considers me a moment. In the dark I can only make out the whites of his eyes, switching places in their sockets while he searches my face for any indication that I may be disingenuous. "You don't yet," he decides. "Not really. But I'll explain in the morning."

He loosens his grip, but his hand remains at rest on my throat a moment longer than necessary. I am still holding on to him. I know this must please him, and perhaps that's why I do not let go. *This is Stockholm syndrome*, I tell myself. It's the only thing that makes sense.

At last, Henry stands. He starts for the door, watching

me over his shoulder to make sure I don't move a muscle. I listen to him lock me inside and lie there taking shallow, shaky breaths, wishing I were drugged again so I did not have to think. Around and around in my mind, I play out what just transpired between us until I arrive at my dire conclusion.

Once, I was in a hotel room in Miami, doing press for the first show my husband and I produced together, and we were waiting for a call from the network publicist. I was sitting cross-legged in the bed with my phone in my lap, facing the bathroom, where I could see myself in the reflection of the full-length mirror above the Jacuzzi bathtub. It was exactly forty-eight hours before our show would premiere, the time when the studios lift their embargos and the media is permitted to publish reviews. The publicist was supposed to be calling with an aggregate snapshot from the critics, but she was five minutes late, and then ten, and I knew it would be bad. If it's all raves, the call comes on the minute.

*Are you sure you're on the Wi-Fi?* my husband had asked. He was pacing the room, and when I looked up to answer him, I caught the reflection of myself in the bathroom mirror. My face looked longer than usual, and my eyes seemed to turn down at the corners, like a frowning mouth. This is what true terror looked like, I saw. I was imagining all kinds of catastrophic headlines—*Emmy Winner Faye Heron Struck Out on Her Own and Struck Out Big-Time* or some punny such—which would snowball into green splats and tipped-over popcorn buckets on Rotten Tomatoes and, the true kiss of death, next to nothing on social media. In the end the reviews were mostly positive, and a small but dedicated fanbase came through on socials, and the publicist had just gotten stuck in another meeting that ran over, but in that moment I saw on my face what I had seen on Henry's as he pulsed my throat in his hand. Something catastrophic is coming.

# Chapter 9

In the tiny bathroom, there are women's sweatpants and a man's fleece, thick wool socks. Drugstore shampoo and conditioner. A bar of soap. A *bar.* One of those very rudimentary toothbrushes they don't sell in drugstores anymore, but for some reason is always a part of the amenity kits on overseas flights. The bristles are so soft that for a paralyzing moment I worry I have his kid's toothbrush in my mouth, before remembering Henry wouldn't do that to me. He will kill me, but he would not give me a used toothbrush.

The first time we came here, Henry said that if I didn't want to bathe in the lake, which I didn't, that I only got three pulls on the shower cord, and everyone would know by the level of the water tank if I took more, and I would be shunned. We laughed but he was serious. This morning, I give myself five pulls, hissing each time the ice-cold water splits my scalp. I get out, shivering, shuddering, really. My chest hitches with painful breaths, and I look in the mirror and I am stunned to see I am sobbing. I usually only cry when I'm angry, when I'm shouting at my husband and begging him to do something to save our marriage. I dry myself with a tattered towel that catches in the clasp of the spiky bracelet I wear always. I blink off my tears and stare at the underside of my wrist a long moment. With the edge of my fingernail, I flick the double-pronged clasp with my thumb, and I wonder, could I use this?

He has left me a weak hairbrush with plastic bristles that snag and break my hair, which he knows I am very precious about. I work through it in small sections. My arm is heavy by the time I'm done, but it is a task that required enough concentration that my panic has momentarily subsided.

When I come out of the bathroom, he is there, standing by the window, his hands in his pockets like he's waiting to take me on a date. He's made the bed with pathological precision, the fold in the quilt at the exact place where the pattern breaks.

"You need to eat," he says. He takes me by the elbow and ushers me outside and toward the main house. I'm barefoot, and he goes carefully, pausing so I can skip from stone to stone on the rough path. "We'll get you shoes," he says, bafflingly apologetic.

My phone sits on the kitchen table in a blast of sunlight, the once-finger-smudged screen pristine, like Henry spent the morning wiping it down with his tongue sticking out of the corner of his mouth in concentration. I just know he has a big plastic tub of electronic screen wipes from Staples, a stocking stuffer he bought for himself and had his wife wrap last Christmas. Tragic, that image.

Henry toes the leg of an empty chair, angling it toward

me with a jut of his chin. *Sit.* I comply, my heart beating in my back. The appearance of my phone, a tether to the outside world, is a thrilling development.

"Do you want to tell me what's going on?"

"Faye," Henry says in a soft, sinister voice, "I will do whatever I want."

My blood betrays me, moving in all the wrong directions. It should be draining, running cold, not surging in the places it is surging, warm as the sun on my skin. It is too much to look at Henry, and so I concentrate on the imperfections in the wooden floorboards that people pay a lot of money for back in LA—it's called hand-scratched, and I'm the dummy who paid for someone to brutalize shiny new floorboards by hand—wishing for this moment to end but knowing that when it does, I will return to it forever.

"Don't look like that."

"Like what?"

"Like you're scared."

I raise my eyes to his. "I am scared."

Henry's astounding face shows all his years of unforgiveness. "Maybe now you are."

I blink slowly, thinking I might understand. "So you know, I was never afraid of you that day in the car. I was afraid of missing my flight and not making my interview. The episode was about ambition, but people interpreted it the way they wanted to interpret it."

"And you let them."

"I'll take responsibility for that, yes."

"How very noble of you," Henry says, each word clipped and clean.

Anger churns in my chest. Anger feels so much better than fear. Fear is something I like to experience when I know I am safe, and I don't know what the hell I am at this moment. "I was angry and I had a right to be. You wanted me to miss my flight. You did not want me going to LA. You did not want to lose your hold over me. And you know what, Henry? PT was the one who told me to write about it."

Henry studies me, his pupils that unusually dark blue and the whites of his eyes veined red, like he's been crying, or trying not to. "I disabled your facial ID and changed your passcode."

It takes me a moment to register that we've moved on. Henry must know I'm right, that there is nothing he can say to defend himself. I stare at the dead face of my phone, dejected.

"You should really have some more discretion when it comes to saving your famous friends' names. I mean, the full name, Faye. What, do you just go around hoping people see your phone light up with messages from Oscar-winning pedophiles so everyone is aware of how important you are?"

"Spoken like a card-carrying member of whatever backwoods society you were born into."

Henry raises his hand and I cower, though he's only reaching for my phone, not winding up to backhand me. There is the smallest sliver of disappointment on my face, and Henry raises his eyebrows and then bunches them together in a broad performance of pity. "I have no interest in smacking you around anymore, though you may want to see someone about yours." He picks up my phone and punches in my new passcode. "I've changed the passwords to all your social media accounts. I'd hate to see you post about the wrong side of it."

"The wrong side of what?"

"The war, the election, Taylor Swift."

I laugh, suddenly elated. "Henry, I've made it abundantly clear where I stand on those issues. It's part of the job of appeasing the public, and I'm very good at appeasement, as you well know. If I suddenly go full Karen instead of my usual carousel of vanilla press photos thanking my hair and makeup teams, you're going to draw attention to me in a way you can't even begin to comprehend. It will be a shitstorm. My husband, my representation, will be all over me, demanding an explanation, crafting a crisis response. And when I don't answer them, they are going to realize something is wrong."

Henry regards me with supreme boredom. "Do you think your *representation* will be so keen to help when they learn you are thinking of leaving them for their direct competition?"

A cold tremor pulses through me. Henry has found the conversation between me and the agent who is trying to poach me. *I enjoyed our meeting*, she wrote to me, just a few days ago, and I have yet to respond. Agents are always trying to poach. But you should never engage unless you are prepared for it to make its way back to your current representation, for them to drop you before you drop them. A few weeks ago, I not only engaged—I met my rival recruiter for lunch in her sun-drenched living room in the flats of Beverly Hills.

"Faye," Henry sighs contentedly, like a lucky man who wants for nothing. "I've gone through every last one of your conversations while you slumbered your roofie slumber. You told everyone to leave you alone this week. You canceled all your meetings. You have an out of office set until May. Your husband is in London in another time zone, and honestly? Not that many people are checking on you, sweetheart." *Sweetheart.* I feel like I've been tased between my legs. "I know because I've been going to shore in the morning to keep up with your correspondence. My thumbs have barely moved a muscle, I'm afraid. Though I'm sure that's by design. You always were a bit of a lone wolf."

I used to ask Henry to humiliate me in all sorts of ways that at the time felt arbitrary. But now I know they were not. I wanted him to tell me things I did not necessarily believe about myself. That I was a whore, a piece of white trash, that I looked better with a cock in my mouth than without. Never in a million years would I ask him to remind me of the first birthday party I had for myself in Los Angeles. My husband, who was still my boyfriend at the time, had looked at the guest list and mentioned that I seemed to have only invited his friends. *Don't you want to invite any of your own?* he had asked, innocently enough. I pointed out that my best friend was on the list, to which he pointed out that she was my agent and I should be careful about conflating the two. I had been in Los Angeles enough years by then that I did not have the excuse of saying that I had just moved there and was still in the process of finding my people. I don't remember what I mumbled in response, but I do remember feeling like I had been slashed across the throat. Slowly, I bring my hand to my neck and squeeze, hold my head in place. It is my oldest wound that Henry has unstitched at the seams.

"What do you want?" I say, feebly. "What the fuck *is* all this, Henry?"

"I want you to understand the consequences."

There is a sudden tightness to the air, the pressurized feeling before a storm. It's that word. *Consequences.* Christ. My body aches. "The consequences to what?"

"Not doing what I tell you to do." Henry has a way of saying things like this, with an offhand ease that belies the sting of his certain follow-through. He may sound unserious, but he means what he says. You will be sorry. You will be scared. But you will also feel elated. There is no word for this feeling, but you will miss it, mourn it, stress-dream about it when it's gone.

Henry revives my phone with a pat of his finger. "This is an Instagram post that I have scheduled to release on your account later today." He begins to read. There is no context. No point. It is just a curated collection of catty things I've said in private conversations over the years, about friends to other friends, about executives to writers, about writers to executives, about actors to writers, about writers to other writers. It is no worse than what any of these people have undoubtedly said about me, but it is bad, and even if I get out of here and explain I've been drugged, kidnapped, starved, forced to wash my hair with Pert Plus, I will be ruined.

"So this is about revenge," I deduce. Ascribing a motive

feels good. It calms me. My brain is doing the thing it does when I miss even one day of my medication, bouncing around my skull like a rubber ball. Dizzying me, dulling me. "I broke your heart. I wrote about you and got famous. And you've been lying in wait all this time, and finally you got the chance to grab me by the balls."

"Some mouth on you," Henry says, tsking. He goes over to the bookshelf outside his parents' bedroom. From the middle shelf, he removes a Scott Turow novel, revealing a safe I'd forgotten was there. He slides my phone inside. "This is going in here, for now. Don't be a hero, Faye. If you stab me in the neck with a fork and I bleed out and die, yeah, sure, you might get away if you remember how to drive the boat, or if you want to risk your life in the woods—there's high black bear activity at the moment—but that thing will post, and I imagine you will lose everything." He slams the door to the safe and covers the keypad with one hand while he enters the code with the other. "Now." He turns to me, slides a hand through his sandy hair in a boyish manner that inflames me painfully. "If you listen to me, if you behave, I will open the safe at the same time every day and delay it another twenty-four hours. And we will continue like that until we are done here."

"Done with *what*?"

"This conversation is over now," Henry informs me. "You need to eat." He goes over to the kitchen counter and begins to crack eggs into a silver mixing bowl. Using something he thinks is healthy but is probably full of GMOs, he sprays a pan and waits for it to heat while he whisks the eggs with a fork. In the sink is a bowl of frozen berries, thawing in lukewarm water. No bread. No butter. Henry has kept himself lean, something I know takes womanly effort for him, and he has obviously retained those early aughts ideas about what makes a person fat. He brings me my breakfast on a silicone kid's plate, the kind that sticks to the tabletop, and as much as I want to throw it in his face, it's really stuck on there and I am ravenous. I finish everything and Henry goes back into the kitchen and makes me more, and when I finish that, he tells me to go sit on the couch.

"Why?"

"Because I know the code to the safe and you don't."

I go over and sit down on the couch. Henry perches on the edge of the coffee table, across from me, and though the table is lower than the couch, I still have to tilt my chin up to meet his eye. "Hold out your hands."

Instinctively, I curl my fingers into fists and hold them tightly to my chest.

"I'm not going to hurt you."

"Why stop now?"

Henry stares at me with heavy brows, liquid eyes. He speaks to me in an impossibly kind voice. "I always hated hurting you."

My throat is gnarled with something like grief. "Then you've lost your edge."

Henry looks away from me a moment, shakes his head slightly. When he turns back to me, he's wiped clean of any unnecessary nostalgia. "Hands, Faye."

One at a time, I float my hands, palms down, fingers

soft, like a dancer. It only looks like I'm shaking because there is so much tension from my elbows, pressed tightly into my sides.

"What's this?"

I turn my right wrist over in confusion. "A bracelet?"

"What kind?"

I look at him like he's given me no time to solve a riddle. "Gold? A gold bracelet?"

"Who makes it, Faye?"

I narrow my eyes at him and speak in a haughty tone. "Cartier."

"Who got it for you?"

"I did," I say defiantly. "It was a birthday present to myself." I made the appointment for one at the flagship store on Rodeo Drive. I wanted something weird-shaped and borderline ugly, something that didn't look like what anyone else had. *You are the first person to ever purchase this bracelet from this store*, said the sales associate with unmissable approval as he presented me with the red leather billfold that contained my authentication documents.

"You got it for yourself, did you?" Henry isn't smiling, but I can tell he finds this hysterical. "It looks like something you might try to hurt me with, so take it off."

I hold his eye bitterly as I flick open the clasp, wiggle my wrist free, and place the very thing I was considering hurting him with into his open hand.

"Put your hair behind your ears," he says.

"Fuck you." But I do what he tells me. "They're not anything you've ever heard of," I taunt through my smashed lips. He's got my chin in his hand, and he's crushing my cheeks together, forcing my face down and to the side.

In a hick voice, "'Cause we go to Jared round these parts, right?"

"Because you're the cheapest snob I've ever met," I sneer.

"It's called class. Take them out before I rip them through your fucking earlobes." Off come the invertebrate-like gold climbers, the blackened diamond studs in the second hole I got in the ninth grade, along with a month of silent treatment from my mother.

Henry uses both hands to split wide the lapels of the old Patagonia pullover he's given me. He stares at the skin on my chest longer than he should. *You are the softest thing I've ever touched*, he once told me. Later, when I went in for a liposuction consult, I would learn I had hypermobility. The doctor asking me if anyone had ever commented on how soft my skin is, because it's one of the symptoms, and I would flash crimson, thinking of where Henry's fingers were when he said that.

Henry pinches the gold-and-diamond locket at my clavicle.

"I have a picture of my grandmother inside," I say. Then, rather pathetically, "Please. How am I going to hurt you with a locket?"

Henry slips his fingers under the heavy rolo chain off which the locket dangles. "Maybe I just don't like looking at you wearing all this."

"Because it reminds you that I don't need you?" I retort. There is fiery friction at the nape of my neck, a final-sounding snap. I feel the chain slither between my breasts and land in my lap. Henry pockets the locket. I lift a knee and aim for his balls, but I freeze, thinking about my phone in the safe. Henry gives me a diabolical smile. "I admire your restraint," he says. He takes my stilled, airborne foot in his hand. I feel his fingers on my ankle like hot poker sticks.

"We used to have some good times," he says, twisting my ankle so that instinctively I curl up on my side, trying to follow the angle to mitigate the damage to my ligaments. I am in the fetal position, whimpering like a cornered animal. "Remember? I could get you to do anything. Never a sparkly thing you wouldn't bend over for."

"I assume," I say in a mocking, strained voice, because my ankle is radiating with pain, "you are referring to that mall-rat heart necklace from Tiffany. But, Henry? You should know you could never afford me now." At that, Henry's face goes purple with rage. He grabs me by my wrists and pulls me up from the couch. We are struggling, touching, breathing hotly on each other. I want him to restrain me, *subdue* me. I want him to do things to me that will split me in two. What is this? What *is* this?

"You're going to get yourself killed, Faye," Henry spits at me, and then he tries to drag me back to the cabin, but my ankle, the one he twisted, buckles. I stumble forward, and Henry hooks an arm around my waist, pulling me into him in an unintended embrace, embarrassing for both of us. He bends at the knees to gather me up, and for a moment, his face buries in the crook of my neck, and I feel the warm muzzle of his mouth. He carries me into the cabin and tosses me on the bed like he used to, only, in this new lifetime, he doesn't grab my ankles and yank me toward him. I don't wrap my legs around him and raise my hips to meet his, our faces sick with need. In this lifetime, Henry leaves me untouched in a flash flood of my own blood and locks the door behind him.

# Chapter 10

Henry and I were together for two and a half years, from the night I sat on his hand until the summer following our college graduation. I don't remember at what point we conceived our perverse layaway plan, but I'm sure I could narrow the time frame by digging through my archived Facebook albums and finding the first appearance of the silver heart necklace from Tiffany.

I had started using Henry's laptop for all my writing assignments. It was not a decade-old Dell and therefore compatible with the Final Draft screenwriting software I'd purchased in a vain attempt to impress Jonathan Granger. And on Henry's laptop I developed a bad habit that continues to plague me to this day, which entails losing long hours to finding the perfect free porn clip when I do not know where to go next with the story I am trying to write.

The name of the site I like to visit has changed over the years, but it's essentially a massive search engine for all kinds of porn and every porn-hosting site. I cannot recall how I stumbled upon it, but I imagine it was by typing something like *girls getting spanked*, because that's what

I thought I was into. And I am, but in a very particular way, and some of what I found led me to other things I realized I might like too.

Over time, Henry started doing to me the things the men were doing to the women on his computer screen. I realized he was going into his history after I returned his laptop and watching what I had watched, and this was how he knew that I liked to be folded over his lap and that while his hand was fine, his belt was better, and also that he was not just allowed to hit me anywhere, but encouraged. Then one day I stumbled onto this series between a husband and wife that documented her pursuit of a designer handbag. He would have her clean the kitchen floors on her hands and knees using a toothbrush and not wearing underwear. He'd fuck her in church clothes before they went to mass on Sunday so that he knew she was leaking next to him while she recited the words to Our Father. And then, for the grand finale, he bought her the bag and had her unwrap it with his cock in her ass. Pure *cinema*, I tell you.

I showed Henry one clip and he grabbed me by my ponytail, bent me over, and took me from behind. We watched the rest as our bodies slid and slapped together and our throats made strange, nearly soundless sounds. After, we lay in bed and devised the rules to our game. Henry would buy me anything I wanted but not that hideous bag. Why was it hideous? I wanted to know. I listened, propped up on one elbow, while he outlined the contours of his fascinating and foreign world. There were appropriate things to spend money on, respectable even. Travel, leisure, and real estate. Clothes should be worn to death and food unfussy—full of chemicals designed to keep you thin, I'd soon discover while rifling through his parents' cabinets for a midnight snack. Jewelry appreciated, so that was fine too, but it should be kept relatively simple. Designer purses, even the unassuming ones but especially the ones with the labels smeared all over like dog feces, signaled the carrier was of the lowest form of human intelligence.

Though I had always admired those bags from afar, none of this I took personally. I was intrigued by the way other people thought, the way they behaved, their beliefs and their prejudices. I have always been more curious than contemptuous, and later, when I was approached about acting, when I said, *But I don't know how to act*, I was told that it was my curiosity about the human condition that mattered more than technique.

A couple of girls on campus had those Tiffany heart necklaces, and they were pretty and inexpensive compared to the pearls Corrine wore and even that so-called hideous bag, which somehow retailed for over two thousand dollars at the time. It was less about the price of the object and more about the financial imbalance between Henry and me, anyway. In how many ways can I say I was a scholarship kid while Henry knew how to sail, shuck oysters, to not wear your sunglasses on your head because it would weaken the hinges and, just as important, never place them face down on the table, because that's how the lenses end up scratched. Henry had nice things and he knew how to take care of them, and I liked the idea of being another one of his nice things. I wanted to be objectified and infantilized. This was the crux of what I was into, I realized with Henry. And Henry was excellent at coming up with ways to manufacture my helplessness.

He bought me that Tiffany necklace, but I never got the chance to wear it. He showed it to me, in the little blue bag and everything, and I was supposed to earn it outright before we broke up. I might think he brought me here to collect if I had not heard what he said right before he locked the door behind him.

*I'm trying to save your stupid fucking life.*

# Chapter 11

That's what Henry muttered to himself, from behind the door, after he stripped me of everything that identified me as an ostentatious twat living east of the 405 in Los Angeles.

*I'm trying to save your stupid fucking life.*

Has Henry undergone a religious conversion? Is he participating in some sort of twelve-step program for whatever it is we used to engage in? We weren't even that hardcore. It wasn't like we had leather masks and ball gags and electromagnetic wands and safe words and consent. No. Ew. Would you look at us? We didn't need all the bells and whistles.

There is a flash in my peripheral vision, and I sit up to see Henry has left the main house, that he's walking down the dock and freeing the side of the boat from the spring line. He hops in, twists open the ventilation cap, and submerges the motor. Yes, I remember this now. I watch him closely as he loops the lanyard attached to the kill switch over his wrist, squeezes the primer bulb to get gas into the motor, and shifts the gearshift into neutral.

He drifts through the water with the choke on, then starts the ignition. He is wearing a salt-stained denim hat and a fleece vest over a light-gray crewneck sweatshirt, and I know his huge dick is snug against his leg. I would still let him annihilate me if he tried, like a feminist fucking scab.

I limp around the room and study the walls, the places where all the fish paintings have been removed so that I cannot take out Henry's eye with the corner of a frame. I'm checking to see if I can find an impression of a cross somewhere. His wife has that Catholic look about her. Maybe she got to him.

I brush my hair again for something to do. I hit a bad tangle and I'm working at it, gingerly, when the little plastic bristles separate from the brush pad and go tinkling all over the bathroom floor. I roar in a way that matches my angry sea monster hair.

Henry leaves me overnight, with no water and no food. I can handle hunger, and toxic diet culture is, by nature, toxic, an absorption of nasty chemical solvents with chronic effects, so I can find the upside to the hollowness between my hip bones. But I really start to panic when I turn the bathroom faucet on and manage only a mouthful before the stream slows to a drip. Henry turned the water off. He turned the fucking water off.

It rains that night, in a nice, soothing way, the branches of the trees caressing the windowpanes, a steady pattering on the gable roof. I am certain Henry has left me to die, that if he really wanted to punish me, this is exactly how he'd do it. Anything else would feel too passionate.

Thumbs in the soft tissues of my neck, a knife splitting my flesh. He wouldn't give me the satisfaction of liking it a little.

I am approaching twenty-four hours without water. My ankle is throbbing with hammy effect, and my head is on a wild ride through the failures of titration. I am heartened to find that the most comfortable position is the one I favor anyway: lying flat on my stomach, head turned to the side, leg pulled up along my torso. It's called the crab position, and my husband has used it to justify his behavior. *You sleep all pointy*, he says, *like you don't even want me to touch you.*

I have a tortured, broken sleep, and when the door opens in the morning, Henry on the other side holding a liter of Smartwater, I openly sob. He comes over and stands above me, the water bottle perspiring lavishly, and I already know before I reach for it that he will jerk it away.

"Beg," he says.

"Please," I beg.

"You know what I mean."

"Henry, *please—*"

He turns to go.

"Okay!" I shout. I peel back the covers, scooch to the edge. I flatten my palms on the bed, push myself to a flamingo's stand. From here, I have to think about it a moment. My ankle is swollen and unstable. I grip the quilt behind me, lower myself into a deep, left-legged lunge until I am on one knee, then the other. Tentatively, I look up at him. He's waiting with affected nonchalance, a few steps over by the door.

I crawl on all fours, fitting my hands and kneecaps into all my old grooves in the red plaid carpet, feeling and seeing and hearing everything in Technicolor. The way Henry holds his chin high, watching me with lowered eyes until I arrive at his feet, his face glassed over with imperial claim. The cushion of the carpet beneath my knees, the little involuntary muscle twitches of Henry's long toes, the rooted heaviness of his calves and thighs. I am thinking about the story of Mary Magdalene washing Jesus's feet with her hair. I went to Catholic grade school, and when we got to this story in the Bible, I had to excuse myself to the restroom, where I silently masturbated. I assumed all the girls in my class found the imagery erotic, the way we all agreed Justin Timberlake was the hot one. But I was socially ostracized after admitting to it at a sleepover. Since the fifth grade, I've known I was different enough to start masking who I was. It was only ever in these moments, bowing before Henry, that I knew I found my congregation, my faith.

I rise up on my knees, wrap my arms around him, press my cheek to his thighs. "Please, Henry." I make myself cry for a little bit, until he feels my tears on his skin, through his jeans.

"Look at me," he says, oh so gently.

I lift my chin until my neck is exposed, open my mouth. Henry unscrews the cap, traces my dry mouth with the wet mouth of the bottle. I lick my lips, whimper.

"What do I get for this?"

My pulse is pounding between my legs. What. *Is*. This. "Anything you want."

Henry is looking down at me with a warm and doting expression. He has crow's-feet now, freckles in the same pattern over the bridge of his nose. When I knew him, he looked like a rich kid you wanted to punch in the mouth. If he came to LA, if he left the boat shoes behind, twenty-five-year-old Instagram models with big shiny lips would throw themselves at him. I might not stand a chance.

He says, "I want you to have dinner with me and be normal. Drink wine. Talk to me."

I nod desperately. "Yes. Okay. I'd like that."

"Don't fucking do that either." *That*, patronize him.

I sit back on my heels and admit, "I think about this room more than I should."

Henry holds my eye a long moment, finds me sincere, though he has no idea how much. He nods. Okay. He motions—chin up again. Then he tips water into my mouth, a capful at a time, until the bottle is empty.

He brings me clean clothes—a worn linen button-down, a six-pack of underwear, a cozy old fleece zip-up. I get moisturizer too, lip balm, Kiehl's shampoo and conditioner, which I just know he believes is the height of nouveau riche luxury, plus a hair tie. He has always liked me with my hair up.

He comes to let me out around six, and I follow him across the stone path. He holds open the door to the main house like it is a restaurant and we are there to celebrate our wedding anniversary.

A bottle of red wine breathes in a glass decanter on the kitchen counter, next to a pair of raw steaks, seasoned with salt, pepper, and fresh rosemary. I rarely eat red meat, and when I was with Henry, I was a dedicated vegetarian.

"You need iron, Faye," he says, offering me a glass of wine. "You're so pale I barely recognized you."

"I stopped going into the sun a long time ago."

He has cut up some cheese and fruit to snack on while he cooks, and I make a gouda and apple sandwich.

"You look so pretty with a tan." He turns on the gas dial, strikes a match.

"I wouldn't look pretty at all if I still lay out."

"You look incredible," he says sadly, his back to me.

"Oh," I say, uncomfortable by his easy display of sincerity. "Thank you."

Henry uses tongs to transfer the fillets into the old copper pan, and we listen to the popping and hissing, inhale the scent of fat and char. I am hungry enough to be hungry for steak.

"Last night," he says, checking the minute hand on his grandfather's military trench watch, "a tree came down on a power line and the road was closed while they removed it. I wasn't punishing you."

"You turned the water off," I remind him.

"I had to repair something and I guess I forgot to turn it back on. It wasn't intentional, and nothing went out online that would put you at risk. I was actually worried about you, out here all alone. Especially since"—he brings his watch under his nose, watches it tick—"well, never mind." He flips the steaks.

"Especially since what?"

"You're afraid of everything."

"There's a pill for that. It's called Lexapro. If you're so worried about me, you can let me have my medication."

"I know all about Lexapro," Henry says curtly.

I stare at him, wondering if I heard him right. "You do?"

Henry lifts a corner of the steak with the tongs, checking the color at the edges. "Go sit down. Dinner will be ready soon."

I make my way over to the table, double-checking that the brass hook next to the side door is still the place Henry hangs the boat keys.

Henry tents the steaks with tinfoil. He sweeps a bunch of broccolini into the same pan, tosses it in the fat and the oil, adds a squeeze of lemon. I realize I am forgetting to drink, and I take two large gulps, so that when Henry comes over it will have looked like I am relaxing and enjoying myself.

Henry cuts up our steak and vegetables on the counter, then carries over our plates. I'm allowed an adult fork. "I cooked them a minute longer than I usually would," he says as he sits down across from me. "Bloody might be a little too much to ask of you."

"Never," I tell him, and our eyes catch. Weapons down. We are us again.

"How much closer are we?" I ask him. "To being done here."

He turns his eyes down. Spears a bite of steak. "Let's not talk about all that."

"What do you want to talk about, then?"

Henry reaches into his pocket. For a moment I'm rigid with terror. I have something in the pocket of my fleece that I should not have, and I think maybe I dropped it and that's what he has found. But then he removes his hand and drops two white pills on the table.

"I don't know how much you take," he says.

I swallow one pill and tear the other in half with my front teeth. "Fifteen."

Henry nods. "I just went up to twenty."

It's like when a hissy house cat comes and sits in your lap. You are afraid to move, to breathe wrong, to do anything that might make it change its mind about choosing you. I adjust my tone accordingly. This is fascinating, that we are speaking about this, like this, and I want to know more about when Henry realized he needed Lexapro and what happened that made him increase his dosage, but I do not want to scare him off either. "I go up to twenty sometimes. Usually when I have a bunch of press to do."

Henry sets down his fork. His hair looks blonder than usual, artfully tossed without any effort, and his cheeks are dewy and flushed from the wine. Lovely, a repugnant word, but he looks lovely. "I really did think I was dying that day, Faye." He is speaking about the day we broke up. The air in my lungs feels sharp and cold. I have the sudden urge to hold him, which disgusts me.

"You were having a panic attack," I say.

"I never would have thought to put those words to it. I know that must sound idiotic to you."

I lean forward and I nearly put my hand on his. "It doesn't, actually. I didn't know that was happening to me either. I just thought, this is normal. Everyone feels like this at times."

"When did you realize not everyone does?"

"You're not going to like this," I warn him.

"I'll live."

I fold my hands on the table primly. Take a beat to figure out how I want to say this. "It was after the episode came out. And it got so much attention. And I was asked to speak about it ad fucking nauseum. There were so many stars on that show but *that* was what made me pop. That episode and the fact that I wrote it became this, like, feminist battle cry that I resented to my core. Talking about coercive control in relationships, and the inference was that I had written it so realistically that of course I must have had some experience with that sort of thing when really, what we had, it was what *I* wanted. And it felt horrible, like I was pretending to be a victim. I felt like the loneliest person on the planet and, really, that there must be something wrong with me for wanting the things I did."

Henry looks at me in a calm and exacting way. "You're far from the only woman who likes that."

I hide my face in my hands. "Oh my God. Kidnap me, starve me, ruin my hair with silicone shampoo, but please don't talk to me about your sex life with your wife." I peek between my fingers, make sure he's not planning on elaborating, then realize something else. "Where does she think you are while you're sitting here eating steak with me?"

"It's her week with the kids." Henry picks up his fork, the pin to the grenade, and resumes eating as though the shock wave he has set off is not still reverberating through the room.

I drop my hands from my face. "You're *divorced*?"

"We're in the process."

*I just went up to twenty*, he said, mere moments ago. "Henry," I say, and I do not need to play my shock. I find it abundantly shocking every time I am reminded I lack the gumption of half the citizens of this country, or whatever the divorce rate is now. "What happened?"

"What happened with yours?" He is looking at my ring finger. Though he took all my jewelry, there wasn't anything on that hand to take. "I've gathered enough from your conversations there is an issue there, though you don't expressly say why to anyone. Does he cheat?"

I force myself to maintain our chatty, civilized tone. "Oh God." I busy myself cutting a piece of my steak. "It's much worse than that."

Henry's eyebrows lift slightly in amusement. He thinks this is hyperbole, I can tell. "I'll get it out of you. Give me time."

"How much time? How long are we going to stay here?"

"Until I tire of you and drown you in the lake."

"Okay, so forever," I quip.

"Let's see what you look like when your Botox wears off." He notices I have cut the perimeter around my steak and left the rare parts. "Can I?" He lifts his fork. I nod. He reaches across the table and his elbow catches in the mouth of the decanter. It toddles, off-balance, and I swear this inanimate object is momentarily imbued with free will, because just when I think it will right itself it decides to spill spectacularly, all over my lap. I leap up from the table, dripping red like a gutted fish.

"Shit," Henry says. And he goes over and grabs a dishrag and hands it to me. I dab and dab at the lap of my borrowed fleece, but soon the dish towel is soaked and I'm still dripping all over the carpet. "Take that off," Henry says. "I'll get you another one."

"It's fine," I say. "It's not that bad."

Henry stares at me with his brow furrowed. "You cannot be comfortable like that."

"It will dry."

"And stain," he says. "It needs to be soaked."

"Okay," I relent. "Just let me go to the bathroom quickly."

Henry reaches for my upper arm as I try to walk past. I collected the bristles from the cheap hairbrush and stuffed them into my pocket so I could put them in Henry's food and watch him choke and claw at his throat in bulge-eyed terror, and when he discovers this, I do not know what he will do to me and so I do not hesitate. I grab the decanter by the neck and swing its fat lower body at Henry's head. Henry stumbles back, landing in a seething sprawl and taking two of the dining room chairs with him.

I grab the boat keys off the brass hook and fly out the door. I feel nothing—not the shiv of the night air nor the delayed scream of my ankle. I clear the steps to the dock, stumble for the far pipe cap, and unravel the spring lines. I dive into the boat, running a mental checklist from the other day: *Ventilation cap—open. Get the motor in the water.* I don't have time to worry about the kill switch. I push away from the dock as Henry comes hammering down it, his light hair soaked dark with Cabernet. He dives gracefully into the cold water and surfaces, reaches the boat's ladder in a few strokes.

"Help!" I am screaming, the word catapulting against the slate walls of the mountains, coming right back to me in a diminished, mocking echo. I am turning the ignition pointlessly. I forgot the primer bulb. There is no gas in the motor. The boat rocks forward as Henry hauls himself onboard, the weight of the water pulling his clothes tight to his furious, panting form.

"I'm sorry!" I scream. "I'm sorry! Henry, don't! I'm sorry!" He stalks toward me in slow-motion horror and grabs me by my ponytail, drags me to the swim step ladder. I have the good sense to suck in one last breath before he buries my head underwater. It is quiet in Lake Wanika, clear and bracing cold. I count. I can hold my breath for a long time. I discovered this special skill with Henry.

Nineteen seconds. I'm usually good for longer than that, but I've never been in water this cold or this panicked. I suck in a breath and scream for help again. Henry shoves me back under, my entire torso this time. It no longer feels cold anymore, and that's how I know I am in trouble. A slinky kind of sleep is calling for me. Sleep has a woman's voice, a voice I recognize but cannot immediately place.

"Faye?" she is calling. "Faye? Are you okay?"

# Chapter 12

I do not remember returning to the cabin, but suddenly I am swaddled in a towel on the carpet where earlier I crawled on all fours. Beneath this towel I am not wearing any clothes. Henry lights a roll of newspaper with a match and waves it around the interior of the fireplace like a torch, a search-party signal to the little lost people who took a wrong turn into the chimney. He lights another match and tucks it under the pile of wood. I expect an explosive whoosh, writhing orange peaks, but a single low flame struggles to convince others to join.

Henry sits back beside me. He is still wearing his wet clothes. “Who else is here?” I ask him in a whisper.

“It’s only us,” he answers in a stunned voice, like he can’t believe everything that just happened happened.

“I heard someone saying my name.”

“You lost consciousness. I . . . I did not mean to hold you under that long. I thought you were dead.” Henry begins to shiver violently. He gets up and leaves me for a while. When he comes back, he’s wearing dry clothes and he offers me some too. He turns away while I put them on, though he must have been the one to undress me, and then he helps me into bed and puts a pillow under my bad ankle before tucking me in. But even with the fire and the flannel sheets, I cannot get warm. My fingers and toes are ice and my teeth won't stop chattering. Henry stares at me, shaking so hard the headboard batters the wall, and then tells me this is to prevent shock. He gets under the covers with me. He reaches for me like he used to. We find our fit—my face jigsawed into his collarbone, his hands sprawled in the small of my back, holding our centers together until the birdsong starts in the dark.

# Chapter 13

The morning is cold, colder than the lake. Henry taught me that's why steam rises off the surface of the water; in retrospect, it makes me sound like an idiot that anyone had to tell me this. Of course that's why steam rises off the water. Joan Didion isn't the only one who was ever so young.

Henry has been gone since dawn. I have showered. I have paced. I have replayed the disembodied voice I heard calling out to me last night. Near-death hallucination or is someone else here? The idea that I could have been that close to death sickens me, but so does the possibility that we are not alone, Henry and I. After a while I curl up into the fetal position in a state of pure and uncut terror, wondering what the consequences will be for my failed one-woman mutiny.

I hear the turn of the key, and when the door opens, I am on my feet, facing Henry resolutely. Henry stands there, the size of the fucking door, my phone in the palm of his hand. Nausea slams into me like a two-ton truck. I'd rather he was holding a gun.

With a long index finger, Henry scrolls, stops, begins to read a message he has composed in my voice.

"Hi, Caroline," he begins. Caroline is the name of the agent who is trying to poach me. My spine curls inward, my stomach burbles. I'm going to be sick. Breathe. *Breathe*, Faye. "I wanted to tell you that while I enjoyed our meeting too, I've decided to stay put. My team has done right by me all these years, and no doubt you are amazing at what you do, but your taste skews a little too commercial for the aspirations I have for myself."

Fuck breathing. Fuck just about everything. For a certain kind of literary agent, which Caroline Hasser most certainly is, there is no greater insult than the word *commercial*. And the way Henry has phrased it—taste *skews*—is the way I speak. It is the way everyone I speak to speaks. Henry Spalding has combed through my messages and delivered a damn-near-flawless performance of Faye Heron. This is not a message but a missive. It will sound the death knell of any sort of future relationship with Caroline. It all but ensures that if I do file for divorce, if I do find myself a persona non grata at the agency that has done more than right by me over the years, has *made* me, really, my options will be severely limited. Caroline is the head of the literary department at the only other big agency out there. I know writers and other creators who do not believe they need the backing of the big ones to make it in the industry, and maybe *they* don't, but I am someone who needs to have the machine behind her. I crave conventional structure in every aspect of my life but the creative one. I need to feel insulated by fast-talking people in pinstripes, cocooned, so that I can set to work spinning all my strange larvae silk.

What's worse—what's actually brilliant—Caroline will read this message and think, *Fuck you, Faye.* It will not elicit phone calls and messages to check on me and make sure I haven't been hacked, lost my mind, been *kidnapped*, the way Henry's scheduled Instagram rant would have. Caroline likely won't even write me back, and there is no one for her to alert. Of course my husband doesn't know I've met with her. Caroline is part of the exit plan I've been quietly assembling while I come to terms with the fact that my marriage is unsalvageable. This is a clean, traceless hit.

"If you send that," I say to Henry in a quiet, pleading way, because I've decided that appealing to the part of him that needs to feel needed by me is the only way out of this, "I'll be trapped."

Henry leans against the walls of my confines with a cavalier arch of an eyebrow. His point is not lost on me.

"This is a stay at the Four Seasons in comparison to what I'm dealing with at home."

Henry puts a hand to his hair, rumples it handsomely, while he considers my plea. "From what I've pieced together, your friend—who is also your agent?—seems to think that if you leave him, you'll have to dissolve your production company, and it could get ugly. I don't doubt it will—divorce is a nasty business—but I don't quite understand why your agency would choose him over you."

"Because his brother is a big shot at the firm."

"Aren't you?"

"I'm Hollywood middle class compared to him."

"Faye," Henry all but purrs, "how modest of you."

I am reminded of that stick of dynamite between my legs. It's the snooty voice, the loose way Henry is leaning against the wall. It's the undeniable reality that he could wreck me with his right thumb. "Okay," I say in the smallest voice I own, hoping it will appease him.

Henry sniffs, his distaste apparent that I would fold so easily. "Okay?"

"Okay," I repeat, stronger, "I'll do what you want." Yes, when it comes to doing the thing I like doing, the thing I'm good at, the thing that earned me entreé into Henry's tax bracket and invites admiration and respect, I will fold easily to protect that. Why does Henry want me to act as though liking what I do and wanting others to like it too is some sort of deeply immoral character flaw?

"You don't even know what I want," Henry says.

"We spent the night together," I remind him. "I felt what you wanted."

"Biology, sweetheart." Henry gives me a small, pitying smile. My stomach twists. I wish I could say in anger.

"I always figured," Henry continues, a bit sorrowfully, "that what we had was like a rubber band. No matter how far it stretched, it would snap back the next time we were together again. But last night, Faye . . ." He sighs and real regret shows on his face. "I slept next to you and I felt for it and it was gone. Whatever has happened to you in the years since we last saw each other, it's made you, I don't know . . ." I know the word he's searching for before he says it. "Untouchable."

I recover, but not quickly enough. Henry catches my grief, and I can see he feels sorry for me.

"I have no desire to fuck you," he says gently, like he's trying to let me down easy. "What I do want is to get into your email. Due to a suspicious sign-in, you've been logged out. Tech support said it could take up to four days, and here we are, on the fourth day. I'm going to shore so I can write down the security questions you need to answer to be able to reset your password. Do that, and then you can go home."

I stare up at him, devastated, uncomprehending. "This is why I'm here?"

"Sorry to burst your bubble, but I have not been sitting around pining for you all these years."

"I heard you," I say. "Back at the hotel. I heard you say you'd been waiting for this for a long time. I don't know what the fuck you want with my email, but that doesn't line up with anything else you've said to me since we've been here." I hear myself, I sound winded and desperate, but I keep going. "It doesn't line up with the way you were with me last night."

"I've said a lot of things I don't mean the last few days," Henry says coolly.

I stare at him, burning with indignation. "Who was that, calling out for me on the water?"

Henry turns to go. "You passed out. It was a dream."

"I don't believe you," I say to his back. "I don't believe anything you're telling me."

Henry steps out the door. "I'll be leaving shortly. This will be over soon."

# Chapter 14

For the next hour, I sit on the bed with a sight line to the house and try in every way I can to make sense of my conversation with Henry. What does he want with my email? Does it have to do with money? Accessing my bank accounts? It's the only scenario I can make fit. If Henry needs money, he would never be able to say so outright, especially not to me.

And what about his reaction, when I asked him about the voice I heard last night? I could not tell if I had imagined it, but his blithe insistence that I did has convinced me of the opposite.

I'm just about to risk a trip to the bathroom when the door to the main house bangs open. Henry bypasses the stone pathway to the cabin and heads straight for the dock. I hurry to the front window to see him off like a girl in an old movie set during wartimes, hand to the glass, sorrow scoring my face. Henry wears a light-colored baseball hat that is darkening by the second, and I look to the lake and see that it's denting with a fast, light rain. Henry pats himself down, checking to make sure he has everything he needs to blow up my life in the pockets of his old waxed chore coat. There was a time he would drape that coat over my shoulders when I was not dressed warmly enough, but that time has long since passed.

I watch Henry untie the dock lines, toss them aside. He steps inside the boat and pushes off the dock. His wake wags like a tail as he motors away. Only then do I retract my hand from the window and stare in a state of giddy delirium. My palm is wet. Not condensation wet, but the kind that comes from a leak.

# Chapter 15

I don't know how I did it. There was a seal? Lining the window frame? It was a rubber or silicone substance. And that was where I found a crack. I scratched and scratched at it, and as I did I felt that the wood beneath was soft and rotted and eventually I got my fingernails in there, and that silicone-rubber-seal-like edge began to peel off in strips. There were still a couple screws holding the window frame in place, but unsealed they were loose enough that I could twist them free with my fingers. I dragged the dresser over to the window so that I could climb up and reach the ones at the top corners. The frame lifted off the wall as a whole piece, and I threw it to the ground, stomped on it until it splintered. Now I am holding one of the pieces like a fencing knife and poking at the panels of glass. They pop out and land on the wet earth outside. If they shatter, I don't hear. The trees are thrashing and the rain riddles the lake like bullets.

I get those men's slippers from the closet, layer on a matted fleece jacket. I climb on top of the dresser again and launch myself from the window, trying to clear any broken glass that may be beneath. I land on my hands and knees in slime and muck, twigs slicing my palms. I've bitten my tongue hard enough to taste copper, but I think, with gasping astonishment, that I've been capable all along. And this renews me.

I get to my feet, smear back the wet hair glued to my forehead, plunge headfirst into the cyclone of the woods. There, I stop. I look around and try to orient myself to find the trail. In the movies, when the captive character escapes, they take off running and they do not stop. But the trees act like an enclosure, shielding me from the sky's bludgeon and containing the noise of the storm to a manageable, thinkable din. That way. The trail is that way, and so is the clubhouse, where there is an office, I remember, with a landline and a desktop, and all of it works, at least in the summertime, when the staff returns for the season. Henry told me the members agreed to outfit the communal space with cable and internet after 9/11, when the possibility of the world ending seemed imminent. It was to be a compromise between the island's Thoreauvian origins and a new world order to have some sort of limited tether to the outside. Everything is powered down after Memorial Day, but they turn it back on for Thanksgiving weekend, and maybe it's not as hard to figure out as I might think. Maybe there is literally a switch that I can flip and the lights will pop on and I'll pick up the phone and hear the dull, invigorating note of a dial tone. Henry and I would occasionally walk to the clubhouse for breakfast, and I don't remember exactly how long it took us, but it wasn't arduous. I think I wore flip-flops. I set off, soaked and mud-crusted, but emboldened by Henry's sloppiness and my ability to outwit him.

Almost immediately I realize the slippers are hopeless. They were big before they were waterlogged and stretched out, and my toes are cramping from curling in their soles. I take them off but carry them with me for a bit, in case I change my mind about walking barefoot. The forest floor is knifed with twigs and jagged rocks, slick as ice with wet leaves. With each passing second the afternoon sky darkens, the trail gets harder to see, and I think about turning back. I think about sitting in that cabin and allowing Henry to find me and see what I've done. Begging for his forgiveness. I won't do it, but I keep imagining it, I keep it alive as a possibility the same way I cling to the slippers. I need to feel like I have options even when I do not. And this buoys me until I come upon the trailhead named after Harpo Marx. It's said he used to cake his body in mud and don a red wig and go screaming along the beaches to scare off lookie-loos who'd gotten word that a famous person was staying somewhere nearby, and under his namesake sign is a mile marker I could kiss on the mouth. Only a quarter of a mile to the clubhouse. I drop the slippers. I run like all the girls in all the movies that climax in pursuit. Because now I am picturing Henry approaching the dock and seeing the busted-out window, his strong, wide strides to the door. His fury, his shame, when he finds I escaped him again. What he will do to me when he realizes I cannot be kept.

*

I am out of breath, and I realize with a bolt of adrenaline that the path has taken on a subtle incline. The clubhouse is built on the highest point of the island, and as it thrusts into view, I have the jarring sensation that I am in two places at the same time. It's a craftsman style, I realize now, a style that celebrates natural elements and handcrafted details that is common all over Los Angeles, and for some reason in that moment I think, *Fuck you, Henry.* I know more about more things now. The woods thin, and I pass the old croquet court where Henry taught me to play and then I got so good he could never beat me.

The clubhouse is a narrow three-story stone structure with sliding barn doors, an iron hook lock on both sides. The inside lock is never latched in the summer, because employees come across the lake at all hours of the night ferrying provisions and groceries. *What's the point of locking it at all?* I once asked Henry. *Bears*, he answered, and I am glad I had forgotten about the bears while I was in the thickest parts of the woods. I cannot believe it when I release the hook on the outside and slide the door open without resistance.

It is dark outside but pitch-black inside. I wheel my arms protectively, feeling for the walls, trying to find my touchpoints. I nick my shin on a pile of heavy ceremonial stones that have been kept next to the door for decades, and then I freeze when something featherlight and many-legged scuttles across my feet. I feel my way to the bend in the hall, then the door to the office. I imagine lifting the phone to my ear, running my fingers over the keyboard of the desktop computer. Civilization, steamed milk in my coffee, forty-two-dollar shampoo—I am so close.

I find the doorknob and experience an almost electrical shock that culminates in a vision of someone on the other side, sitting behind the desk—*It's you, that actress-slash-writer-slash-director I was supposed to know but didn't until you went missing. We've been looking for you.* I cannot believe it when I stumble through the door and find that I am somewhat right.

"Jesus Christ," Campbell is saying as he comes over to me. "Jesus fucking Christ."

We stare at each other, staggered. The small room is partially lit by an open laptop on the desk, next to a rusted metal canister of pens and paper clips. Campbell is dressed sensibly, in hiking boots and jeans. The hood of his windbreaker clings to a hook on the wall. It's dry. I notice that right away because I am standing barefoot in a pool of my own sooty runoff. He's been here at least a couple of hours. It wasn't raining when I woke up.

"What are you doing here?" I gasp.

Campbell gapes at me a moment longer. "I was checking on PT's place. There was a problem with some of the drainage pipes before he died and with the storm—I mean, whatever. What the fuck, Faye? Are you okay? Why are you—"

I throw myself into his arms, babbling about Henry bringing me here, locking me inside the cabin, taunting me, torturing me. Campbell is holding me in one of those swaying hugs, alternating from foot to foot like we're dancing. When he releases me, I note, faintly, that our positions are now reversed. Campbell is the one with his back to the door and I am the one stuck on the inside.

"Did he say *why*?" Campbell asks.

I dig the heels of my hands into my eyes and shake my head. Something inside me screams at me to be evasive, and though I listen, it makes no sense. This is *Campbell.* One of my oldest and only real friends. "Revenge?" I guess. "For writing about him? Humiliating him?"

"Okay." Campbell exhales hard, hands on hips, looking around us like he is trying to come up with a game plan. Under normal circumstances, nothing could be more reassuring, but for some reason my teeth will not stop knocking together and I have to bite down hard to make them stop. "Okay," Campbell repeats. "Where is he now?"

"He went to shore. I got out through a window and ended up here." I go mute with anxiety as I realize that Henry will have to pass the clubhouse on his way back to his property. He will see Campbell's boat docked, he will pull over, investigate ... My tongue sticks to the roof of my mouth.

"We have to go," I say, sounding like I've got a wad of cotton balled up in my throat. "Before he comes back."

Campbell nods, but he stands there, unmoving and in the way. "Yeah," he agrees, the way people do when they're not really listening to you. "The backup battery should be charged soon. Then we can call someone."

"The backup battery?" I stare at Campbell's formerly white T-shirt, now stamped with my mucky silhouette. I must look like a wild thing, roughed up from the storm, and yet Campbell has not moved to offer me his dry windbreaker, or a towel from one of the linen closets. It would be musty and maybe even crawling with something, but it is at least a considerate gesture. And long ago I filed away Campbell as someone with pristine manners.

"The storm knocked out the main generator," he explains.

"But if there's no power, how are you charging a backup battery?" The moment the words are out of my mouth, I wish I could take them back. Campbell gives me a blank stare that renders him utterly unrecognizable to me. Though, that's not really true, is it? I saw something in him the morning I ran into him outside the chapel. Something different. Something black. I begin to shake, hard and uncontrollably.

"What's going on?" I whisper, like the answer is something we are trying to hide from the real bad guys.

Campbell does not speak. He holds out an arm and begins to herd me back behind the desk, and I'm performing an Olympian floor routine in my head to assign a reasonable explanation to all this. This is Campbell. *Campbell*, who installed the window unit in the bedroom of the small yellow house I lived in my senior year, Campbell who paid for things when I was broke and never made a big deal about it, Campbell who sent me flowers after I won my Emmy, Campbell who went on a coke rant about girls and their three-quarter-length-sleeve shirts and made us all howl, Campbell who once dumped a drink on a townie girl in a knockoff Juicy Couture sweatsuit, who cheated on Corrine with a freshman girl and then ostracized her so severely she transferred in the middle of the year, who is older now, and meaner around the eyes. Campbell, who is caging me into the farthest corner of the small office with his chest, which is broader than I remembered it being.

"Does Corrine know you're here?" I ask accusingly.

Campbell gives me a confused look, and for a moment, I imagine him saying she is already here. That it was Corrine who I heard calling out my name and asking if I was okay last night when Henry almost drowned me. But no, it could not be her. It's not like I know Corrine's voice so well after all these years, but I do know that she would not speak my name with concern. The voice I heard was worried for me.

I stammer an explanation for why I am asking about his wife. "I mean. If Henry comes back, and something happens. Corrine will call someone if you don't come home." I am saying this as a reminder to him, but as a reminder to him of what? That he can't hurt me? That's preposterous. Why would Campbell want to hurt me?

"Everyone knows I'm here," he says vaguely. He taps the keyboard. "Internet's working."

I see the home page of Google load, and I relax slightly. I reach for the landline, but Campbell puts his hand on top of mine, stopping me.

"Phone is DSL, and that's down," Campbell says. These are all words that mean nothing to me. In ways I am proud of and ways I am not, I am a stereotypical silly little girl who figured out enough to make it in this world and let everyone who wanted to take care of her when things got hard do just that. Campbell takes out his own phone and makes a show of thumbing the screen, tossing in an irritable sigh here and there meant to convey his frustration.

"Anything?"

"Fucking Verizon," he grumbles. He nods at the screen of the desktop. "If you want to check your email or anything until this loads, be my guest."

A small tremor begins at the base of my spine. I keep my voice steady. "I think let's just get out of here." I pause, give him a chance to agree. When he doesn't, I follow up uselessly, "Please, Campbell."

"Mmmm," Campbell murmurs noncommittally, eyes on the screen of his phone. There is the telltale vibrational chime of one text, then another. Slowly, Campbell puts his phone in his pocket, then lowers his eyes to mine. "You should check your email, Faye."

"Why?" I am scared and hungry, cold and exhausted, but my voice is laced with irritation. What the fuck does everyone want with my email?

Campbell groans with real irritation now. "Please, Faye, make my life fucking easy, for once."

That's hilarious, but I decide against reminding Campbell that he grew up in the wealthiest zip code in Connecticut with a silver spoon in every one of his orifices. "Maybe," I say, "if someone would tell me why my email matters so God damn much, I might be willing to help you out."

"So Henry did try to get into your account."

I debate my answer, decide honesty is best. "Yes."

"And you refused him?" There's something perverted in his tone.

"So far, yes." I'm flushing like I've done something to flush about.

"Good." Campbell gestures impatiently. "Please sign in. It will take two seconds, and then we can get out of here. I promise it's not a big deal."

I don't see another way out, but still I feel like I'm giving in too easily as I sit down in the ugly black rolling office chair from 1997 and navigate to the sign-in page. "I've been locked out of my account for the last few days," I say. "It might not even let me reset my password." But instead of shaking its electronic head at me, my email server informs me that my request to reset my password has been approved. Fuck.

"Hurry," Campbell says, glancing at the door.

The process can't take more than three minutes, but it feels unbearably tedious and drawn out with Campbell standing behind me, taking sharp, shallow breaths that waterboard the same sensitive spot in my scalp. The moment I'm in, Campbell drops to his knees next to me and brushes my hands off the keyboard with his. I hate when people do that to me, but I am also dying to know what the hell he is looking for. I watch as he navigates to the search bar, then types in a name.

The email from PT appears, adorned with the little paperclip icon that indicates an attachment.

**Here's Emma's script. I haven't even read it yet, because she changed her mind about what she wanted to write about at the last minute. She's really great, but it's inexcusable that this is late. Anyway, let's catch up when we've both had a chance to read.**

Campbell selects the message and deletes it. Then he empties my trash and signs me out.

"There," he says, somewhat cheerfully, at the same time I put a pen into his ear canal.

I expected blood, but there is none, not even a trickle. For about five full seconds, Campbell and I just stare at each other, horrified, like neither of us wants to believe that I took things to the next level, that we have to deal with this now. The pen sticks out of Campbell's ear at a perfect right angle. He coughs, like something is stuck in his throat, then brings his hand up to feel the mutilation for himself. His fingers trace the sturdy implant of the pen and he begins to gag aggressively. I push the rolling chair back into the wall so that I can slide off the seat and crawl underneath the desk to the door.

In the doorway I stop and look back at him. Campbell is curled up in a ball, batting at his ear and making small, whimpering noises. Impossibly, I feel embarrassed. *Did I overreact? Is there a simple explanation for all of this?*

"I'll get help," I promise him. He gives no indication that he believes me, let alone can hear me, and I hurry for the sliding barn door.

I had been sure to latch it behind me when I came in—bears—and the iron hook is jammed at an odd angle. I push my hip against the door, trying to dislodge it, and in my peripheral vision I see Campbell coming toward me with his arms raised above his head, like a bear did manage to get inside and now he's trying to scare it off. One of the heavy ceremonial stones that earlier bruised my shin slams into the ground and somehow, miraculously,

I'm staring at it from outside on the covered front patio, the rain roaring all around like a beast disturbed from its hundred-year slumber. I expel one short cloud of breath, and in the time it takes to dissipate, I process the reality that Campbell just tried to kill me.

Campbell hadn't expected me to get the door open, and momentum has sent him skidding onto the wet porch, landing with a bone-breaking crack on his knees. I look down at him and feel a surge of pleasurable, white-hot rage as I reach for the stone and raise it above my head. I did not, in fact, overreact. I have every right to do what I am about to do. I bring down the rock with the force of an axe, and Campbell's skull makes a soft, rotting sound. It can't possibly be enough to kill him, to stop him, but he falls forward on his hands and knees, gurgling in a way that seems disproportionate to the squishy little sound his skull made. His elbows buckle, and he flops flat on the wooden slats of the patio with his head turned to the side, one eye fine and the other discharging a pus-like substance. He does not blink or breathe. I stare at him, amazed. I did not realize it would be that easy to kill someone.

And then.

I feel it. I feel *him*. I raise my eyes. Henry stands at the base of the wide porch stairs, wet clothes clinging to him like plastic wrap, the elements outlining his absurd stature like a warning. *You will not beat him; don't even bother trying.* He's beneath me, and by the laws of scale and perception, he should feel dwarfed. But I am eye to his hawkish eye. I feel like a prairie animal, something small and low on the food chain, like Henry is waiting me out until hunger or thirst forces me into an open field. I take a step back. He steps forward. Something hot and hopeful springs to life inside me.

Fine.

Kill me.

But chase me first.

# Chapter 16

I turn and go crashing through the clubhouse. Inside, the rain is thousands of sharp fingers jabbing the roof, the windows, the walls, jabbing at me. *This way, Henry. She went this way.* The sky pulses purple with lightning, ratting out my ascent on the stairs. Henry bangs up behind me, a tremendous force that avalanches the three-story structure and sends books flying off shelves and my teeth rattling in the sockets of my gums. He says my name. I wish he would shout it, frenzied and furious. But he sounds calm. Like everything that happens next is natural and inevitable. No reason at all to panic.

The gun room is on the third level. That's what I am going for. But I'll never fucking make it. I duck into the game room and slam the door closed, turn the dinky little lock. Immediately the door handle begins to strain and jiggle. "I'm going to get this door open in two seconds, Faye."

I spin in a circle, whimpering. The game room was made the game room because it has those little clerestory windows that wrap around just under the ceiling and the little kids can't reach them and crawl out and fall to their deaths. I can't reach them either, and even if I could I wouldn't fit through. Henry is throwing his huge body against the door, and that's when I see it. A door-shaped seam in the wall, peeking out from behind a chair. I shove furniture out of the way and unlatch the lock. Inside, I find a small storage space cluttered with junk and reeking of mildew. I twist my head and see a tunneled space and, on the other end, the gloomy sky that is still somehow lighter than it is inside, and I realize this strangely shaped room used to be somebody's bedroom, that I'm looking up through a chimney. The door is cracking and splintering behind me, and I stack whatever I can find. Encyclopedias. A decaying cloth suitcase. I flip over one of those old sleds with the metal runners. I put one foot on top of my pile, then another. Miracles of miracles, it holds. Chimneys tend not to be straight. I know this because of the fireplace in my house, the one with the crack that PT immediately recognized. The crack is superficial, we've had it inspected, and I refused to restore the brickwork once PT told me the story of how it got there. It spikes diagonally like a wave in an abnormal EKG reading, and though my husband has been a proponent of gutting the whole wall anyway and building out into the yard, I've gotten him to agree to an annual inspection to ensure the damage does not become structural. It feels like bad luck to do anything about it until we have to. One day our assistant couldn't be there to meet the technician, and the guy roped me into a conversation from which I couldn't politely extract myself, and so now I know everything I never wanted to know about chimneys. They're designed with these little shelves inside; that's how he gets up there to clean everything out. I reach and feel the ridging like one of those polyester bumps on a climbing wall at a gym, and I pull myself up one step, then another, and is a part of me disappointed that Henry didn't catch me? Above the clatter of the storm rises a snappy mechanical sound, later I will understand it was the metal hinges of the door splitting in two. A strong hand snaps closed around my ankle, and as I go down, I get that butterfly feeling in my stomach, like I am riding a roller coaster, one last thrilling shot of euphoria before it all turns to black.

# PART 3

# Chapter 17

Henry floated the idea of a summer at the lake about a month before we graduated. It was April and a hard one. The trees would not bloom. There was a once-in-a-century ice storm that shocked the buds and delayed the dog-woods. At the colleges, the surest sign of spring appeared at the lake, when crew practice transitioned from indoors to out. Sometimes, on your way to class, you would find yourself neck and neck with the needlefish-like body of the racing shell, eight rowers moving as one to cut a neat center seam down the center of Seneca Lake. But that spring was the coldest on record since World War II, and only three weeks earlier, PT's wife had left a suicide note alongside her latest negative pregnancy test and paddled her single scull into the lake in the middle of the night. They said it probably happened in an instant. Something called cold shock response. Falling into water so brac-ing she would have involuntarily gasped, aspirated, and choked, all the while sinking into even colder deep water. They believe Sarah died without surfacing and that the currents carried her to the Erie Canal and eventually out into the Atlantic. The search for her body was called off after only two days.

PT had returned to teaching, though he was scattered and half there. He needed a dedicated assistant, Henry said. Someone to help him sort through Sarah's belongings, decide what should be kept and donate what should be donated. Henry had spoken to him, and PT had agreed to pay me twenty dollars an hour, an ungodly sum I would not come close to clearing if I moved to New York or LA to waitress while I searched for a real job in a fake and fickle industry. Henry told me to think about all the money I would save on rent and incidentals while I simultaneously sent out my résumé and accepted any interview opportunities that came up. The Albany train station was a two-hour drive, and an Amtrak from there to Penn Station took another three hours, but this was not any more inconvenient than if I chose to live at home in Massachusetts while doing all the same things. Plus, Henry said, this was the last summer we could respectably spend free of the demands of adulthood, and we would always look back and remember that we spent it at Lake Wanika, together.

I broke the news to my parents at graduation. I thought it would soften the blow that I'd decided to move in with my boyfriend if I told them in front of Henry's parents. His father was a big, warm man, and his mother a natural blonde with ruddy cheeks, a merciless snob, but she liked me for Henry. I caught a look she gave to him the first time he introduced us—it was a look of droll humility that said, *I take it back, I was wrong*—and I knew he had told her about me and she had asked all kinds of questions about where I was from and the schools I had attended and found his answers lacking. Occasionally, I still wonder what it must have been like to have a son who was so handsome that you also had to worry about in the romance department. Henry should have been the grand slam of offspring—good-looking, tall, monied, and male. But the way his mother embraced me, despite my lack of pedigree, carried with it the distinct whiff of relief.

"Hmmm" was all my mother said when I told her about my postgraduation plans.

"We will be there, of course," Henry's mother jumped in to say.

My mother gave her a hard smile.

"I think this is a nice opportunity for Faye," Henry's mother persisted. "She'll be day-to-day with PT, who is always the first one informed when an assistant or internship position opens up in the space she'd like to be in, and New York is only a train ride away."

My mother did one of her never-ending shrugs then. Her shoulders go up into her ears and they stay there. They do not release. "It's just not appropriate."

Later, in his room, Henry was livid. Who was my mother to judge us, to judge *his* mother? People like her, with their puritanical beliefs, lived limited lives. *Limited*, code for *middle class*. My mother had always worked and made her own money. It wasn't a lot, especially with four mouths to feed, but Henry's life was just as small as hers, two darts on a map, one in the southern Adirondacks and the other pinning his parents' primary residence in New Hampshire. And he had limited ideas about what life should look like too, at least that's what I began to realize when I packed up my things and defied my mother by moving to Lake Wanika one week later.

I don't know if I changed or Henry did, if we both did just enough that our edges stopped fitting together and instead poked and prodded. I went into the city for an interview at a production company at some point in June, and when that didn't pan out and I got another interview at one of the talent agencies, Henry gave me a hard time about going back to the Staples in Mount Emerson for more quality stock paper on which to print my résumé. It was nearly an hour's drive, and that didn't include the ten-minute ride on the boat to the parking lot. Why didn't I just buy a sleeve of it when I was there the first time? He taught me to drive the boat but never actually let me drive it, and his school-bus-yellow Defender was a stick shift that was vintage, temperamental, and he'd rather just drive me himself than risk me blowing out the clutch.

Then, in July, PT sat down to dinner with us and announced that Jonathan had recently decided to promote his assistant and was looking for a replacement ASAP.

"And it would be in LA?" I said. Henry sat next to me, silent, cutting his chicken marsala into smaller and smaller pieces instead of eating any of it. It was Italian night at the clubhouse.

"I know you're trying to focus your search on New York," PT said. He cleared his throat, glanced at Henry. "But this is *the* opportunity, Faye."

New York had been a concession to Henry. We were talking about moving to the city together, and I was applying for assistant positions in the literary departments in the New York offices of all the major talent agencies and the smaller ones too, at the production company run by the man who would later end up behind bars and the one run by the guy who would not ask for hotel room massages but would throw office supplies at your head. Henry's family needed someone to run point on their rustic furniture suppliers from New Jersey to Virginia. New York made a little bit of sense for both of us. There was nothing for Henry in Los Angeles, and it would be easy to blame him for the location limitations I'd set on EntertainmentCareers.net, but the truth is that taking a job in Los Angeles was akin to breaking up with Henry, and I did not want to do that for reasons that were both noble and not. I cared for Henry and I did not want to hurt him, but I also knew that being on my own meant a grimy apartment, freaks for roommates, public transport, and no sides of guacamole in my Chipotle order. At the same time, it thrilled me to think about nights out on the town, wearing high heels and eyeliner, socializing with people other than Henry's parents. Henry was willing to try New York with me while in the same breath proclaiming his loathing for the city. It was dirty and loud and riding the subway made his chest feel squeezed, but those were *his* noble reasons. Henry hated the idea of leaving the lake because he was afraid of losing me out there in the world.

PT sent my résumé to Jonathan, and his recently promoted assistant emailed me to set up the interview for the following week. I had some savings from the four years I worked as a lifeguard for the swim and dive teams at the colleges, money that had remained untouched in my bank account because I lived at the lake those first two months following graduation, but when I went to book my flight and hotel room, Henry said he wanted to come with me, and it made no sense for us to book the flights separately, and he might as well book the hotel while he was at it. I let him, though I had a bad feeling.

On the morning we left for the airport, Henry picked a fight. He was angry that I would not use one of his weekender duffel bags, which would fit into the overhead, that I instead insisted on bringing my massive rolling suitcase that I would have to check. We had an eleven-hour travel day ahead of us, and we were landing late and now we would have to wait at baggage claim. I was not traveling alone. I should think about other people for once. I could be selfish, had anyone ever told me that?

Yes, actually. My mother did all the time, and once I went to my father with tears in my eyes and asked if it was true. I asked because I wanted to be told different. I wanted him to say without hesitation, *Your mother was angry when she said that, she didn't mean it.* Instead he muted the television and furrowed his brow and thought about it. *Sometimes*, he said, *yes, you can be.* I was ten years old, and I hadn't taken the trash out before my parents got home from work, though I must have noticed it was full.

This was obviously years before I employed a famously published therapist, out of network, of course, who told me this was an egregious thing for a parent to say to a child because children are, by nature, selfish, and it is your job, as a parent, to meet the needs of a child and not the other way around. This was before she taught me about patterns. If I had noticed a pattern before this, it was people calling me selfish; heretofore, I must be selfish. But the motif was not that, as it turned out, but that I was seeking out connections with people who made me feel bad about myself in the ways my parents did. This was all beyond my reach on the morning I was trying to leave for Los Angeles, but with Henry hounding me and the clock ticking down, I grasped the essence. I knew Henry was trying to do whatever he could to keep me all to himself, and I also knew if I said any of that to him, it would only agitate the situation. *You're right,* I said to him with as much humility as I could stand to muster, *I'm sorry. I'm so sorry.* He calmed down; he bought it. I knew then it was done, but I also knew I would do whatever it took to make my motherfucking flight.

We got in the boat. We got in the car. Henry was sweating. It was a hot day, and he was the one who had to haul my heavy suitcase around—did I not think of that too? Ten or fifteen minutes into the two-and-a-half-hour drive and he could not cool down. The air-conditioning was roaring and I was sitting on my corpse-cold hands, but he could not stop sweating. *Is this normal?* He looked at me, but I was too panicked and furious to see the real fear in his eyes. He pulled over, curled into a ball, told me he thought he was having a heart attack. But when I went to call 911, he took the phone out of my hand and told me to give him a minute to see if the feeling in his chest might go away.

I sat there, staring at the clock, while Henry hugged his chest with his huge arms. I loved his arms, his wingspan, his height. I was small then and I'm smaller now. Even short Hollywood men are taller than me, but sometimes Henry used to spread his arms and block me when I tried to get past him, swoop down on me, envelop me, throw me on the bed, against the wall, over his shoulder. I would miss all that, but I would not miss this flight.

I turned to him, my face worried, and asked if I could put my hand on his chest. He let me, and I worried my face more. That doesn't sound right, I told him, though his heart felt like any heart, beating a little too hard in its enclosure. His face crumbled. He gripped my hand. We could call Dr. Payne, I suggested. Dr. Payne was a retired pediatrician who had a cabin on Lake Wanika. We thought it fantastic that this was a doctor who administered to frightened children and his last name was pain. Henry handed me my phone then. I did not have service, and so I wandered down the road and called PT and told him what was happening.

Thirty minutes later PT arrived with Dr. Payne in the passenger seat. PT got out and came over to the car and opened the trunk. He put my suitcase into his car. I went over to Henry. Dr. Payne was saying it was good that Henry didn't feel nauseous, that he did not have pain in his jaw. I told him he would be all right and I was sorry and goodbye. He turned his head away from me. That was it.

The drive to the airport was tense. We were up against the clock, and PT suggested that I transfer the essentials from my suitcase into a gym bag he had in his trunk. I was just barely going to make my flight, but not if I had to wait in line to check my bags. I crawled into the back seat and I was editing my things and I felt I had to acknowledge what had just happened.

"I feel terrible for just leaving him," I said.

PT nodded and said nothing. I needed him to know I was not a bad person, and so I started to cry. I learned I could make myself cry when I was in the seventh grade, so long as I was saying something that made me genuinely sad.

"Who knows, maybe down the line, we can figure it out. My parents broke up for nine months and then got back together and got married. I can't picture my life without Henry." I tried to picture it, then sniffled. "It's too sad."

"Can I give you some advice?" PT said. He was wearing his glasses but not sunglasses, and in the rearview mirror I could see he was squinting painfully at the bright road. He left in such a hurry that he didn't grab his sunglasses, and this realization made me enormously sad. Sarah had died only a few months ago. He was fifty and he would never have children though he would have been one of those fathers a child referred to as her best friend, even as a hormone-riddled teenager.

"Okay," I said.

"Don't be afraid to write about this one day."

# Chapter 18

I half wake under a warm blanket, a fire smacking the metal screen. Some of my limbs are asleep and some bunched up tight. My eyelids drop again, and I go to turn over, get comfortable, and this is when I wake-wake with a violent jolt. I am tied to the spindle-back chair in Henry's cabin, and Henry is sitting across from me on the couch, brow furrowed indeterminately, his dark-blond hair ivied around his ears the way it would when we would stop for breakfast after the gym. Our eyes meet, and something in the fire combusts with the energy of a gunshot.

I retrieve my voice, buried somewhere craggy and deep. "How long have I been out?"

"It's the middle of the night," Henry replies, his eyes drifting over me like I am a live specimen, something to be examined and tested with cruelty, if necessary. "You took a pretty nasty fall."

"I forget. Is it medically advised to tie someone up after a potential spinal-cord injury?"

"You should not have run," Henry says simply.

I lean forward as far as my restraints will allow. "What the fuck is going on?"

"You killed your good buddy Campbell, for one."

I glare at Henry, waiting for him to take it back. I wait a long time.

"He's dead?" I say in a dull voice.

"Very dead."

I blink off some tears, then nod stoically. Okay, then. Well. I knew that. Didn't I? "He was going to kill me." I look to Henry for reassurance. Find none. "I had to do it," I say, stressing the impossibility of my predicament.

"Didn't stop you from enjoying it."

"You think I *liked* killing Campbell?"

Henry brushes that lush lower lip with his thumb. "I know what you look like when you enjoy something, Faye."

I refuse to flinch. I refuse to, even though arousal is butchering my middle. Why—*why*—am I like this? "Before I *had* to kill Campbell, he made me sign in to my email."

It takes Henry several seconds to remember to blink.

"He deleted a message from PT. How come?"

Henry settles back into the couch, cocky, comfortable, those tree-trunk thighs spread obnoxiously wide. "If you have to ask," he says, bouncing a knee, "I'm assuming you have not yet read Emma King's script? Poor thing poured her blood, sweat, and tears into that, you know."

"Hadn't even opened the attachment."

"You are a very important woman," Henry says viciously.

"That has nothing to do with it."

Henry laughs because I don't deny it.

"I am overwhelmed easily. I shut down. It's depression. It's how I was raised."

"How were you raised exactly?"

"To focus on one thing and be good at it. Everything else falls by the wayside."

"Not your looks," Henry says with sudden despair. "You stay on top of that shit."

I glance at myself in the reflection of the window. I should look like hell, after these last few days. "The day of the funeral," I say. "When Emma got me alone, said that PT canceled his classes the day before he died, that he had Band-Aids all over his hands, that he emailed her to come over first thing that morning. She was telling the truth."

Henry makes a circular motion with his finger, near his ear. Keep going.

"Whatever she wrote, you guys didn't want me to read."

"Close, Faye. So close."

My mind passes the needle through the loop, completing the stitch. "Something you didn't want PT to read either."

Henry's face turns somber, giving me my answer.

"What could this girl possibly have written that would make PT distressed enough to have a heart attack? That has culminated in *this*?" I push my shins against whatever he has used to confine me to this chair, something rough and bristled that infuriates my skin. Dock lines, I realize, and he has stripped off my sodden clothes, leaving me in nothing but a flimsy old button-down with fraying lapels. He has put warm, clean socks on my feet and because I am bound to my knees, my thighs are spread at a porny angle. Henry has covered my lap with a blanket, a laughable attempt at a gentleman's gesture, then sat here and waited me out.

Henry jiggles one wide-angled knee anxiously, considering how to answer. "Something bad."

"How bad?"

"Oh." Henry lifts a hand. How to possibly put this? "Goodbye, Campbell's casual political aspirations bad. Bye, Wee Burn Country Club membership, Brunswick enrollment for the brats, the annual chartered couples' trip in the Bermudas." Henry pauses. "That sort of stuff doesn't do it for me, but goodbye to everything that does." His voice takes on a wistful note that sounds genuine, but I am in no position to trust anything I hear.

"What did you guys do?"

Henry clears his throat, scratches off a speck of mud on his thigh with a fingernail. "First, I need you to know it was an accident. And I have lived with the pain and guilt of it every single day since then. And sometimes I wonder . . ." He trails off, scrunches up his face like whatever he is wondering is too painful to imagine. "Nah. There's no use, and it wouldn't absolve me of anything anyway." He studies the pale spot he's left on his pants. Along with the dirt, he scratched off some of the khaki color too. "Sarah did not drown herself in Seneca Lake."

It takes me a second to process this utterly explosive statement. "How do you know that?" I ask tremulously.

Henry closes his eyes and shakes his head. Shakes, shakes, shakes his head.

"Oh my God," I hear myself say. "Henry. Oh my God."

Henry heaves an agonized sigh. Opens his eyes. Stares unblinking at the fire. "We were driving. *I* was driving. It was five in the morning? I don't know. We were going home. Or I was trying to. But Campbell wanted to go somewhere else. He wanted me to drop him and he wanted my coke and I told him no, you know, you need to fucking call it. We both did. And he started reaching, like, into my pockets. Trying to find my cigarettes, my shit. And I was pushing him off me and I didn't see her. Obviously," he groans, lightly, "I didn't see her. But that was what time the crew team met for practice, and Sarah always walked."

I wish I had my hands. I wish I could cover my mouth.

"She was gone. You know. No question. But we could see. In my headlights. We could see that along one side of my car, the paint was, like, sheared off, and she was covered in it. It was in her hair, under her fingernails. That fucking yellow paint. Everyone knew I drove that car." Henry lifts his foot to the edge of the coffee table. Pushes it away, then hooks his toes under to pull it back. He can't quite make it fit in the grooves of the rug and he leans forward and tries to line everything up with his hands, then makes a tossing motion, like throwing something out in the trash. What's the point? It will never look as it was again.

"I wanted to call the police," he continues, a defensive edge to his voice, like I have asked why he did not immediately get Sarah help, "but Campbell knocked the phone out of my hand. He said she was dead. It wasn't like there was anything we could do at this point, why ruin our lives on top of it? I was . . ." He looks at me, his dark eyes utterly haunted. "I couldn't breathe, Faye. I was a mess. I just clung to Campbell, who kept promising me everything would be okay. We put her in my car and then he said let's think about this. PT was in LA for the week. We had a key to the house. We knew she wanted a baby and it wasn't happening. There was a fucking negative test in the trash like it was ordained by God. Campbell wrote something short and sweet on her computer and we pushed her scull into the water. Then we started driving for the lake. This area, it's so vast, but it's someone's, you know? The land either belongs to the government or some off-gridder who will shoot you if he finds you trespassing. You can't leave a dead body in the lake—it will float. I mean, that's why they searched for her. Because bodies float. It doesn't always mean you find them, but we couldn't take the risk. It was safer—it was smarter—to bury her on our land. But you will never, ever believe what happened when we got here." He lets out a brittle-sounding laugh. "The lake was frozen, but only on *our* side. It's not like it had never happened before, our side is slightly more elevated, but not since our parents were kids." Henry stares hard at his hands a moment, turns them over in his lap, and frowns at them, like he is looking at an imposter's hands. "We weren't trying to be cruel, burying her on PT's land. And I chose a nice spot. The little tear-dropped clearing by the Dorothy Parker tree. I mean, it's eleven thousand acres, he was never going to find her. He never should have found her."

I'm aware of my breathing suddenly. Short, hot breaths, in and out, like I've just been sick over the toilet.

"A week ago," Henry says. "Two weeks ago? Who fucking knows anymore. PT called. He needed to speak to me, in person." Henry runs his hands down his face, pulls at the skin under his eyes so that I can see the pink, moist membrane underneath. "I thought he was going to tell me he was diagnosed with cancer or something."

When Henry arrived, he found Campbell already there. PT had bandages all over his hands. His skin had a gray tint to it. He told them to sit at the dining room table and he turned his laptop around and there it was, the title page. *The Accident* by Emma King. He made them read the story of what they did to Sarah, and he watched them with his small, kind eyes, his breathing growing ever more shallow.

PT had decided he would not speak to anyone until he knew if it was true. He canceled class to drive to the lake and dig. He dug and he dug and then, he hit bone. He fucking found her. Not all of her. But a piece that was most definitely human. He drove back to campus in a daze.

"He wanted us to be men and own up to everything," Henry says with this stunned, distant look in his eyes, like he is remembering something from a very long time ago. "He wanted to know how Emma knew about this and why the fuck she would choose to write about it."

I find I am regarding Henry with anger, with disgust, but not necessarily for what he's done. I resent that he is telling the story in a way that forces me to pepper him with questions, like some kind of wide-eyed damsel tied to the train tracks, like a female character written by a man not that long ago. "But how did she know?"

Henry taps out an irregular rhythm on his knee, trying

to decide how to answer. "She used to go out with Win, Corrine's younger brother. Did you know that?"

I did not. But I should have. The tit-for-tat way they spoke to each other that night at the fraternity house. I was so focused on my own history with Henry that I could not see they had one of their own too. "So, what, Campbell told Win? And then Win told Emma?"

Henry stops tapping his knee. He goes very still and he holds my eye. "Emma knew because Campbell told her. Because he was fucking his little brother's girlfriend for the last year."

I gasp. A sharp, stereotypical inhalation. In a flash, I remember looking over at Emma that night at the fraternity house and finding she had reapplied a coat of lip gloss sometime between when we spoke to Win outside and when he took us to the room where Campbell was. She was trying to look nice for him. And—oh my God. Oh my *God*. That voice. Calling out to me on the lake. I knew I knew that voice. "She's here," I say, and there is a pressure in my ears, a piercing whistle in my skull, like a kettle come to boil.

Henry sighs heavily, like he wishes he could tell me otherwise.

"What the fuck? What does she think happened to Campbell? What are we going to do?"

"I have it under control for now."

My laugh is shrill. "You call this *under control*?"

"I went to see her," Henry speaks over me, but he somehow manages not to raise his voice, to sound like the reasonable one. "After I got you back here." *After I stripped you naked and tied you up*, he cannot say, certainly not in the excessively calm tone he's affected. "I explained Campbell had to head back home unexpectedly and that I'll take her to the train station so she can get back to the colleges in the morning."

I am irritable and impatient that I still do not understand. "But why would Emma write about this? Why would Campbell *tell* her about this?"

"You know what he's like when he's fucked up. He blabs. He tells you things to keep you close. He took Emma for a ride. One day he loved her, he was confessing his deepest, darkest secrets to her, he was leaving his family for her, the next he was dodging her. She was hurt. She wanted to hurt him back."

Fine. Passable answer. Next terrible question. "Did PT die in front of you?"

Henry bows his head as though the answer itself is a holy one. "He was crying. We were all crying. In one breath he would be gasping how much he hated us for letting him think Sarah had taken her own life, and in the next he would ask us what he was supposed to do now. If he was supposed to go to the police and send us away from our children, and if he didn't, what kind of husband did that make him to Sarah?" Henry stares into the black hole of hurt he created a long moment, looking lost and resigned to staying that way. "It was late. He told us to go get a hotel. Get some rest. We'd have to figure this out, some way, somehow. He'd have to talk to Emma. He had to see where her head was at, what she was thinking, just, how the hell to handle this."

"How could you leave him alone like that?" I am seething with disdain. "You knew he had a heart problem. You knew he had overexerted himself, that he had just had the shock of his life. You knew what would happen."

Henry does not look away from me. He takes it—my judgment, my scorn. "It is one of two things in my life," Henry says, "that I will never forgive myself for."

I search the firelit contours of Henry's face. I thoroughly vet him. I think about our time at the lake when we were younger; only a few months before, Henry's earthly axis had shifted. I had chalked it up to more quotidian change. Graduating college. Living together in all but isolation. Not knowing what we were going to do with our lives and how we would make it work between us. Henry had always been someone with control issues, but they had kicked up during our time here and turned our relationship untenable. What he has told me has made sense of things. It has a ring of truth to it. I've always wondered if that's the phrase because it's like searching for a ringing phone in a strange house with a long corridor of seemingly endless rooms. You get closer, the ringing gets louder. The caller is persistent, the message urgent—they will keep trying until you pick up. I am nearer to an answer; that much I am sure is true.

Henry clears his throat roughly. "After we learned he had died," he says, "Campbell made this comment."

I tense, knowing it will be bad.

*"'Two birds, one stone.'"*

My insides slop around my stomach. "Because I would come back for the funeral?"

"He asked you to speak, for added insurance." Henry fingers a loose thread in the faded needlework on a throw pillow. Wraps it around his finger as many times as it will go, cutting off circulation and turning the top of his finger purple with trapped blood. "That night that I apologized to you. You looked so surprised. Disappointed almost. Like you expected more of a challenge. But I needed a reason to leave while your hotel room was unoccupied. Campbell wanted to drug you right there, but I thought we could sort this out without you getting hurt. My hope was that I'd get into your room, find your laptop, just, make sure you hadn't read it and recognized anything and then delete the thing and you'd at least be one less person we had to worry about."

The scuff marks at the base of my hotel room door. "You actually got in," I say, astounded.

Henry says, somewhat wryly, "Not that it mattered. You were locked out of your account." He presses the top of his finger, the one he has coiled in the pillow's thread. It must be numb by now. It must be dead. "You keep telling me you've changed, but."

"Some things still feel too hard for me to figure out," I concede. Again I test my braided black restraints, with more curiosity than fight. They have a sharp, plasticky feel to them, like those clear heels that briefly came back into style and made my legs look a million miles long in red carpet photos. "You spoke to someone," I remember, "the day you came to my hotel room. You said to come back later. I thought it was maybe a hotel employee."

"Campbell," Henry says.

"But why come back later? He must have helped you get me to the car."

"Because he was on a very short fuse. I did not want him knowing yet that I could not access your account, that I didn't know what you knew. He was panicked. I was panicked. I just said, okay. I'll bring you here. I'll figure it out. Every day, I went to shore, hoping, praying that would be the day I could recover your account. When I came back and found the window popped out, I was terrified for you, Faye. Campbell was coming undone." He snaps the loose thread free of the pillow and I watch, with immense satisfaction, as his finger returns to its normal size and fleshy color. When I look up, I find Henry's eyes fastened on mine. "For the record, Faye, I carried you out to the car alone. I told Campbell I didn't need his help, because I did not want him laying a finger on you. He kept saying it would take two people and I said will you look at her?"

*Jesus, you're light*, Campbell had said to me before we said goodbye at the dock. He had picked me up. He had *weighed* me.

A shudder jerks my shoulders and moves to tingle the top of my scalp. I am thinking about speaking to Campbell outside the church, the way he held my bag for me and how warm that moment felt, and all the while he must have been looking at me as an impediment to blast right through. "What's going to happen when Campbell doesn't come home?"

"Corrine isn't expecting him until Monday. When that doesn't happen, I assume she will start calling around, and when no one knows where he is, they will look for him. What they find . . ." Henry takes a deep breath, as though envisioning their grisly discovery. "It will look like an accident."

"Emma *knows* we're here," I remind him angrily. "Isn't she going to wonder why you told her he was okay when he was *dead*? What if she goes to the police?"

"She won't."

"How do you know?"

"Because tomorrow morning, you are going to talk to her."

I stare at Henry, agog. "About?"

"Her future. How talented she is. How much you would like to help her, but you are going to need her to keep quiet about some things."

I am speechless a moment. Then I hit each note in an impeccable demonstration of a guffaw—high, and higher still. "Henry," I say. "You've lost it if you think I'm doing that. You need to call the police. This has gone too far to try to cover up."

Henry does not budge. "That isn't an option."

"Campbell is *dead*. Corrine is going to push for answers when he doesn't come home. The longer you wait, the worse things are going to get. And when Emma learns you lied about where Campbell went that night, don't you think she will go to the police herself? And tell them not just about this, but Sarah too?"

"If Emma planned on going to the police," Henry counters, "she would have done it already. It's too late now. She had information about a crime and she used it to punish the married man she was having an affair with. She's too involved. She's *guilty*."

I lift my chin with defiance. "Well, I am not. And the second I can, I'm going to the police."

Henry stares at me with especially cold eyes.

"Please," I scoff. "If you were going to kill me, you'd have done it already."

"I don't want to kill you, Faye."

"Then what do you *want*?"

"I want you to trust me."

"Trust you?" I repeat harshly.

"Trust me to take care of this. To keep you clear of it. To protect you."

"Sure, okay," I agree sarcastically. "Tell me what that looks like."

"That looks like speaking to Emma tomorrow, then hunkering down here for another day or two while I take care of a few more things."

I look at Henry like he has sprouted an additional head. "What *things*?"

"You need to trust me."

"I don't!" I shout this, and Henry presses his lips together stubbornly.

"The other night," he says after a moment, "when we slept next to each other. And I said I could not feel what we once had? That was a lie."

"*Don't*," I say, twisting my wrists raw in my restraints. "Don't do that."

Henry ignores me. "I *did* feel something different. Something that made me crazy."

"Stop," I say, but my voice sounds weak and ineffective.

He does not stop. His face is pleading and guileless. "I was bursting out of my skin trying not to touch you."

I close my eyes in one final act of self-preservation. I feel like one of those street cobras, dumped onto the hot pavement, too sluggish and malnourished to attack my charmer, easily tamed, soothed, tricked. "You will say anything at this point," I insist, mostly for myself.

"I could say that if you decide not to trust me, if you decide not to let me take care of this my way, I will go ahead and I will ruin everything you have worked so hard to accomplish."

I open my eyes to find Henry looking at me with what I can only describe as anticipatory regret. *Do not make me do this to you* is what his face is saying. I curl my hands into fists, furious. "Then do it. I know you want to. Or is that the grand fucking finale to this elaborate revenge plot?"

Henry leans forward to stress what he is about to say. "I promise you, there is a way out of this, for both of us, unscathed, if you just trust me. And if it all goes to shit, I will say you were coerced into doing this, and you will have your episode to prove I was always a controlling piece of shit."

"You would never."

"I would. A thousand times over I would. Because I still love you."

I turn my head like he has slapped me. The windows show a black as solid as a brick wall, hiding the surface of the lake, though I imagine its frightened, gooseflesh appearance in the rain. I can only see myself in the window's reflection, the struggle on my face to hide my same sobby feelings. Yes, I went to PT's funeral because I wanted to pay my respects to the man who helped me get my start, who was *kind* to me on top of it, but also because when Campbell told me Henry would be there, my body lurched like a creature brought back to life to destroy the person who created it.

I face Henry. Find his eyes like one of those old carousel projectors, blinking fuzzy, precious memories. Before the word is even out of my mouth, I regret it.

"Beg," I say to him.

Surprise softens Henry's features. Then, I watch as understanding sets in, rearranges him molecule by molecule. He leans forward, stares at me with his hands bracing his upper body on his knees, long enough for me to take back what I said. He is giving that to me, I realize. A chance to change my mind. Even if I wanted to, my mouth is sandpaper. Now it is too late; he is rising from the couch. There is an unreal quality to the room, its golden romantic cast, its cold drumbeat of rain, as he steps around the coffee table and comes to loom over me in a way that reminds me I am tied to a chair in the middle of nowhere with a murderer who has already gotten away with it once.

"You asked for this," Henry reminds me. He drops down to his knees, putting us at eye level. He is so much more daunting at eye level than he is standing. I can see myself reflected in his exploding pupils, seamed blue and then black again, a miniature, petrified version of myself. "I am begging you, Faye," he says. "Please. Trust me."

I stare at him, unyielding.

"Faye." Something splinters in Henry's smooth voice. "If we go through all this, and I don't ever get to touch you again—" He breaks off and stares at my lap, where under the blanket I am not wearing underwear. His cheeks are flushed. His mouth is pink, his eyes are soft and downturned and a wretched blue. "I will never forgive myself." Beneath the blanket I am beating a loud and lonely percussion for him. He hears it, he must.

"Please," Henry says. He *begs*. "Faye. Please."

I make myself count to three before I ruin my life, to be sure this is really what I want. Yes. With Henry, the answer is always yes. "You never bothered to ask before."

Henry's absurdly full lips part in disbelief. "Because that's not what you like."

I am shackled like a prisoner and dizzy with freedom as I say, "Then do what I like."

The rain has stopped. The house is silent and waiting.

Then, methodically, Henry folds back the blanket, lets it slip off my knees and bunch on the ground. I am thinking that the sight of my thighs forced wide by the restraints is nearly intolerable until Henry slides his cool hand under my shirt and puts his thumb on my clit, obliterating the physical barrier we've been testing and pushing up against these last few days. We stare at each other, astonished. When all of this is over, when I am stuck in stock-still traffic on Sunset at three forty-five in the afternoon, when I am staring at the pink dusk, wondering if it is nature or pollution I am enjoying, this will be the moment I return to again and again: Henry's thumb printed on my center and our shared awe that we get to have this again.

"You're still so soft." He says this with a slight gasp, with total grief. He leans in, brushes my bottom lip with his. We open our mouths, do not use tongue. He groans a curse deep into my throat, thumbing my clit in small, delicate circles. "Does he tell you how soft you are?"

I press my forehead against his with a whimper. No, my husband does not tell me how soft I am.

"How pink you are? How perfect?"

"Fuck."

"You still like it when I hold you there?"

I melt into his hand. Nod with my bottom lip in my teeth.

And so Henry cups me between the legs, snugly, in the way I still like, the heel of his hand firm against my clit, fingertips digging into my ass. I am a nuclear button to which only he has the code.

"You're in my dreams," Henry says, kissing the tip of my nose, the dip in my cupid's bow. "Sometimes you refuse to talk to me. Sometimes I'm chasing you, trying to stop you from leaving again. But sometimes you are like this." He sits back on his heels, strokes my pussy lightly, thoughtfully. Watches, his beautiful face mesmerized by his ability to stir up all the ugly, undisguised desperation on my own. I feel full and empty at the same time, an irreconcilable pain that binds me to Henry still. His eyes leave mine, travel the length of my body, stop at the place where my long shirt cuts off his hand at the wrist. I follow his sightline to see his hand roving under my shirt. Such a small movement, barely a rotation, to be so vulgar. We stare at what his hand is doing to me with slack jaws, looking like two druggy dumbfucks who are almost certainly going to jail. But, you know what? Hard time might give me an edge. I'd have a good lawyer; I bet Gloria Allred would take me as a client, she'd make sure I was sent to one of those cushy prisons where they do yoga and eat organic, that I was out in less than a year. I raise my chin, open my mouth in a silent groan. Release blasts through me, shrapnel lodging in my nerves and fibers, embedding a bright new everywhere burn that makes kindling of the lie I've been telling myself over the years. That I could ever be okay without this.

I am a limp, leaking mess as Henry unties my ankles, my rug- burned wrists. I reach for him like a child, and he picks me up, hooks my legs around his waist, carries me into the bedroom. He pulls back the sheets and packs us tightly inside. I fall asleep on top of Henry's chest, listening to the private conversations in the chambers of his heart.

# Chapter 19

I wake alone, the room infused with harsh, high-noon light. I feel melty and warm, my mind untangled and clear. *You killed Campbell yesterday*, I am reminding myself when Henry comes out of the bathroom, patting his face dry with a hand towel.

"Hi," he says, almost shyly.

I sit up in bed slowly. "Hi," I say.

"Did you sleep okay?"

I nod. "You?"

Henry nods too. We are being careful with each other, polite and distant.

"I was going to make some breakfast," Henry says, and starts for the kitchen. I catch his hand as he passes, tug him back to me. I get on my knees and tilt my face up to his. Henry is backlit and precisely rendered, his shadow falling to the side and broken by the wall, too long to fit the floor. He looks down at me with his deep-water-blue eyes, his face twisted in pain. I put my hands on places where he is furrowed, frowning, try to smooth him into what it is I am feeling. *Alive* doesn't begin to capture it. I feel younger than I am, more beautiful, my wits sharp as knives. I awoke a completely idealized version of myself.

"I'm sorry," he says, burying his face in my hands.

"Sorry?" I repeat.

"I don't know how to say this without sounding patronizing, but I'm just so fucking proud of you, Faye. Sometimes I'm so proud it turns into envy. Sometimes panic. I think about that day in the car and what would have happened if you hadn't gotten away from me, and it makes it hard to breathe. And I'm like . . ." Henry is having trouble breathing now. "Should I just let you go? Am I going to ruin you? I don't want to ruin you, Faye."

My heart is flipping around like a fish on land. Henry is giving me an out, but the crevices of my fingers are collecting his tears like rainwater, and my body is aching from the briefest of use. I put my mouth on his and shake my head. No, no, no. I am not being ruined. I am being reminded of what I am capable of. "I want to do this for you," I say, and I kiss his neck, his collarbone, the backs of his hands and the fronts.

Henry grasps my hands in his own. I can see the question shaping his lips into a small O. Why? Why would I want to do this? How can I be so willing to risk everything? I give a small shake of my head. Please don't ask. Not yet, anyway.

Where the inlet narrows with tall granite rocks on either side, the current curls around us like a fist. Henry does something to the gears that throws our heads back then snaps them forward on our necks. My hair is sticky with the spray of lake water by the time we reach the cabin where Campbell and Corrine spend the smallest fraction of their summers possible. Corrine much prefers her parents' shingled estate that clings to the cliffs of Newport, though Campbell did what he could to make the property on Lake Wanika more appealing to her, going so far as to install a tankless water heater that caused such an uproar an addendum had to be added to the community guidelines regarding property permits. It confirmed for the members a bias they'd harbored against Corrine before they had any evidence to support it: she wasn't all in on this place. She didn't want to see flabby old bodies bathing in the lake, and when something needed repair, she hired people to fix it.

Inside, I track Emma's silhouette moving away from the window and disappearing into the back of the house. She was watching, waiting for us, and I think she ducked into the bathroom to reapply a coat of her emotional-support lip gloss, because when she lets us in the side door, her lips are once again that cheap shade of pearly pink that makes her appear tanner than she already is. I can smell the dry shampoo on her, and she is wearing black slacks and a button-down, like we have a scheduled job interview.

"Come in," she says with an expansive sweep of her arm. I stomp my feet on the braided jute doormat and step inside Corrine's version of Connecticut in the burly mountains. Beige rugs and beige couches. Those woven navy-and-white barstools at the countertop. Matching light-oak coffee and farm table. Bland on ever more bland.

"I'm so glad to see you," Emma says to me with relief, then directs a chiding glance at Henry. "You had me worried the other night."

"Oh God." I laugh like I am embarrassed and tuck myself into Henry's side. "We were just messing around. I had no idea anyone else was here."

Emma eyes me, then Henry, like she is a social worker assessing for signs that I am protecting my abuser. But I am snug under Henry's arm, fitted into his firm torso, and I do not have to perform my content.

Emma gestures for us to sit down on the linen couch, having no choice but to find us genuine. "Can I get you anything to drink?"

"I am dying for a seltzer if you have." I hate seltzer but I just know Emma's got a whole case of it in the fridge, that it is as much a part of her personality as her winter tan.

"Yes!" Emma cries. "Grapefruit or lime?"

"Grapefruit." Gross. "You are a godsend."

"Henry?"

"I'm fine, thanks."

Emma sweeps into the kitchen, reaches for two highball glasses, presses each into the ice maker (an ice maker!—the Wanikans must love that), then pours our drinks at the angle that kids pump beer from the keg into their party cups. She presents mine to me with a small bronze coaster underneath.

"Thank you."

Emma sits down next to us in an oatmeal-colored boucle chair and watches me sip my seltzer like she has cooked an extravagant meal for me and now she has the pleasure of watching me savor my first bites.

"Crisp," I say to her, and Emma beams with pride.

Last night, while I was tied up and probably bleeding

from my brain, Henry came to see Emma to let her know that Campbell's son, the quiet red-haired boy I met outside the chapel, had a severe asthma attack and was taken to the hospital in an ambulance. Corrine had called the caretaker, who lives a mile from the parking lot, and he rushed over and spotted Campbell's boat docked outside the clubhouse. He'd gone inside and found Campbell and chauffeured him straight to the Yale New Haven emergency room. Campbell had left his car for Emma so she could drive herself to the train station in Albany and catch a ride back to the colleges. He'd told Corrine he was low on gas and he hadn't wanted to waste any time stopping.

"Is Tookie okay?" Emma asks, her tone turned mothering and grave.

"I stopped by the clubhouse this morning to call Campbell and check in," Henry says. "Tookie is going to be released later today."

"Thank *God*," Emma says. She puts her hand over her heart, exhales hard. She waits just long enough to ask, "Did Campbell say anything else?" She slurps from her drink, her eyes trained eagerly on Henry. She's wearing winged eyeliner, and one side is drawn longer than the other, like a lopsided Cleopatra.

"He said he loves you and thank you for understanding," Henry says.

There is a blast of color to Emma's cheeks. "Of *course*," she emphasizes. "I just feel so bad for him. And for Tookie. Corrine is, ugh, well . . ." Emma looks to me as though I might have the word for what Corrine is.

"He's lucky to have Campbell for a father," I say, and

in that moment I remember how Tookie had slipped his hand into Campbell's the day I met him outside the chapel and leaned into him shyly, hiding half his face behind Campbell's leg. My heart beats slower, lower, thinking about his freckled face falling when he learns his father is gone.

"So lucky," Emma agrees, but I can tell she's bored of speaking about Campbell's kid and ready to return to the subject of herself. She sets her glass on a coaster and crosses her legs, clasping her hands around her knees with a patient, expectant look. Last night Henry also told Emma to hang tight, that we'd come by to ferry her to the parking lot in the morning, and that I had something I wanted to talk to her about, writer to writer, a vomitous lie that Emma looks ready to lick up on her hands and knees.

"This is awkward," I say to her, shrinking into myself and grimacing like I am embarrassed. "Because it's going to come across like a quid pro quo, but you should know that quid pro quos happen all the time in my industry and you only make them with people whose contributions you value."

Emma stares at me hungrily with her uneven eyes.

"I'm obviously mortified that you found out I was here with Henry—"

"I would never judge you," Emma insists magnanimously.

"Unfortunately, you would be the only one, should this get out."

Henry reaches for my hand in a show of support. I glance at him with gratitude, face Emma bravely, as though I have called a press conference to share some harrowing health update with the public.

"Women cannot win."

"Mmmm," I agree, though this is one of those sayings I detest coming from women like Emma, someone who has not yet lost anything, who does not understand it is this very consensus that has made it possible for me to win sometimes. If the world were fair to us, what would I have to write about? "I would like to offer you a role as a production assistant on my next project. We are in conversation with someone very exciting to star, and if she attaches, preproduction would begin this summer, likely in Los Angeles, though it could be Atlanta. In addition to your salary, I would cover your travel and living expenses for the entirety of the forty-seven-day shoot, which will shake out to about four months."

Emma doesn't say anything, and after a long moment, when it becomes clear that's the offer, she releases her knees and eases back into the chair. "Oh," she says, surprised and ever so slightly insulted.

Henry must feel that my hand has gone cold in his. He gives it two quick squeezes, like a defibrillator supplying an electrical current to my failing heart. *Look alive.* "A lot of very successful people got their start as PAs," I add in a perky tone.

"Not you, though." Emma's wet lips curl into a rather sinister smile.

"I started as an assistant to Jonathan," I say, my chest hot. "If you would prefer an opportunity like that, I can help to arrange it. It just means a much longer commitment, and you likely won't get production experience for a while. It took me three years to step on set."

Emma has her hands on the arms of the chair, and she picks at the nubby fabric, flicking the fuzz onto the floor for Corrine to clean up at some point. "I thought you were coming here to make me an offer on my script."

I give her an incredulous look to which she has to concede.

"I mean, okay, I get it, we can't use *that* script for obvious reasons. But to make an offer for me to write something else."

"It doesn't work like that."

"How does it work?"

"If you've written something I like and think is viable, I would attach as a producer and shop it around to the studios. If it's a fit for them, they are the ones who make us a financial offer to option it as we develop it together."

"Great," Emma says brightly. "Let's do that."

I keep my voice even. "But you don't have anything for me to take out."

"I'll start working on something."

"But I can't promise you it's going to be something I want to attach myself to."

"Ummm." Emma winces apologetically. "I think you kinda do."

My face turns terrifying.

"Sorry," she adds quickly. "Never mind."

"No. Go on."

"It's just"—Emma scrambles to win me back—"I know

you and your husband have built something really cool together. I'd love to be a part of that."

"That is what I'm offering you."

"I can't go to Los Angeles right now. Or Atlanta."

"How come?"

"Well." Emma jams her hands between her legs and squirms girlishly. "Campbell. He's divorcing Corrine. So I need a sort of work-from-home situation."

Next to me, Henry stays silent, listening to our seltzers fizz frantically in their glasses. He has told me the less I know the better. That the only thing I need to do is offer Emma something tantalizing enough that she will promise her discretion for the next few days.

"Emma, as much as I would love to lock myself in my office, work on something for a few months, then sit back, let it sell, and get back to my regular life, this industry does not work like that, not even for someone like me who has already established herself."

"Really?" Emma scrunches her cute little nose dubiously.

"*Really.* First, you have to write something that is even good enough to be picked apart by your agent and producers, and then you have to collate all their notes and take another stab at it, and then you do that again and again until you hate the project so much you're not even sure if you want it made at all. And then, when everyone agrees it's ready for market, you may or may not get an offer, and if you do, you have to be prepared to do that over and over again with studio notes, and each time you earn a little bit more money.

"But that's getting way ahead of ourselves, because

your priority at the moment should be getting a foot in the door. That looks like being on set. With an address in Los Angeles. You need to meet people your age who will grow up to become the agents and producers and studio execs who will deign to pick your work apart. You need to make connections and trade favors and eat some fucking crow every now and then. Being good is not good enough."

"You said yourself the world has changed. That everything is remote now. That you have to know what the rules are to break them." Emma cringes slightly at herself. "I read that in your interview in the style section. I loved it, by the way."

"But you don't know what the rules are yet."

"You just told me."

"Me telling you and you experiencing them are not the same."

Emma shrugs. "I'm not taking a blood oath to never move to Los Angeles and do all the things you're talking about. I just want to sell something I've written." On my face, she must see some sort of fading, that I am close to folding, because she grins. "It will be good. I promise. I'm really good, Faye. I won't let you down."

She will. Anyone who wants it like this is deficient in the magic needed to make something good. The fondest months of my life are those I spent carving out time to write on set, surrounded by people who had accomplished more than me. Squeezing in a single exchange while a makeup artist dusted my T-zone with mattifying powder, finding the words to put to the terror and rage my character felt when she realized she might miss her flight, then going back and finding better words, and better words still. The angst I felt waiting for my agent to read it before I dared show it to anyone else. *FAYE!!!!* she had written me, and my angst grew wings, busted out of its protective shell, and took vibrant flight. *HOLY SHIT.* Emma will not get that from me or from anyone. There is nothing holy about doing things this way.

And yet.

There is a sunny confidence about Emma, sitting there on her boucle throne, the lady of another lady's manor, that all but guts me. I'd bet anything she has one of those *they're just jealous* mothers. Any time someone was mean to her, any time she wasn't invited somewhere, she didn't make the team, she didn't get what she wanted—her mother, who definitely had Emma young, who probably wears her hair long and half up in a scrunchie, put her arms around her daughter and assured her it was because she was so exceptional, not just in her talents but as a person, that others found her too threatening to include. Emma believes she deserves good things in life not because she has put in the time or effort but because she is good. Some might call this entitlement, but the older I get the more I think it might be nice, to be so assured of your solid human gold. I would not have what I have if I had a mother like that, but maybe, I'd manage to survive without it. Maybe my magic is a black one.

I smile defeatedly at Emma. "Okay, then."

Emma slides her hand into the space between us so that we can shake on it. Her skin is cool and dry and her grip loose, as though there was never a need to worry to begin with. Of course things would work out in her favor. This was the outcome Henry needed, and so the relief I feel is mainly tied to that, but also, a little bit, to this tactile reminder that Emma is Emma and I am me. Emma won't ever feel as low as I do on my lowest days, but then again, there will be few occasions to fly.

The three of us pile into Henry's runabout and spend the ten-minute ride to the parking lot in companionable silence. The plan is for Emma to drive Campbell's car to the Albany train station, Henry and I following in Henry's car, and then one of us will return Campbell's three-row jetliner on wheels to the parking lot at the lake. We say goodbye and climb into our respective vehicles. As we exit the leafy, unpaved private drive onto a two-lane road, the radio catches a signal and the dim interior of Henry's Tahoe gooses with a nineties boy-band song I know by heart.

"I'm not attaching myself to anything she writes," I tell Henry.

"You won't have to," he says. "I promise."

"How can you promise that?"

Before Henry can answer, the treacly chorus cuts out, and the display screen shows an incoming call from an impossible name from my life back in California. Henry ends it with a sharp jab of his pointer finger.

"Your phone must have connected," he says, staring straight ahead. "Call him back once we are closer to the city. It's just going to keep cutting out here."

*

In the rearview mirror of Henry's car, there are more mirrors, fastened around the headrests, ostensibly so that Henry can keep an eye on his kids while he drives. Here and there, we pass squat, rundown homes situated next to massive farming structures on sprawls of land so green it makes my eyes hurt. We don't get green like this in Los Angeles. Trucks and battered SUVs are parked in the driveways, lights on in the windows. The speed limit is only thirty-five. I could open the door, protect the back of my head, roll onto the side of the road, and listen to the stifled voice in my head. *Run*, it is saying, *I* am saying, however faintly. I could say that last night was about doing what I had to do to survive. About Stockholm syndrome. About PTSD. I could convince the authorities and probably my therapist too, and that's how I would live with myself. But the thought of leaving Henry makes me feel hollowed out and black, drained of a life in color.

I remove my hand from the door handle. There is no green like this in Los Angeles.

Two hours and seventeen minutes after we started, we see our first sign for the Albany-Rensselaer train station. Henry pulls up alongside Emma at a traffic light and rolls down my window, gestures for her to do the same.

"We have to grab some groceries," he tells her. "Park in the lower lot, and we'll pick up the car on the way out."

Emma nods and lifts her hand in a neighborly wave. I flutter my fingers at her. The light turns green. We turn in different directions.

"What's that about?" I ask Henry.

"I thought you could cook for me tonight, since you turn green whenever I put a plate in front of you."

"I generally try to avoid blowing through my sodium allotment within the first minutes of waking."

Henry actually laughs. "Fair." Up ahead, I see the familiar white font of a Whole Foods sign. But Henry does not slow down.

"What are you doing?"

"We can't go there."

"Why?"

"Because they have security cameras. And I don't want anyone knowing we were in Albany today."

"But what about the train station? Aren't there security cameras there?"

"We aren't going back for Campbell's car."

I lean my head against the window. Stare at my excessive green surroundings until my eyes water. I don't bother asking why we wouldn't go back for the car. The less I know and all that.

Henry turns on a single-lane state road, driving with a low, underhand grip on the wheel, elbow resting on the window ledge, his fingers pinching and releasing the light-brown hair at his temples. In the back seat our groceries clink and bump into one another. We went to a super Walmart at some point between Albany and the lake, a place with wide mopped floors and ice-cold tomatoes. Now we are two miles to a town called Eggs, according to a green mileage sign approaching in the distance.

"You need to call your husband back," Henry says

suddenly. "This area is good for reception for a few minutes." He scoots back and hunches over, rooting around in the map pocket before producing my phone. He plugs in the new passcode he's assigned me, and then the screen opens a portal back to my life.

My husband answers, speaking to someone else. "It's Faye," he's saying to the people he is with. "I've gotta take this." Then, "Hey, babe. Give me a sec." Some chatter in the background. "Howie and Anne say hi."

In my peripheral vision, I see the seams of Henry's fingernails redden on the wheel. Never, in a million lifetimes, would he resort to calling me babe. "Tell them hi," I say cheerfully. My husband tosses back the greeting on his way out of the conference room where they are probably gathered. I can picture the modern but outdated production office they've rented in the financial district of London. Glass walls. Flat, gray carpeting. One of those coffee makers that spits out cappuccinos and doesn't fully mix the powdered milk.

"Hey," he says again, once he's alone, and his voice sounds different. Lower. Somber, like he has bad news to deliver. "I need to ask you something."

My blood crashes in my ears, deafening me a moment. Next to me, Henry sits up straighter, at attention. "Okay," I say.

"Is it true you took a meeting with Caroline Hasser?"

In my peripheral vision, the trees blur like I'm drunk. I look to Henry, open-mouthed. He shakes his head, mouths, *No. No. It wasn't me.* I cover my face with my hands a moment, try to think. I don't know how my husband found out, but denying it will only make things worse.

"I did," I admit.

"Faye," my husband says, hurt. "Why the hell would you do something like that?"

"Why do you think?" I say back indignantly.

There is a long silence. "We're making a movie together," he reminds me. "My brother set meetings for when you get back and talked you up to these guys."

"I don't think we need to pursue independent financing for this one."

"No studio is going to give you what you're asking for, even with A-list talent attached. And anyway, how do you propose all this works if we have split representation?"

"People do it all the time."

"Not married people."

"Well," I say, and let him sit with that a moment.

"I see," my husband says in a stranger's voice that makes me feel like gravity doesn't exist for me anymore.

"How did you hear about this?" I ask, feeling scolded and small.

"Did you really think I wouldn't?"

"I guess I knew there was a chance," I say. Part of me wondered if I took the meeting hoping he would find out, so that I would be forced to make a decision, one way or another. I swallow nervously. It's a gulp, Faye. Just say it's a gulp. "Does anyone else know?"

"Not that I know of, no, and I'll do my best to keep it that way, but I can't make any promises." In the background, someone opens a door and asks my husband something. He tells them he will be there in a minute, waits a moment, then speaks close to the receiver. "All I ever asked, Faye," my husband says, lowly, sounding every bit as far away as he is, "is that you don't pull the rug out from beneath me."

I'm so angry I see stars. "I asked you to take care of this last year, and the year before that, and the—"

"I got the name of someone from my brother. I have an appointment for next month."

*Why bother now?* That's what I'm thinking. I'm angrier, actually, that he waited until I was pushed to the brink. Now I'm the one who will be the bad guy. "Wow," I say, in a tone that is up for interpretation.

"What we have is too important for me to throw away."

But he has. He won't agree with me, but he has. It's been too many years of trying. What we had is in a junkyard, buried under several hundred tons of scrap metal and hazardous waste. I'll poison myself trying to find it.

"Just give me a chance to do what you asked, Faye."

I stare out the window at the many mossy mountains that separate us. "Okay," I say eventually. Look up Groundhog Day in the dictionary, and there will be an image of me, Faye Heron, giving her husband one last chance.

My husband exhales, relieved, and I find I can be angrier still. This is always what happens. He ends up reassured, and nothing changes for me. "How's the writing going?" he asks.

"I've hit a wall."

"We told her we'd send it Monday."

"I may need a few more days."

"Do your best."

"Never occurred to me," I say.

My husband laughs appreciatively. "I miss you. I'm so ready to come home."

I hesitate a moment, and an exciting charge ripples through the car. "I miss you too."

# Chapter 20

Twenty hours after I ditched Henry on the side of the road, I met my husband for the first time.

I was sitting on a slim black leather couch in the middle of what felt like an airport hangar, surrounded by fit and frowning people wearing headsets inside their glass-walled offices. I was sleep-deprived and ragged with regret over the way things had ended with Henry. I had arrived an hour early for my interview with Jonathan, figuring I'd find a coffee shop and sit and wait. Jonathan's office was located in what looked like an old warehouse in Culver City, immediately off the highway on a street that did not even have sidewalks. I'd gone around the corner and sat on the pavement for forty minutes until it was time to go and check in.

Ten minutes after my interview was supposed to start, a guy came out of one of the glass-walled offices and strode toward me with his headset around his neck. "Faye?" he asked.

I stood and shook his hand. He was mid-to-late twenties, a grown-up wearing a pressed shirt and tailored jeans.

Light scruff on his jaw. Hazel eyes. He asked me if my trip had gone all right, if I had hit any of the legendary Los Angeles traffic on my way to their offices that morning. He said he had a terrible commute himself but it was worth it to live on Ocean Avenue in Santa Monica and walk to the beach barefoot every morning to surf. I could immediately picture him paddling into the Pacific, whipping wet hair out of his eyes, his phone back on sand, rattling with reminders about important meetings with important people. He was easygoing but successful in a way that made me want to split him open for answers. How did you do it? How do I?

"I'm just happy I made it," I said.

Jonathan's former assistant continued to smile at me. He hadn't stopped smiling since the moment he laid eyes on me. "Jonathan is almost ready for you. Can I get you anything? Water? Coffee?"

"Maybe some water," I said, and he motioned me to follow him into the kitchen area. On our way he pointed out various corners of the office and explained who worked where and what they were doing. They had two shows currently in production and seven in development. Jonathan had recently promoted him from assistant to production coordinator after three years on the desk. He was trying to get this role filled quickly so he could fly to Cincinnati, where they were in the last month of production on something, and he started to tell me about the project but stopped abruptly.

"You brought a copy of your résumé, right?" He glanced from the small bag hanging on my shoulder to my empty hands and back to the small bag again.

"Shit," I said. "Oh my God. Shit." I clapped a hand over my mouth. I had printed out five copies of my résumé on sturdy stock paper in the office of the clubhouse, enclosed them in a plastic file folder, then left that file folder in the suitcase I unpacked in the back seat of PT's car on the way to the airport.

He put his hand on my arm, stopping me and glancing around the office to make sure no one was watching. "Come with me." He took me over to his desk and had me sign in to my email while he ravaged the supply closet for the good paper.

"Thank you," I said as we stood next to each other at the printer. It was 2014, and the surest sign that you could be trusted to get someone's coffee and make a dinner reservation was if you remembered to bring a hard copy of your résumé to your interview and then followed up with a handwritten thank-you note within forty-eight hours. "*Thank you*," I said again, near tears this time, because I had barely slept, and I had hurt the person I loved and obliterated the brief but comfortable existence we had created at the lake, and I was imagining what it would feel like to go into Jonathan's office and see the look on his face when he realized I had forgotten a copy of my résumé—like I was raised in a barn—and the idea that this person I had just met saved me from such a devastating fate had left me weepy with gratitude.

"Hey," my husband said softly. "I'm happy to help."

I was a good assistant. Not great. Occasionally bad, though my husband helped cover for me in an instance where I screwed up a car service and booked Jonathan in a window seat instead of the aisle. I spoke to Henry once more, when I returned home after the interview. Home-home, to my parents' place in Massachusetts. I had accepted the job, and he wanted to know where he could mail my things. I told him I would reach out when I found a place in Los Angeles, then never did. I felt bad for him, and it made me angry to feel bad for someone else when my life was taking off in the way I'd hoped it would.

My husband went to Cincinnati. He came back and soon left for Toronto. There was a lull in production after that, things tied up in development, and that's when things started up between us.

The office was full of young people who were friends with other young people who worked at other production offices, talent agencies, management companies, studios. We went to happy hours together. I made best friends, enemies, had crushes, and eventually made out with my husband in an Uber ride home from an LCD Soundsystem concert at the Greek. We hid our relationship from everyone. There wasn't a strict no-dating-your-coworker policy, but my husband was paranoid about his private life. Jonathan had passed on two ideas my husband felt strongly about, and around my two-year anniversary as Jonathan's assistant, he was toying with the idea of leaving and starting his own thing. When people hear this story, they picture a Jerry Maguire situation. Me as Renée Zellweger, willing to follow a boisterous Tom Cruise anywhere. But it was never so much an act of faith as that.

My husband bided his time. Waited for the right

moment. His brother, the superstar agent, was in the process of putting together a merger that would turbocharge executive pay at the agency that now represents me. When it went through, he not only became rich himself but because he had made other, more senior people rich, an umbrella of untouchability opened over him and he got to decide who stood under it and not. That was when my husband decided it was safe to start something that would potentially put him in competition with Jonathan.

Not long after, he got one of the projects Jonathan passed on greenlit by a major studio. It was a show about young women making their way in Los Angeles created and written by a young woman trying to make her way in Los Angeles, and one day she came over to talk to my husband about something, and we met for the second time, but it was the first she really clocked me. “Well, you’re pretty,” she said. “Have you ever acted before?”

I thought about the tears I produced in the back of PT’s car, my profuse apologies the morning I had to leave for my interview that I had not meant but had pacified Henry long enough for me to escape. “Not professionally.”

She laughed. She thought that was interesting. She wanted actors on her show who were not actors. It wasn’t like she handed it to me on the spot. There were auditions, chemistry tests. Test screenings and rewrites and reshoots. I quit my job with Jonathan, and he was mostly annoyed he had to find a new assistant, but there was no bad blood, and now when we see each other out in the world, he greets me warmly and not just because I made something of myself. It’s because, as the sister-in-law to the superstar agent, I get to stand under the umbrella of untouchability too. And people who break his kid brother's heart by serving him with divorce papers face a far worse fate than simply standing out in the rain.

My brother-in-law is a bully. He's crude and money-obsessed and vengeful. I've seen what he's done to actresses he believes have spurned him. I saw what he did to the creator of my show, who is no longer in my life, who is now living in her parents' attic back home in Indiana.

I don't really know what happened between them. They dated casually for a few months, and from what I can gather, he was the one who broke up with her because he believed she was cheating on him with someone on her set. I don't know if she was, but I do know that even if she had been, she did not deserve what came next.

Some mouthy mouthpiece with a large and furious Twitter following dug up old tweets that were brazenly anti-Semitic. The creator swore she'd never written them. They were doctored; part of a smear campaign against her. So many of our peers and decision-makers in Hollywood are Jewish—did I not find it suspicious that it was this group in particular that she had allegedly offended? *I don't know*, I had said to her, feeling exhausted. I had no idea who to believe. My husband balked when I asked if he thought his brother had anything to do with it, and the creator refused to apologize for things she didn't say, which of course only inflamed the situation more. Suddenly I was being asked to take a stand—if I still supported the creator, that meant I supported bigotry. Which one was it?

I had to make a statement. I had to disavow her. I

thought I was doing the right thing at the time. It was only later, on my wedding day, that my brother-in-law put his cards on the table. He had asked to take me for a spin on the dance floor, and there, his hand a little too low on my back, he whispered in my ear, *Break his heart and I'll bury you in Indiana too.* He spun me wide, and so I saw he was grinning at me in his sneaky game show–host way, those veneers like white bricks in his mouth. I went pigeon-toed, knock-kneed. This was the slick new reality of my slick new life.

I can imagine exactly how it would happen for me. It would start online in the comments section, where well-compensated trolls would blaze a deadly fire. Did I cheat? Did my sweet husband want a baby but I was too vain and selfish to give him one? Am I actually not that pretty and did I only get this far because I had the privilege of receiving a scholarship that allowed me to attend the same college as a successful producer twenty years my senior? Jonathan is gay, so at least no one can say I slept with him. Some people might defend me. Because all I am is a woman who asked for a divorce, right? Phase two will go for the jugular. Some set designer from some production I worked on will come out of the woodwork and say I was a toxic employer. Once there was a clash between our director and line producer and we sided with the director, who was a white man. The line producer was not. It will not matter that my husband's name is also on our LLC. I'm the woman. I should protect other women, even when they are demonstrably in the wrong. I should do better, *know* better. And for anyone who may feel bad for me, they will be reminded that I have my millions to cry into, millions that will be drained and divided by the divorce and legal battles over who gets ownership of which project and why, and by the time all is said and done, my financial adviser will have little to advise me on.

It does not matter that I have more to offer, more I want to do, that I'm talented and shrewd and bankable. This life is on loan. And truthfully? Knowing that keeps me sharp. I am someone who needs the fear.

# Chapter 21

In the parking lot, a sudden, strong panic grips me to my bones.

"Henry," I say, paralyzed with dread, "wasn't Campbell's boat docked over there when we left?"

Henry follows my eyeline to the white runabout with sporty green stripes. I swear it had been one over from the boat slip when we first arrived, and now it's not.

"It's only because you're looking at it from the inverse direction," Henry says. Does he sound unsure? I cannot tell. A shiver goes through me. The temperature has dropped to somewhere in the sixties, though it's difficult to gauge after so long living in a desert climate. The humidity does this thing, traps you in a disorienting, sticky web. We are walking back over to the boat slip, our boots scuffing the packed-sand parking lot, and now I stop and fold my arms over my chest and look out at the clear water, the low, dark sky. It's going to rain any minute now.

"How long are we going back there?" I jut my chin over Henry's shoulder. There. The cabin. Our rotten slice of paradise.

"Corrine is expecting to hear from Campbell on Monday. I imagine that's when she'll start calling around, asking people if they've seen him."

Monday is three days away. I look up at Henry, my eyes smarting under the harsh gray clouds. I'm remembering Susanna Moore's novel *In the Cut*, which I finished on the plane to New York not even a week ago. I read it as a middle finger to anyone who would believe a smart, self-sufficient woman could be turned so stupid by lust.

"I have so much to lose, Henry," I whisper.

The look on Henry's face rips me in two. "I have more," he says.

I sigh. Drop my head. Nod. *Let's go*. We start walking toward our slip, and I help Henry load the grocery bags into the boat. He steps onto the deck and turns around to offer me his hand. Stupidly, I take it.

I spend a long time in the old copper tub with the wood-covered bottom painted something called Japan green. It was site-made nearly one hundred years ago, in front of the fireplace, so that the metal could absorb the heat and keep the water hot enough for multiple family members to take a soak. I had forgotten the very particular smell I'd sometimes pick up on Henry's skin, that dissonant combination of smoky and squeaky clean.

Now I sink into the bathwater and think. I think about the tone of Henry's voice when he assured me Campbell's boat was parked in the same place as where we'd left it. I am of course rattled by the conversation I had with my husband, by the thought of what would happen to me if he were to find out where I really am, but even when I set that aside, I can't shake the sense that Henry is hiding something from me that I need to know.

I rub my legs together, feeling how smooth they are, relieved I committed to all eight appointments of laser even though my husband no longer touches my legs. Sometimes, I can't believe this is my lot in life. I have a therapist, obviously, with whom I've spoken about my marriage at length. We've dissected my parents' marriage, my husband's parents' marriage; we agree that nothing is happenstance. I'm playing out something that I experienced young, some vital need of mine being unmet, misunderstood, frustrated. I used to think that if I could make sense of it I could fix it. *No, no*, my therapist had said, shaking her head. Fixing is not how this works. You either decide you can accept this, live like this, or you cannot.

In the kitchen, I can hear Henry rinsing things in the sink and placing pots on burners. He's getting started on dinner. I step out of the bathtub and wrap myself in a towel. I freeze, hold my breath, listen to make sure Henry is still occupied. Then I start to open drawers. This room used to belong to Henry's parents, but now the surfaces are covered with photographs of Henry and his wife with their girls doing outdoorsy, fresh-air things. They watch me with their freckles and gummy baby smiles as I go through their parents' belongings, looking for I don't know what, but something that will assuage my fears that I'm being had so I can go out into the kitchen and have sex for the first time in two years.

I open the nightstand drawer, and I must be on the

wife's side, because there is a little porcelain dish cluttered with ticky-tacky jewelry, greenish from wear. My eye immediately goes to the small blue pouch that should be faded with age but somehow isn't. Tiffany must use some crazy dye preservatives. I unsnap the button and turn the pouch upside down. The long silver chain unspools first, the open silver heart tumbling after. I brush the signature twisted metal of the old Elsa Peretti design with my thumb. I'd never officially earned it, and it makes me queasy to think what his wife did that maybe I did not. I wonder how Henry can stomach it, looking at his wife wearing a piece of jewelry that was meant for me, or maybe it's like reminiscing about a loved one you've lost, a way for the living to connect with the dead.

Henry is standing at the kitchen counter, holding a knife. He looks like a scolded little boy when he sees me, with his ruddy cheeks and pouty pink lips, put in time-out for playing with a toy that does not belong to him. There is no full-length mirror in the cabin, but the floor-to-ceiling picture windows capture my reflection. I am once again wearing one of Henry's button-downs, bunchy thick socks, and nothing else, like here on the island we are stuck attending a purgatorial *Risky Business* costume party. My hair is wet and my skin is dewy and radiant from the bath, and around my neck I'm wearing the necklace Henry bought for me twelve years ago.

"Did you really give this to your wife?"

"Did you really go through my shit?"

"I looked under the mattress too. Your turn."

Henry turns his attention back to the onion on the cutting board. "She found the gift bag when she first moved in with me," he said. "I told her I'd bought it for an ex, but it was from Tiffany and you'd never worn it, so she didn't care that much."

"Did she know the ex was me?"

"She knows all about you."

*This* is intriguing. "I want to know all about her."

Henry brings the knife down on his index finger, opening a thin red seam above his knuckle. "Fuck." He turns from me, reaches for the roll of paper towels on the counter behind him.

"Put it under water," I tell him.

He flicks the faucet on and jams his finger into the stream.

I go over to him and peer into the sink. "Is it deep?"

"I'll live."

"Why don't I take over?"

I can already tell that Henry has no idea how to make an adult pasta, only the buttered kind for his kids. I push him aside, pluck the tomatoes from the vine, rinse and dry them thoroughly, then toss them in a hot, dry pan. I mince a few cloves of garlic while the tomatoes blister, then add the aromatics and olive oil, a few splashes of sweet, tangy vinegar and salty pasta water. I drain the ziti two minutes before the package instructions and finish everything off with grated parmesan cheese and a pat of butter. I've always been a good cook, but for whatever reason, the men I am with don't like the kind of food I make. There's never enough meat or it's too much lemon or they're afraid it will make them fat.

"Low carb is a very provincial way to eat," I tell Henry as we sit. When he knew me, I did not know how to cook. He fed me, clothed me, housed me, then we called it love.

"Entertainment is the original provincial profession." Henry inserts a single tine of his fork into the ziti's tunnel, holds it aloft, and examines it warily.

I sip the red wine he's poured into short, mismatched water glasses. There was once a blistering conversation between the Spaldings at this very table about the burgeoning trend of stemless wine glasses, what an affront they were to civilized society. "Tell me, what is your wife's honorable profession?"

Henry takes a slow sip of wine, eyes on mine. "She used to be the deputy director of philanthropy at the Gates Foundation."

My face reveals my utter surprise that Henry has a wife who held such a prestigious position. "Did she quit when you had kids?"

"She didn't quit," Henry says. Then, before I can probe more, "Does your husband have a drug problem?"

I chew my food. Swallow. Smile. "He's never so much as smoked a cigarette in his life."

"Never smoked a cigarette and calls you *babe*. I'd stop wearing my wedding ring too."

I sit back. Settle cross-legged in my chair. Okay. Now is as good a time as any to have this conversation. "There's a little more to it than that."

"Are you going to make me guess?"

"You could never. Not in a million years."

Henry puts down his fork. "He cheated on you."

That's funny. "No."

"You cheated on him."

"Are we counting this right now?"

"No."

"Then, no."

"He's threatened by your success."

"We are successful together."

"He wants kids and you don't."

"He wants whatever makes me happy."

"He's gay."

I sip my wine, shake my head. Try again. I am deriving immense pleasure from this. You may be unique, but your problems are not. I've heard this in therapy, on podcasts, from sober friends who have turned to AA. But I do feel unique and so does my problem, and it feels good, it feels validating, to see that reflected in Henry's inability to guess what the problem is.

"I already know you're a little bit gay," Henry says. Something alights in his eyes. "He doesn't like that *you're* a little bit gay."

I pause. Press my lips together. It's not quite it.

"Okay, so I'm warm." Henry pulls at his pretty lower lip. Thinks. Starts to say something, then thinks some more. "He doesn't like that you're a little bit gay, but he also doesn't cheat on you," he repeats back to himself. He frowns. "He's too vanilla for you?"

"I would take vanilla. God. I would take vanilla."

Henry stares at me. "But it's your sex life?"

I swirl my wine in my glass. Do not dispute it.

"Faye." Henry draws out my name, the way you do the word *ohhhh. Ohhhh*, this is bad. "Is he impotent?"

"Sometimes that would happen, before we stopped trying. But that was a long time ago now."

"How long?"

I scoff. That is the question married people who have normal sex lives ask, because normal sex ebbs and flows. The answer, for those married people who have normal sex lives, is somewhere in the vicinity of three weeks and a year, and then these married people with normal sex lives assume this is the range in which we are operating and assure me that I am normal too, that dry spells are a normal part of normal marriages. Shimmy into a pair of crotchless panties, and have I ever tried role play? I give them a trouper's smile and thank them for the advice, as though I have not been rejected in all manner of confounding and vulnerable positions: in slutty nurse costumes, in private Jacuzzis, at night and in the morning, on his birthday and mine.

"A better question," I say, "would be how many times in the near seven years we've been married."

Henry openly gapes at me. "Is it that low that you actually know?"

"Three times a year before I finally gave up? I could easily calculate it."

"Faye," Henry says with one of those gasp-laughs that empties your diaphragm. "How does that happen? Why would you marry someone like that?"

"My therapist tells me that I got into this relationship

for a reason," I say, "that there is something about my husband that soothed me and felt familiar and safe to me. I didn't know he had all these hang-ups when we got married. We had sex when we first started dating. Not like you and I had, but it felt taboo in its own way because we worked together and we were hiding it from everyone. But once that was gone, once we started our own thing and got so busy, I just couldn't seem to get him interested anymore."

"What is his problem?" Henry asks, and his quiet indignation is indeed the balm I've been looking for all this time.

"Well, to start, he won't admit there *is* a problem. I've been asking him for years to go to therapy, to figure out why sex makes him so uncomfortable. And he looks at me like I have three heads and insists sex doesn't make him uncomfortable. He's so convincing I believe him. But then we go on vacation and I come out of the bathroom in the most ridiculous underwear they make and he's too full from dinner to do anything but cuddle. Role play is for weirdos, sex toys are for masturbation, which should always be done in private. The girls in porn aren't hot enough. Sex at night is for people who don't get up at five a.m. to take a Barry's class before work, and sex in the morning is for people who don't get up at five a.m. for a Barry's class as well.

"He does not cheat," I continue, "and I'm the one with the addiction to porn. He does not see a gorgeous woman on the street and stretch his arms over his head with a yawn and a clandestine glance. I stopped initiating because he can't always get hard, or he can't last long enough for me to get off, and he gets so down on himself that I end up having to comfort and reassure him that it's okay and I still love him, all the while feeling like the loneliest soul in the world. I've heard women who struggle with infertility talk about this, how it feels like everyone around them just breathes and gets pregnant, and it's how I feel about this. Everywhere, all around me, are women complaining about how much sex their husbands want or the acts that their Tinder dates expect them to do because of all the dehumanizing porn they watch. *You have no idea how scary it is out there*, they tell me, but I do, because I watch all that porn too. And then I get these pop-up messages in my inbox all day long about horny sluts looking to fuck five miles away from me, and I want to cry because even my computer thinks I am a man who is not getting any from his wife, and of course it does. That is the way the world works for everyone but me." I gulp my water. My throat is dry, and there is still so much more to say.

"I can't cheat, obviously. Not in Los Angeles, not with anyone on set in any of the places we go. It would get out. A few months ago, I told him that I can't live the rest of my life like this. I gave him a deadline to get into therapy. Six months to find someone and book his first session. He didn't even have to go! Just have proof he sent an email to set it up. He missed it; of course he missed it, and yet I still cannot bring myself to divorce him, because divorce is for people who married assholes. I wish he was an asshole. I wish he cheated on me. I wish he was like you and wanted to control and isolate and punish me, and I wanted to resist him, because then we'd finally have some friction."

Henry regards me, stunned. "That's not where our friction came from. Is that seriously what you've told yourself all this time?"

I study the dumbfounded part of his lovely lips, his wide eyes that are both light and dark, all blinking and disbelieving that I've misunderstood what transpired between us an eternity ago. His cheeks are pinkish from the sun—the term *high health* flashes in my mind—and he's wearing a chambray button-down that he owned in college that is now splattered with bleach spots, the collar flimsy with wear. He looks like a college lacrosse player, and not the one who would so obviously roofie you. He's the one parents love, teachers and small children too. Completely, utterly harmless.

"Where did it come from, then?" I ask, deciding to take him in good faith. "What is it you tell yourself?"

"I gave you what you needed, but you refused to give it back to me. Same shit that happened with my mother."

I gape right back at him. "Are you in therapy?"

Henry sips his wine and he *winks* at me. I am speechless. My West Coast–wellness-chasing husband does not have a therapist but Henry does. "For how long? What made you go?"

"I just . . . noticed some patterns."

*"Patterns."*

"Will you please stop looking at me like that."

"Like what?"

"Like I'm some kind of hashtag men's rights dickhead."

"You are a dickhead. That's why I liked you."

"You ever talk to your therapist about that?"

"All the time."

"And?"

I stare at the table contemplatively. I cleaned my plate; what's left on Henry's has gone cold. We finished our wine and our water. In the far corner, the fire is down to embers. I know what happens next, and it is almost too much to bear. I thread my fingers together and twist them back at painful angles, trying to centrally focus my discomfort, to somehow contain it.

I shrug. Answer broadly, cowardly, "From an evolutionary standpoint—"

"An *evolutionary* standpoint?" Henry is jiggling his knee, grinning at me like I've got to be kidding him. He's reclined comfortably in his chair, legs spread in that way that spawned ragey Instagram accounts featuring men on the subway in the 2010s. He is once again barefoot, the bottoms of his pants rolled just above his ankles. His heels bounce in the thick old carpet. Most people think of money and they think of the private choppers landing on an East River pier to return the cast of *Succession* to their earth-toned penthouses, but Henry sitting there in his father's hideous windbreaker from the eighties, in his fusty summer home to which he will never have to earn the deed, which he will never feel pressure to update, that is money to me. That is a power that makes me want to crawl on hot coals.

I roll my eyes. "Yes. From an evolutionary standpoint, being on good terms with a dominant person increases your chances of keeping the resources you need to survive."

"And I'm the dominant person in this situation?"

"You know you are. Most men are."

Henry raises his chin and narrows his eyes, staring at me down the bridge of his nose. *Ahhh.* He gets it now. "I'm picturing little twenty-two-year-old Faye, thinking she would shatter my heart and she would be fine. That she'd have her pick of the litter."

"I did think that, yes."

"And now you know how good you had it?" That cocky grin again, the one that makes my skin feel too tight for my body.

"Ha-ha," I say. "I'll take my licks."

"Oh, I know you will."

Warmth surges through me, as much a cardiac shock to the system as jumping into the half-frozen lake in the wintertime.

Henry drops his head, scratches the back of his neck, his face all screwed up from thinking. "But if that's what you like, then why marry your husband?"

"Because in a weird way, this is control. This is how he wants things, for reasons neither of us understand, because he doesn't want to go there, and I'm the one who is falling in line."

"Last night," Henry says. "How long had it been?"

"Since someone else got me off? I don't actually know."

"Ballpark."

"Eight."

"Eight months?"

"Don't be obtuse."

"Faye," Henry says sternly, like I've told him an outlandish lie.

"I mean we've had some sex in that time. But me getting off with him?"

"Eight fucking years, Faye?"

"Please stop. I'm mortified."

"What do you have to be mortified about? He's the one who should be mortified."

I glance at the bedroom door, my cheeks flaming. "Because I don't even know what I'm doing anymore. Last night was easy. Last night my hands were literally tied. But the person I was when we were together, I don't recognize her anymore. I don't really remember how we used to do things, just that it was good, and I'm scared it's not going to be good now, because I feel like such a freak and I've . . . given up." I lift a hand. What more is there to say? I don't know why people call it an unburdening. Nothing about me feels lighter for saying this. I want to weep from the exhaustion of carrying something so huge and shameful, which now feels close to colossal for putting words to it. Before, it was merely a free-floating abstraction of unhappiness I could bat away like a bad odor while I barked at people about the lens I wanted, to kick up the audio in the edit room. *Not that actor*, I got to write back to my casting director, *I don't believe he's ever really struggled in his life, find me someone with yellow teeth and acne scars, someone I buy*. I did an all right job of fashioning a way to say what I want and get it, to tunnel around the truth: I'm still in here. I cannot be deleted.

"It would be so easy," Henry says in his posh, appealing voice, "for me to make it easy for you."

My stomach contracts, hot and tight. I reach for my

water, drain what's left, then roll the empty glass around in my hands for something to do.

"Do you want me to?"

I stare at my glass, give an almost imperceptible nod. Outside, the sky pulses with heat lightning, the kind they say is not dangerous.

Henry does not move, but his voice changes like he's risen to his full and towering height. "I didn't like it when you told him you missed him today."

I sit very still and think about my answer. "If I didn't say it back," I say, and I can hear how nervous I am in my quaky prepubescent voice, "he would have been suspicious."

Henry's face is stone. "I didn't like it, Faye."

More harmless lightning, revealing the empty black stage of the lake.

"I can't imagine it was easy for you to hear," I submit. "I'm sorry."

Henry puckers his lips in a show of consideration, sliding his plate back and forth on the table with his wounded index finger, a big cat toying with its prey. "What if I said that's not good enough?"

I raise my chin, hold Henry's eye, force myself to withstand the discomfort. Sometimes, I think that it is these moments, the ones between the moments he tells me what to do, that I miss the most.

Henry nudges the plate in my direction. "I'd like you to clean up now."

I am weightless and warm as I gather our dishes and carry them to the sink. I turn on the faucet, squeeze a generic brand of blue dish soap into a sponge, an everyday domestic act turned tightwire act under the tension of Henry's storm-blue stare.

I dry the plates. Open a cabinet door, return them to their stack. A light, irregular rain begins to streak the windows, and then thunder cracks so near it feels like an unruly child has shaken our little snow globe, rattling the miniaturized scene of us.

"There are crumbs on the table," Henry says.

I tug the dish towel off its hook.

Henry flicks his hand. No need for that. "You can use your mouth."

I fold the dish towel silently, my hands shaking, and return it to its hook with the borders lined up neatly. I approach Henry, aware that I am retracing an old, sacred path. Lust rises in the back of my throat like bile.

With one foot, Henry slides a chair out of the way and angles his own so that he is sitting perpendicular to the table, creating a small space just big enough for me to slip inside. Our bodies brush—my outer thigh, his inner—and then, impossibly, I am bending over the edge of the table and crumbs are adhering to my tongue like a lint roller. Henry puts an elbow on the table and rests his temple on his fist, watching me with that combination of contempt and fascination that has always been my undoing. He takes the tail of my light-colored shirt and passes it between my legs, exhaling long and slow when it comes away wet.

He fingers the damp fabric with a low, incredulous laugh. "I haven't even touched you yet."

I rest one cheek on the table, look up at him with all

my stupid, embarrassing need. His nostrils flare once, like he might cry.

"Okay," he says, because he has always been inside my head, hearing and understanding everything. "Okay," he says again.

He stands, placing the wide sprawl of his fingertips on the small of my back. I hear the clang of metal hitting metal, leather rustling belt loops. Henry slips his big toe under my instep and nudges. Wider. He wants my legs wider.

For a while, he strikes me in silence. I imagine his face, his grim concentration as he waits for one of us to break and say I've had enough. But nothing he's done to me has ever felt like enough.

"Say you're sorry, Faye." Henry's voice is tight with anger and yet in it I hear the heartbreak he is asking me to soothe.

I curve my torso on the table, turn my head to the side with the pad of my thumb tugging down my lower lip, taking in Henry with heavy, hooded eyes. His fresh-looking face is soft with devotion, a flip of light hair in an eye. His shirt is untucked, buttoned all wrong at the bottom so that it hangs haphazardly at his collarbone. He looks undone, tormented in exactly the way I hoped he might be after all these long years without me.

"I'm sorry I told my husband I missed him," I say. The expression on Henry's face tells me this is not nearly enough. I stare at the pained part in his lips and I realize what it is he needs to hear. "I'm sorry I have a husband." That's it, isn't it? My gravest offense.

With an anguished groan, Henry collects me by my hair, stands me up, turns me around, walks me backward into the bedroom with his mouth on mine. If I stopped suddenly or turned around to run, he wouldn't let me. It is this thought that propels me over the threshold of the door. I want to feel so wanted I have no choice, though of course this is everything I choose.

The lights are off, the drapes open, the moonlight casting everything in silver. Henry lifts me by the wrists and throws me on the bed, slips off his shirt, steps out of his jeans.

The snap of his boxer band, and then he stands before me, naked, godlike and indestructible, something knowing and merciful on his face. The fire and the moonlight are too romantic. I need to be tossed around, sordidly fucked while still half dressed. He grabs my ankles and slides me under him.

"I'm not on birth control anymore," I suddenly remember to say out loud.

Henry wraps my legs around his waist and gives no indication that he hears me or cares. He rubs the head of his erection over the seam of me until I'm wet enough for him to push partially inside. I'm mortified by how much it hurts, and tears prick my eyes, not from the pain but because the pain indicates something I've found ways to manage before now.

"Fuck, Faye." Henry doesn't go any deeper. He scooches us farther back on the bed so he can climb on top of me and put his thumbs in the damp corners of my eyes. He's staring down at me in astonishment, like he can't believe everything I told him was true. "I felt that. I'll go slow."

I try to turn my head, but he holds me still between

his hands, watching me chew a hole through my lip as he slides the rest of the way into me. I make a sound without opening my mouth, like I've just been given some piece of terrible but inevitable news. Henry moves slow and shallow until I start to relax, and then he rolls over onto his back, bringing me with him. He puts a pillow in his lap, bunches it down, giving me something textural to rub against. I think about the time he gave me his credit card to buy a new dress, how he gave me a limit and said that for every dollar I spent over it, he would hurt me that many times. I think about how I spent an extra thirty-one dollars, just to see if he meant it, and how I remembered that he did every time I sat down for the next week—

"You're so pretty when you're about to come," Henry says, because I am damp at the small of my back and my pleasure is concentrated in a perfect little knot at the top of my pussy.

I am nearly horizontal on top of Henry, the silver heart pooled in his clavicle. I'm grinding on him when I should be bouncing. There's no way he's not bored. I start to straighten, but Henry hooks his finger through the charm and holds me down.

"I want it from behind," I protest.

"No, you don't."

Henry works his hand between our bodies, pushes the pillow into me. "I want you to keep rubbing your clit on me. I want to be inside you when you come."

He sounds so earnest, looking up at me with his sweet serial-killer face. I squeeze him between my thighs and I fuck and I fuck and I fuck.

"You get so tight," Henry says. "Like you don't want to let me go." He does this, he tells me beautiful stories about us that would otherwise turn my stomach. Like some kind of exposure therapy for true love. I come for a long time, shaking my head *no* as Henry insists it's true, it's true. We love each other.

Henry rolls me onto my back. I'm exhausted, malleable, slick behind my knees and at the nape of my neck. He braces himself on his knuckles above me, his hair flopping at his forehead as he pushes in and out of me. I brush it out of his face, tenderly, because maybe it's all a little bit true. Henry's lips part and his eyes turn to sleepy, twilight slits.

"Let me love you, Faye." He manages to make it sound like a kingly order. He holds my chin in his hand, he forces me to look at him, and I promise him I will try. Then he comes with his mouth on mine, kissing me softly like I am a normal girl, someone who says things like *soulmates* and *making love*. It is as repugnant as it ever was, but I take it. For Henry, I take it.

# Chapter 22

I shove open a window and breathe in the pristine morning. Henry's golden head bobs in the lake, his hands working suds through his hair. I make coffee for us like a dutiful little wife, head out barefoot into the thick, noisy morning, alternating the length of my stride to spare the worms and critters stranded after the storm. The crickets are chirping at a frenetic pace, and I remember Henry telling me that there is a way to calculate the temperature outside by counting their chirps in fourteen- or fifteen-second increments, then adding some number I can longer remember.

I pause in the skimpy shade at the base of the dock and try not to squint. The trees are flowering with small white and purple flowers, beautiful but ineffectual when it comes to my concerns—aging and melanoma, in that order. Henry hauls himself up the ladder, biceps corded and dazzled with wet. He steps naked onto the dock, a hulking, streaming sea creature. He reaches for a towel and dries his hair as he strides over to me at an unhurried, unselfconscious pace, his cock swinging mightily between his legs.

"Why are you cowering back here?"

I hand him a mug. “Shade.”

He considers me with an up-and-down swoop of his eyes as he sips the coffee. “How do you manage living in California?”

“Hats, mineral sunscreen, depression.”

“Depression?”

“It makes it hard to leave the house during the day. I actually think it’s my best-kept beauty secret.”

Henry removes my mug from my hands and sets it on the floorboards of the dock. I know what he’s going to do before he does it, and I turn to get a head start. He gets me by my bouncy cheerleader ponytail, picks me up in a bear hug, and marches us to the end of the dock while I kick and protest.

Henry lays me down on the degraded gray floorboards and pins me in place with his knees. From the shower caddy next to the ladder, he produces a slimy bottle of Hawaiian Tropic dark tanning oil with an SPF of two. It is possibly the same bottle Henry used when we were in our twenties. Despite all his preciousness when it comes to his diet and his teeth and his hair, Henry has always been reckless about the sun. I watch from beneath him, appalled, as he lubes his coconut-sized shoulders, somehow nut brown though it is not even May yet.

“How are you not dead of melanoma?” I ask.

“The sun is not bad for you here,” Henry replies, completely serious.

I laugh. Here. Like the Adirondacks have a special kind of sun, one that doesn’t spot and wrinkle and metastasize to your brain.

Henry drags an oiled finger down the bridge of my nose. "Do you still get freckles?"

"They're called sunspots in your thirties."

Henry looks crestfallen a moment. "How did you celebrate it?"

"Thirty?"

"No," Henry retorts, "your first sunspot."

I squirm beneath him as he knots my T-shirt under my breasts. "You really want to know?"

"You're not the only masochist on this dock." Henry drizzles my middle with more oil. I am trying not to think of everything I will have to do to undo this—probably more of those tiny little needles with the electric microcurrent that makes my limbs involuntarily flail. The thing they do with my own blood: extracting it, spinning it, injecting it right back into my face.

"We did a dinner," I say as Henry bastes my thighs next, "at this old-school steakhouse in Hollywood that's been around since the 1920s. You know, iceberg salad with creamy dressing and tiny martinis that go down in three sips."

"What did you wear?"

I smile. I like that Henry cares about what I wear. "Black leather pants and a black tank top. No bra."

"Unimaginative slut," Henry says, despondent, then rolls off like he's taken a bullet. He folds his arms behind his head. I turn to study him in profile. The heavy, furrowed brows, the bead of sweat in the fluffy bow of his lips, sand and grit in the hair at his temples. That one tendon in his jaw, right next to his ear, keeps popping out like a broken bone.

"Which famous friends attended?" he wants to know.

"All of them," I say. "But they're not my friends."

"Are they all as brutal as they seem?"

"Some of them are about as normal as they can be, given their circumstances, and I would go so far as to say they're good people. The fun ones are really fun." I close my eyes to the sun, not because it feels good but because I'm worried about squinting, wrinkles, that crepe-like texturing. "It's just, you can't get close with people like that. They're guarded; they have to be." Henry exhales through his nostrils, a nearly soundless snort. I hear it too. The second I say it, I hear it. That I was drawn into a world of walls, of parties and pleasantries and protections.

"What did you do for yours?" I ask him.

"My daughter had just been born."

"She was the most precious gift," I intone.

"Kids aren't like that, actually."

"Are you one of those who just talks about how hard it is all the time?"

"No, that's the height of childishness. If you're surprised that it's hard, you're probably not much smarter than a fifth grader."

"So what are kids like, then?"

"They love remote controls."

I laugh. How random. "Remote controls?"

Remote controls, sunglasses, and keys, Henry says. And yet somehow the house feels haunted by a poltergeist with an affinity for beautiful wooden blocks and ugly plastic stackers, books about belly buttons and berserk hippos. He is never too tired to clean up even though he is unbelievably tired. Some days he is sure his children hate him. Or don't hate him, exactly, but don't feel any special attachment to him. He loves them and that's nice, but a lot of other people do too. Some of those people, like their aunt with the trampoline in her backyard, they might miss more than him if they were to go away. And other days they take a wrong step and whack their heads on the edge of the coffee table and he is the only one they want, the only one who can soothe them, and they nuzzle their heads under his chin and cling to him with shuddering, shaky breaths, and it feels so good he wonders if he is suffering from that Munchausen by proxy thing. He spends more time on the floor than he ever thought he would. He changes his clothes three times a day because he never feels clean with two under four running around with hummus in their hair and someone else's snot on their sleeves. He is relieved his daughters take after him and not his wife in the looks department, but terrified that they also contain the same reject quality that Henry has grappled with his whole life. His wife joined a baby group with their first, and slowly over the years the invitations to the birthday parties have fallen off. It happens, she assures him. But Henry has met the other mothers, and he detected a core clique that excludes his wife. Their children played well together even as babies. They didn't cling and cry. They didn't puke constantly the way his first did. Too many times a day to count, until she turned one. Not all babies puke, it turns out. And if they do, it's a tiny dribble. His daughter was constantly wet under the neck. He was afraid to pass her to strangers. Afraid no one would think she was cute anymore if they saw how much she barfed, and it matters to him more than it should that other people think his children are cute. When people say that having a child is like having your heart beat outside your chest, he thought that had to do with love. But it doesn't. It has to do with all your own wounds and shame. Because the biggest revelation Henry has had since becoming a father is that he would never, for one second, consider locking his baby in the cabin while he posted up at the main house without a monitor, which is what his mother did to him.

I don't know what to say and so I say nothing. I reach for his hand and squeeze. We lie next to each other, ruining our skin for some time. Tomorrow is Sunday. The day after that, I'll go back to Los Angeles with a tan.

# Chapter 23

That night, we eat leftovers warmed up on the stove, and after we've washed and dried the dishes, Henry tells me to put on a coat. The day stayed hot, but now the windows are pebbled with rain. When I ask him where we're going, he pretends not to hear.

We get into the boat, and instead of following the back-bend curve of the lake's shores, Henry steers us diagonally across. We used to do this drive with Henry's parents on Friday nights. I would be entrusted with the shopping bag containing bottles of Merlot and disks of soft cheese, Henry's mother repeatedly reminding me to keep it in my lap so that the bottom did not get wet and tear. The first time I carried that intact shopping bag down the dock and up the stairs to the front door where PT was waiting for us with a warm smile and an immediate offer to take the bag from me, I did not understand why the other residents spoke of *PT's place* in such breathless tones. His cabin looked like all the other cabins on Lake Wanika: cozy and unassuming with a dash of intentional kitsch. It was only after Henry took me to see the tree that Dorothy Parker engraved, a winding but mostly flat mile from PT's back door, that I understood. In the distance Henry pointed out peaks of open rock to five thousand feet and said that from up there you could look down and feel like you were king of an entire continent. That's that's how vast PT's property was, how wildly the terrain varied, from sandy hills with conifer cover to private ponds of screaming frogs to stretches of boulder and, in the spring, pockets of what everyone referred to as "lovely black goo," actually some kind of fungus that can almost act as quicksand. And all of it belonged to PT, an unpatrolled hunk of private, howling real estate.

It's been years since I've been in this house, but Henry opens the doors and twists the switches of the gas sconces, and I reacquaint myself with the tatty tribal rugs, the art on the walls that is not fish, and I remember the relief I used to feel when PT opened the door and invited me inside. Here, it didn't matter that I didn't know how to check a boat's engine oil or bushwhack a trail. There were old films to watch and discuss, meaty pours of Italian reds, PT asking me what I thought about *Jaws*—the book, not the movie, told from the perspective of the shark.

PT never had a television. No one on Wanika Lake does. He would use a battery-operated projector, which Henry removes now from the low wood console pushed into a white wall, the only painted wall in the cabin, on which I watched *Casablanca* for the first time.

"What are we watching?"

"Pick out a bottle," Henry answers without answering. "You'll see in a minute."

I go through the kitchen and into the pantry, find a white Burgundy with a scrawly old label. I hear a few chords of a theme song that freezes me in my tracks, and just as quickly it cuts out. I come back into the kitchen area and stare at Henry.

"I've never seen it," he admits. "Other than that episode, I mean."

I'm flooded with my favorite kind of feeling. It is a full-body rush to get to watch something you've made with someone who has never seen it before. Though I've seen my show dozens of times between writing it, shooting it, editing it, screening it, and editing it again, the thing always feels brand-new again when I am with someone who does not know what happens next.

"Why start now?" I say. I'm trying to play it cool but I am profusely happy.

"Because it won't be painful to watch you when you're sitting here next to me," Henry says.

We start with season three, the season I finally raised my hand and ended up writing and directing four of the nine episodes. Henry laughs at the parts that I intended to be funny. He claps when my name comes on the screen. *It's so good, Faye,* he keeps saying to my utter delight, *I get it.*

"I have to know," he says, when we take a break to use the bathroom and scrounge around in the kitchen cabinets for snacks. "What do your parents think?"

"Oh," I say, my hand in a box of stale Cheez-Its. "They stopped watching after the second episode."

"I'm shocked they got that far."

"Yeah, well. I used to get links to the episodes early. And they begged me to send them. And I did and then I just never heard anything, and after a while I checked in and my mother said, and I quote, she was worried I was making a mistake that would hurt my future prospects in life. Also that there was no way she could recommend the show to her friends in good faith because some of the things we spoke about, some of the things we did, were private things, things between a husband and a wife, that should not ever be discussed out in the open and especially not by people who were not married to each other."

Henry holds out a hand. I pass him the box of Cheez-Its. "I can't say I'm surprised. Your parents always struck me as a little repressed."

"A little?" I laugh. Hook my finger through the heart charm on my new-old necklace, saw it back and forth obsessively. "You know, part of me could respect it. If those were their values, and they just stuck to them. But when the show came out, it was immediately this zeitgeisty, awardsy thing. And then I started writing for it. And directing it. And then I won a very prestigious award. And they wanted to be invited to everything. And I did. I invited them. To all the premieres and the parties. Because I wanted them to be proud of me. And they are, so proud. But it's like . . . they're proud of my success but ashamed of what I do. Does that make sense?"

Henry offers me the box of Cheez-Its as a consolation. We nibble and crunch for a moment, not talking.

"Do you think," Henry says, "you are the way you are because of them?"

"I don't think there's one thing that happened to make me the way I am. I think it's a bunch of things and whatever sneaky internal damage occurred when everything collided."

"Like?"

"Well, I think I have a thing about being taken care of." When I was a child, my parents did nearly everything for me. I hated the mornings, and so they laid out my clothes at the foot of the bed. In the bathroom, a slug of toothpaste coated my toothbrush. When math and science made me want to lie down and never wake up, my mother took on algebra, my father acid-base definitions, and let me return the A's in English. This was a precarious deal, I'd come to find, because any time I did anything to displease them, which was often, they threw it back in my face. They did everything for me. Did I have any idea how good I had it, how ungrateful and selfish I must be at my innermost core to not see that on my own?

"And you have a thing with taking care of people," I say. "So we plug in there."

Quietly, Henry says, "Hurting you is the opposite of taking care of you."

"Oh," I muse, offering him the box again, but he waves it away. I set it down on the counter and dust salt from my palms. "The daycare thing is definitely tied up with that."

Henry frowns. "The daycare thing?"

"I told you about that."

"Uh," Henry says. "No, you did not. A daycare thing? I would remember a daycare thing."

Henry would. Henry would remember this. "I really

thought I told you this." I uncross my arms, cross my feet. I suddenly cannot find a position that feels comfortable.

"What the fuck happened?"

I clasp my hands at my pelvis. That still feels wrong. I jam my hands into my pockets. Better. "I went to this daycare where they spanked you." I laugh a little; Henry does not.

"What would you get spanked for?"

"Like, if you did something wrong."

"What would you do wrong?"

"The first time. The main time. I got lost."

"You got lost? How is that a three-year-old's fault?"

"I wandered off," I say. "Or I didn't wander off, exactly, but I didn't keep up." I'm falling all over my words, struggling to explain. I take a deep breath. Center myself. Start from the beginning. "There was a stable not too far from the school. You could get there through a path in the woods. They would take us there to visit a horse named Nickles. It was my turn to pet him or feed him a carrot or whatever, and I was doing that, and all of a sudden I realized it had gotten very quiet. I looked over my shoulder, and everyone was gone. I was all alone in the middle of the woods. I stumbled around until I found a house and knocked on the door. They brought me back to the daycare center, and the owner dragged me into the middle of the room, pulled down my pants, and told all the kids to gather around."

Henry stares at me in horror. "She made the other kids watch."

"She always did. Sometimes she would just put a kid

in her lap and cross their arms over their chest and hold them by their wrists and, like, turn them, in a circle, telling all the other kids, like, 'Look at so-and-so, he's been very bad. He did something wrong. Stare at him.' She owned the daycare, this woman. Her name was Mrs. Worther. She could be so mean, but then after she would punish you like that, she'd, like, dote on you. Cuddle you. Stroke your hair. It was all extremely fucked up, and so yeah, that's probably at play here."

Henry is staring at me, appalled. "Uh, ya think?"

Something about the way he says this is funny to me. *Uh, ya think?* Extremely funny, actually. I start to laugh.

"Jesus," Henry says, shaking his head in disgust. "That's almost as fucked up as the fact that I didn't talk for, like, a year."

"What?" I stop laughing. "Henry, wait. What? You didn't talk for a *year*?"

"Faye," Henry says, in the same admonishing tone I used when I insisted I'd told him about what happened to me at daycare. "I told you this."

"No," I say firmly, and then I burst into laughter again. This conversation is absurd. "No. Henry. Come on. I would remember if you told me you did not say a word for an entire year. What the fuck? What the fuck happened?"

"Oh," he says, his eyebrows raised, realizing maybe he hadn't told me about this either. "I told my mom I had to use the bathroom. We were running errands or something, and the store we were in wouldn't let us use the bathroom, and she was like, 'Can you just hold it? We can be home in ten minutes.' And I probably could have, but I told her I couldn't. So she took me across the street to the McDonald's, and she got hit by a car."

"Henry! No. Stop. *Stop.*" I'm wiping tears from my eyes with my knuckles.

"Yeah. I mean. She was fine, in the end. But she was in the hospital for like a week." Henry stares off into space, shell-shocked all over again. "And I was like, I almost killed my mom because I told her I needed the bathroom, so I should probably just never speak again."

We stare at each other with stricken faces. "Why didn't we ever tell each other this stuff before?" Henry asks.

"I guess we just didn't think it was important then, but now we realize it's so important we thought, of course we told the other about this."

We stand there in the kitchen a moment, not saying anything else, not looking at each other. Henry notices some crumbs on the counter and sweeps them into his palm, deposits them in the sink. He looks up. Fixates on something over my shoulder. I turn to see my face, frozen on the white-painted wall. I'm twenty-seven, pouty, positively lethal.

"Remember the time we stayed here?" Henry poses the question to my old face, though the memory is so vivid it feels new. PT had a wedding in Europe and asked us to housesit for the week. I told Henry I wanted to fall asleep alone. I wanted him to enter the room in the middle of the night. I wanted to be surprised and scared. I wanted him to be a stranger who felt nothing for me at first, but began to feel bad when I started to cry, who dried my tears with the corners of the sheets and kissed me on the mouth until

I gave in and stopped fighting him. *This is rape you're asking for*, he said, impressively neutral. It was like a waiter repeating your order back to you to make sure he'd written it down correctly. Henry wanted to make sure I would get what I was asking for. We had been strolling back from breakfast and he had come around in front of me to say this, to stop me and make me stand still and take in what I was asking for. I had given him a light shove in the chest, and he had grabbed my wrist, pulled me close. *Should I care if you come?*

I thought about my answer as though he were again my waiter, asking me how I'd like my steak cooked. *I don't think I should*, I said after a moment, *not if I want this to feel real*. Henry nodded, his face serious and already frightening. *Wear your hair in a ponytail*, he said. That was that. My steak was as I asked.

I used to think that the things we did together were possible because of me. I was taught all the tired clichés, that men were pigs, that they only had one thing on their minds. I assumed most would kill for a woman with an appetite like mine, that there were a million Henrys out there and only one of me. But now I know.

There is only one of him too.

# Chapter 24

Our last full day is a stunner. Piercing blue sky and the sun shining through to the bedrock bottom of the lake. We have a cannonball contest. We take turns straddling the other on the dock. We go inside and artfully design a snack plate. We make cocktails, screwdrivers. Tomorrow we will leave. Why not get drunk and walk around naked and fuck like the nubile survivors of a shipwreck from that famous eighties movie, discovering what's between our legs for the first time? We do all that and we doze in the sun and we wake up and do all that again. At some point Henry pries himself away from me to take the toolbox I always made fun of him for having into the cabin to fix the window I broke. I offer to make us another round. From the freezer I remove a frosty bottle of vodka. True WASPs know nothing of quiet luxury or the debatable metabolic merits of tequila. They dress unfashionably, and their Grey Goose is always cold and half empty.

The second cocktail of the day burns a slow, syrupy trail from my throat to the pit in my stomach. I am boozy and besotted with just about everyone and everything, waltzing around the house, humming happily under my breath. Inexplicably, I find myself drawn to the wall of bookshelves. I run my fingers over the spines of procedural crime novels and guides to hiking trails in the Northeast. I see the safe and think nothing of it at first, and then I remember that yesterday, before we left to meet Emma, Henry had opened it to get my phone, and I caught his fingers plug in the last two digits to the combination: *13*. I was born on the thirteenth. And now I want to know if Henry used my birthday as the combination to the safe, because if he did I will tease him about it. I'm not really trying to go through his shit again. And I believe this until 12/13, my birthday, works to pop open the door, and inside I find some envelopes containing legal documents that fuzz before my eyes and an orangey prescription bottle for a medication with instructions for Patrick Toner to place a tablet under his tongue at the first sign of an angina attack. The typeface blurs and focuses in my vision. I guess you can murder someone with a heart attack if you pry their life-saving pills from their cold, dying hands, the same hands that once held your bottle and bathed your velvety baby skin.

I walk the stone path between the main house and the cabin with soft feet, my face serene and my heart ramming my ears. I mosey inside with a fresh screwdriver, finding Henry on his knees, blotting the edges of the window frame with a small spongey paintbrush. I rap on the open door to get his attention.

"How's it going?"

"Just waiting for the caulk to dry so I can repaint."

"What does the caulk do?"

"Seals the window to the wall."

"How long does it take to dry?"

Henry sits back on his heels, cranes his neck to check his phone. It's resting face up on the bed, and I see there are seven minutes left on the timer he's set. I don't know how long it will take him to repaint, but once the caulk is set, he won't be able to get back out the window. Seven minutes. I have to keep this up for seven minutes. I offer Henry the glass. He takes a long swig, stares at the pulpy surface a moment. "I want to see you, after all this is over." He looks up at me with his ink-blot eyes, terrified. "Do you want to see me too?"

I won't ever recover from this, I decide. "Henry," I say, like I can't believe he had to ask, "of course."

Henry expels all the air from his lungs, wide shoulders sagging with relief. It winds me too, to watch someone so big act so small. "I can come to you. Or we can come here."

"We'd need to be very careful."

Henry nods. Then, "You don't think you'd ever leave him?"

"I just don't know . . . how we untangle things."

"People do it all the time."

"Yeah. And people lose everything."

"You wouldn't lose me," Henry says with a sad smile.

"You say that now."

Henry gives me a startled look.

"We're living in a bubble here." I gesture. Here. The

cabin. The lake on all sides. No one but us and the crickets to tell us if we need a jacket before going outside. "I don't know yet how this translates in the real world."

"I'm just talking about trying. You want to try, don't you?"

"I said I did."

"You *did*?" Henry sets his drink down on the floor. Begins to get up. Shit. I glance at his phone on the bed. Six minutes.

"I do," I say, correcting myself, but this does not diffuse the suspicion on Henry's face.

"Did something happen?" Henry wants to know, edging close, worrying his hair with his hand. "Did something change?"

I shake my head vehemently. "It's just hitting me that we're leaving. That I should be scared. Really fucking scared."

Henry reaches for me. He tugs me to him, cheek to chest. I let him. I don't have a choice. He smells too good.

Henry burrows his face in the crook of my neck. "What aren't you saying?" he whispers warmly into my skin. The room has a chemical, trippy odor. My mind feels jumbled, distorted. Something. I have to give him something to pass these next five minutes and thirty-four seconds.

"I'm different," I attempt haltingly, "out there. I'm not like *this*. I'm not soft."

Henry draws back, scrutinizes me all over. He picks something out of my hair, shows it to me as though to assure me it's not anything with legs. Just a small, fleecy white bloom. "Faye, no offense"—he blows the bud from his fingertip—"but if you think this is you being soft, we've got some work to do."

I say to him, unsmiling, "I think you'll still want me out there. I could be wrong, but I think you will. What I mean is that I don't know what *I'll* feel."

Henry stares down at me, the tenderness in his eyes turning over into something else.

"There is something tempting," I rush to explain, "about feeling small." I look down at my feet, wishing I had thought to put on shoes before I came in here. "I've gotten to be that again with you, here, but back home"—I glance out the window. Who knows in what direction. East, south, Canada. If my architecturally significant post and beam with a view of the observatory lies due west, it is only by luck. "I am too big for that. I do not need you the way I once did."

"Faye," Henry says, my name smooth on his tongue, "there are ways I can give you what you need that have nothing to do with who has the bigger mortgage now."

I look up at him, crinkle my nose in disgust. "You have a mortgage?"

There is a subtle darkening in the room. Cloud cover, though last time I noticed, the sky was an unblemished blue. My heart kicks my chest. This is our third rail. Who has the money. Who has the power. And I've just reached out, gloveless and death-wishing, to touch it.

"Your bravado," Henry says, cool and remote, "is actually revolting."

"Nothing I've said is untrue."

"You don't need to say everything that is true," Henry says. "That you don't know that yet, that's the revolting part. Show some fucking humility."

I glance at the timer on the bed, back at Henry. "Make me."

Henry stares at me with livid calm. Lightly, he runs a hand up my back, gathers my hair in his fist. "Easy, Faye. It's so easy with you."

My head jerks back. I expel a guttural sound from my diaphragm, like a tennis player at Wimbledon returning a tough serve. Henry adjusts his stance, shifting his weight so that he can slide one of his considerably thick thighs between my legs. My pelvis is instantly flush and frantic with blood.

"I want you to fuck yourself on my leg," he says. "Don't be cute or sexy about it. You know what I want."

It is what I want, actually, but what I want is what Henry wants and around and around we go. I sink down on Henry's thigh with a groan that will haunt me until the end of my days. I can barely stand to hear myself so needful. Henry watches me with something like curiosity, but as I squeeze my thighs around his thigh and seek my relief, I realize the look on his face is nearer to pity. A warm panic squeezes my lungs. How can I leave Henry? How can I leave *this*? And so instead I leave my body to watch what I am doing from the outside, the gruesome spectacle I am making of myself while Henry stands, unmoving and benevolent, scanning my face for signs I'm about to bust all over his J.Crew chinos.

"I could watch this all day," he says fondly. "Are you going to come, sweetheart? I see it in your face. That's fast, even for you."

I grunt with my bottom lip in my top teeth.

Henry cups my chin in his hand and brings his face close to mine. "The thing is, Faye? You can't get away from me." Then, almost apologetically, "No matter where you go and what else you accomplish, I will always know you like this." I gasp in his face, a disastrous admission. Beneath all the other hollow and painted versions of myself, Henry has found the innermost doll in the nesting set, the smallest, most solid me.

On the bed, the timer counts down the final few seconds. We notify Henry that we are done at the same time. I stand there, in the shrill blare of the alarm, straddling Henry's leg, spots swimming in front of my eyes, trying to find my footing again. I am a bad, bad person, I have to be, for being able to do that, for doing what I do next.

I go over to the bed and stab the alarm silent. Then I lift Henry's screwdriver to my lips to take a sip. The glass is slippery with condensation, and it falls from my fingers just as easily as it shatters on the floor. "Shit," I say. "Sorry. I'll get a towel."

"Don't move," Henry says, as I hoped he would. He turns and disappears into the bathroom, and I grab the toolbox—there are hammers in there, things he could use to break down the door—and I take wide, leaping steps to freedom, slam the door behind me quick, lock it with numb, shaking hands. From the other side, Henry calls out my name in confusion. I take a step back from the door in disbelief, and when I realize I did it, I locked Henry inside, I lunge forward furiously.

"You're a fucking liar!" The words come roaring out of me. Something small and fast goes tearing through the woods.

"Liar?" Henry repeats, bewildered. "What the hell are you talking about?"

"Why is PT's heart medication in your safe?"

For a moment, only silence. Then the doorknob begins to rattle menacingly. "Open the door, Faye. I mean it. You should not have found that. You should not be out there alone. Please. Just open up and I'll explain."

"Explain to me now."

Henry hits the door with the flat of his hand in frustration. "Campbell took it."

I shake my head. Try to think straight. "When?"

"The night PT had us over. He went upstairs to use the bathroom, and Campbell pocketed it then. He had no way of knowing for sure that PT might need it, but he had a pretty good idea. A man with a heart condition who overexerted himself and found out his wife was murdered? Campbell took his shot."

"Why? Why would he do that?" I am close to crying, thinking how little PT mattered to Campbell in the end, how little any of us did.

"Because PT was talking about going to the police and outing us. Why else?"

"Then why do you have it?"

Another pause. "Corrine found it."

I take one big step back from the door, my shock necessitating a physical response. “Corrine?”

“Yes, Corrine.”

“But . . . what did she say? How did Campbell explain himself to her?”

“He didn’t have to, just. Open the fucking door, Faye.”

“No. Answer my question. Why wouldn’t he have to explain himself to her?”

In the silence that stretches, I’m sure Henry is about to tell me. But then there is a vicious crack from the inside. I hug myself in horror, realizing Henry is throwing himself at the door, that we did this once already the night he chased me down at the clubhouse and he managed to blow the hinges off the door then too. I turn. I run.

# Chapter 25

I rip the boat keys from their hook and stumble back outside. Henry is still crashing into the door and shouting my name at a terrifying tenor. I break into a sprint and vault myself onto the deck of the boat.

Key in the ignition. Key right-side *up* in the ignition. Wait for the engine warning lights to turn off. A minute that feels like an hour, and then finally, I shift into reverse. I clench the steering wheel with all my might, try to make my hands forget to shake. Is it terror or grief? I am leaving.

The sun glares at the water, punch-bright and sinister. My hair flaps around, tickling the back of my neck like ghost children playing a malevolent game. I keep whipping around, eyeing my wake made wavy and mirage-like by the boat's motor, every cell in my body tweaking with the sensation of being followed, though that would be impossible. I took Henry's only mode of transportation, and there is no one else on the island but us.

I push through the inlet at a higher speed, my hands sweating and my teeth chattering. I have no idea why they call it "driving" a boat. A car and a boat have steering wheels, and that's about where the similarities end. Boats do not always go where you steer them. Boats are not easier to handle at lower speeds. Boats do not have *brakes*. The only way to slow down is to reverse, and I do that now because as I emerge from the inlet, I come upon another boat, bobbing listlessly like a car on the shoulder of a highway. Inside, someone waves their arms frantically for help. It's Corrine. Fuck. It's Corrine.

# Chapter 26

My heart is going berserk as I choke up on the throttle, maneuver jerkily alongside the shipwrecked vessel. Corrine watches me over the rims of her small gold sunglasses, her face intermittently betraying her surprise and disgust at the implications inherent to my presence on the island, all between repeated declarations of gratitude, that she is such an idiot for not checking to make sure she had enough gas before she left the lot, that she was this close to abandoning the boat and swimming to shore, that Campbell would have killed her if she'd left the boat. A stilted laugh, at the mention of Campbell's name. My tongue tastes sour.

Corrine coaches me through dropping my fenders and untying and retying lines so that we can raft up without dinging the paint, because Campbell will also kill her if she dings the paint. Another tinny and unconvincing laugh I wouldn't believe Corrine capable of producing if I had not heard it for myself. She must know he's cheating. She must have come here to catch him out. I recognize the hallmark forces of humiliation tugging down the corners of her mouth. I've seen gravity take premature hold of my beautiful Hollywood friends who have been scammed by men who wear lifts in their loafers. It is anatomy-changing, to know that others know you have been cast aside.

There is a spare tank of gas at the back of the runabout, and I have decided that I will share that with Corrine and also let her know that I am going to shore to call the police and she should come with me. She will undoubtedly ask why, to which I will tell her she has two choices—to come with me or not, but that I cannot answer her question just yet. I have no idea how she will react to the truth—that Campbell and Henry were responsible for Sarah's death all those years ago, that this set off a chain of events that left PT dead and, now, her husband, whom I will tell the police I killed in self-defense. Then I will somehow get to Emma before they get to her, and I will self-finance her shitty unwritten script if that's what it takes for her to back up my story. She'll probably never finish it. I have that going for me.

"That should do it," Corrine says after we've tied the lines in an X shape from bow to stern, stern to bow. I'm sweating from the labor, from the strange and unseasonably strong sun, but Corrine's T-zone is matte and her deeply tanned skin shows no signs of pinkness or agitation. "I have to admit," she says with another hollow laugh, "when I heard another motor on the lake, you were the last person I expected to see."

We are barely clear of the inlet, bobbing dangerously on deep-water currents, and at various intervals, I rise above Corrine and she above me, like we are girls on a seesaw, ribbons fluttering in our hair. My stomach has that roller-coaster feeling, impossible to tell what is gravity and what is gut. Do I feel queasy because my organs are in free fall or because my body knows something my conscious mind won't yet acknowledge? I swallow down the urge to retch over the side of the boat. The last thing I ate was a screwdriver at noon.

"Not my proudest moment," I admit to Corrine on my way down.

Corrine stares at me obliquely behind her small sunglasses. "None of this is," she says, though in a tone that is not unkind toward me. I hear it in her voice. She knows. She's known since the first time Campbell came home smelling like Emma's dry shampoo, probably.

"Corrine," I start, suddenly flush with generosity toward her, "I know I've never been your cup of tea—"

Corrine laughs sharply. "That's how you see it?"

Some sneaker wave rolls underfoot. The water smacks the sides of the boat, sloshes overboard, sends my feet slipping in opposite directions. I hook an arm around the back of the captain's chair and catch myself before I fall.

"I tried to help you," Corrine says, steady on her feet.

I study the natural expression in her forehead, a map of her commitment to the sun over the years. "When? When exactly did you try to help me?"

"Back then," she insists, with a vague flick of her hand. "In school. I told you about Henry. I told you how he treated Berry. And you laughed like I was some kind of narc."

In my mind's eye, I see Corrine standing on the patio, unlit Pall Mall in her hand, her blond hair longer and tucked into the collar of her fleece, telling me that Henry used to handcuff her best friend to the radiator before he left for class.

"It didn't feel like that," I say to her now.

"That's fair," Corrine says in a surprise show of compromise. She is quiet a moment, gazing out at the blueberry-colored water. "I'm sure everything was a bit of a . . . culture shock to you. I would have been wary of all of us too. But at eighteen years old, Faye?" She looks me square in the face. "I thought you were about the biggest asshole I'd ever met."

A sloppy formation of birds sails overhead. I watch the weakest link struggle to straighten the line.

Corrine murmurs something I can't quite make out.

"I'm sorry?"

Corrine pushes her small sunglasses into her thin blond hair, scrunches up her eyes. "I said, *Joke's on me*."

We catch the same current, Corrine and I, plunge downward at the same time. I stumble, grip the ledge. "It was all a long time ago," I assure her. I know where she is going with this, and we simply don't have time.

"It was Campbell who should have come with a warning," Corrine says.

I feel a spirited flash of camaraderie with Corrine in that moment. Pigs fly. I'll need a down coat in hell. "We need to get out of here," I say urgently to her. "Something very bad is going on."

Corrine blinks once, then not again for a long time. This is a sign of trust in some species of animals, isn't it? "Something bad," she repeats, almost sadly. She thinks I'm about to tell her Campbell is here with another woman. She has no idea that we are beyond that ordinary kind of bad.

"I can't explain right now, but we need to go to shore together, and then I'm calling the police." I let go of the captain's headrest, take flat, careful steps toward the back of the boat, where a jerry can of backup fuel is strapped to the swim deck. Here it occurs to me that this is the one way a boat *is* like a car. The gas tank is concealed within the body of the vehicle, there is actually no way for me to know if Corrine is on empty, and now I am turning over what she said to me, wondering if that is the sick in my stomach—*When I heard another motor on the lake, you were the last person I expected to see.* She knew someone else was on the water before she saw them. She had time. To turn off the engine. To drift toward the embankment. To stage this whole scene—

"Took you long enough," Corrine says in a revived voice, a cunning one that suits her much better than the voice of a woman who has been stranded and humiliated. I turn slowly, woozy with sun and my own latent stupidity. Corrine is pointing a pistol at me, of course she is.

"Where's Henry?" she asks.

There is a long silence between us. Corrine seems to understand that I need a moment to process this question. Not *Where's Campbell?* But Henry. *Henry.* The sun is suddenly too much of a strain on my eyes. I close them. I see Campbell twitching on the deck of the clubhouse, one eye seeping something yellow. Open is better, actually.

"I just want to go home," I say to Corrine, and then I

laugh at the futility of this statement. I am very far from going home.

"Then you should have made a run for it in Albany," Corrine says without sympathy. Albany. She knows we went to Albany. My stomach burns with vodka and citrus, and now my chest, my throat—I lurch over the edge of the boat and vomit bright bile into the clear water. I sink down on my knees, rest my head on the back of my hand, take deep, raspy breaths.

"Where's Henry?" Corrine asks again.

"The cabin," I manage to answer.

"You locked him in?"

I raise my head. Wipe my nose on the back of my sleeve. Nod.

"Idiot," Corrine seethes under her breath. There is something right about seeing her with a gun in her hand. It's the reddish, reckless color of her skin, like one of those maverick Florida men with YouTube channels that secure them political appointments. "Okay," she says, scanning the inlet behind me, thinking, thinking. "Here's what we're going to do. You're going to drop anchor and climb in with me. Don't do something stupid like jump. You see this water, right? It's clearer than plastic. I won't miss."

"I don't know how to drop the anchor," I say, outmaneuvered.

"I'm going to tell you what to do, just like Henry does. You like that, don't you?"

I stare at her, my stomach still churning, and I think, whatever happens, she is taking me back to Henry. I am suddenly desperate to see him. To look into his wide eyes with my own. *Corrine is here, and she is ordering me around at gunpoint. Can you believe it?* My brain writes a prescription for this scenario, over and over, until I am drugged into believing it as memory. Any other outcome is not just neurologically out of reach, but simply not what happened. Henry will be just as shocked as I am. He will be concerned for my safety. He will want to save me. This is what will happen, what practically already has; otherwise my legs will give out when I stand. I will fall overboard and I will be shot dead by a Connecticut housewife with a prized collection of bento boxes, and that is not how I plan to go.

# Chapter 27

Henry must see us coming. He must be standing at the front windows, the same as I did when we first arrived, watching his captor return to him. Corrine goads me down the dock with the gun at my back and has me unlock the door, and then, standing face-to-face with him, I nearly vomit again. Henry regards me clinically, almost politely, as though I am no more than a stranger off the street. He would not want to see me hurt, but if he did, he would also go home and make dinner and think no more about it. I've been a fool.

"Don't look at me like that," Henry says, but the statement is directed at Corrine.

"Like you can't handle your shit?" Corrine snots back. She jerks her head. "Let's go. Might as well get this taken care of since I'm here."

Henry sighs in the way you do when someone is right but there is no way in hell you'd give them the satisfaction of admitting to it.

"Henry," I try, though I know it is useless. He steps around me like I am simply in the way.

*

I sit on the back bench of the boat, knees pulled to my chest, watching as PT's shoreline nears. Corrine and Henry are having some kind of hushed argument at the bow of the boat, glancing back at me every so often to make sure I have not thrown myself overboard. I have eliminated the possibility that they are having an affair. Their dealings with each other are laced with a familial kind of tension, like siblings fighting over the cost of a care home for a declining parent. With every spike of my pulse, I nearly say it—*Corrine, Campbell is dead.* But I don't know if she knows. I don't know if this is a card I should hold close for now.

We get out of the boat, and I walk down the dock sandwiched between Corrine and Henry. Corrine keeps stopping to check that I am still following, despite Henry bringing up the rear, and I could project all kind of meaning onto this, but I need to keep a cool head. Still, it seems an important detail—Corrine doesn't trust Henry.

We bypass the house, go instead to the small shed with a thatched, hobbit-like roof sprouting new spring grass, that shock-green, like vegetables tossed in boiling water. Henry goes in and comes back out with shovels. Shovels. Panic squeezes my chest. I stand there and I refuse to move, even when Corrine needles me between my shoulder blades with her index finger.

"No," I keep saying. "No." It seems the only word my mouth is willing to form, and then my knees rubberize and I'm sitting on the cool carpet of the woods with my legs straight out in front of me like a dummy whose ventriloquist has removed his hand from my back. I'm suddenly reminded of horror nights at Universal Studios, one of my favorite things about living in Los Angeles—the unmatched production quality around the holidays. I'd gotten tickets for the haunted house. It was a replica of the house from *Halloween*, wasn't it? And around every turn, Michael Myers was waiting, and when my husband and I made it through to the end, he turned to me and he was laughing and he said, *Do you realize you just kept screaming the word* no? *No*. I will not die. *No*. Not yet.

"We're not going to kill you," Henry says with far more impatience than reassurance.

"Don't make promises you can't keep," Corrine tells him over my head. I sit there, feeling like the child of divorced parents fighting over whose weekend it is with the child they don't really want. It's about winning, about ego.

"The two of us should just go," Henry says. "Look at her. She's in bad shape."

"I'm not leaving the little escape artist alone."

"Then you go and I'll keep an eye on her."

"So you two can run off and pin the whole thing on me?" Corrine says with an incredulous laugh.

*Pin the whole thing on me*. Corrine, glancing back at me and Henry to make sure we were still following her, that we weren't conspiring behind her back. Corrine doesn't know where she stands with Henry. She is off-balance. Time to knock her flat. "Campbell is dead," I say. My ace, on the table.

"What did you say?" she all but gasps.

"Campbell is dead," I repeat, articulating each appalling syllable.

"Campbell is not dead," Corrine insists through tight lips. "Campbell was *murdered*. By that little slut in polyester pants. The love of my life." Corrine sniffs. She pushes out her lower lip, makes it quiver. "I don't know how I'll live without him." A knuckle into dry eyes; end scene. "How'd I do? In your professional opinion, of course."

I stare up at her, bested, disgusted. Corrine is wearing navy leggings and a long-sleeve T-shirt from some watering hole in Newport, one of the last "authentic" spots that summer people gatekeep from the tourists so they may get bombed with the locals who water their hydrangeas in peace, and she has thrown a sweatshirt over her shoulders like it is a cashmere cardigan. Her wispy blond hair is pulled into a low loop at her neck, and as ever, there is not a stitch of makeup on her face, the features of which are young because she is still young, though the overall effect is hard and weathered from so much sun. The only piece of jewelry she wears is her gold wedding band. Techincally, she no longer has a husband, and she is planning on blaming the slut in polyester pants, who must be Emma, and now I'm thinking about what Henry said, about the CCTV footage, about how no one could know we were in Albany, and I'm realizing that when the police go to check it, they will see Emma driving a dead man's car, and that this has somehow been the plan all along. I'm realizing the depravity that the two of them are capable of, and my stomach clenches my organs like a hostage negotiation—give me something to eat and I'll release your kidney.

"We'll get you a menthol tear stick," I tell Corrine.

She rolls her eyes. “Good one, Faye.” She points the pistol at my scalp. “Now get the fuck *up*.”

Henry offers me his hand, but I slap it away. I get up fast. Too fast. My vision craters, and a small part of me is pleased when the spots multiply instead of clearing. Fainting will slow them down, and it will certainly piss off Corrine. My eyes flip into the back of my head, seeking the dark.

# Chapter 28

I sit, slumped and hurting, at PT's elaborate hickory table with thick logs for legs, watching Corrine bang around the kitchen, seeking anything with carbs. Henry is across from me, monitoring me without expression. I can't look at him looking at me like that, and so I stare at the lines in the wood of the table until they swirl like I've microdosed too many times to have any business using the made-up word. I am, at the moment, tripping all over my mutinous unconsciousness. My feet catching on the corners of everything I refused to see before. Henry has always been my captor, even when I thought I was free.

"Cereal." Corrine retrieves a box from the cabinet next to the refrigerator, turns it over in her hands, looking for the best-by date. "I bet that's a real treat for you, Faye."

My vision throbs like a second pulse. "Will someone tell me what the fuck is going on?"

Corrine sighs. "See," she says, "the problem is you're an actress. So I don't know what to make of this whole wide-eyed thing you've got going on."

"Campbell's dead and you seem pretty okay with it. I am unclear what to make of that as well."

"*Pretty okay*?" Corrine repeats in a rage. "You think I'm *pretty okay*?"

"You don't seem all that torn up."

"I'm furious."

"He attacked me first. I had no choice."

"Jesus, Faye." Corrine groans, exasperated. "We were planning on offing him anyway, is that what you need to hear me say?"

Outside, the frogs are shrieking incessantly. *What is that?* I asked, the first time I came here, and then they dulled to background noise that I stopped noticing until now.

"It's *Henry* I'm furious with," Corrine clarifies, "for thinking with his dick when he's the one who needs this to work out more than anyone."

I allow my eyes to drift to Henry at that. There are freckles over the bridge of his nose that were not there when we arrived. Did that happen when we were lying on the dock and he gave me his battered heart to hold? My chest feels hot and cold, a strange menthol sensation, remembering the wounds we bared and then what we did to each other to anesthetize the pain. Henry stares back at me with the indifferent gaze of a sunning house cat.

"I'd argue," Henry says idly, "that you need me more than I need you. You're the spouse. Everyone will be looking at you."

"Which is why *I'm* covering all my tracks. You should

try it, Hen!" Corrine slams the cabinet door shut. "See, Faye, when I called the caretaker to ask if he'd seen Campbell—I'm playing a part here, you know. I have to look like I was worried I hadn't heard from him—he said no, but that he did see Henry at the super Walmart, groping hothouse tomatoes with a woman who was *not* his wife."

"Fuck," I say.

"*Fuck*," Corrine agrees, opening and closing the cabinet drawers until she finds the one with the utensils.

"He didn't recognize her," Henry says to Corrine about me, as though I am not sitting right there. "And he's promised not to say anything."

"For a price," Corrine reminds Henry furiously. She gets out a bowl, and into it she shakes a generous serving of stale cereal. I know it's stale by the sound it makes when it hits the porcelain; like broken glass. "That's coming off the top of yours, by the way."

I gape at Henry. This is about something as cheap as money? "Is it a life-insurance thing?"

Corrine snorts. She has found a carton of shelf-stable milk in the pantry, and she's sniffing from the spout, making a putrid face. "Henry? Would you like to be the one to elaborate?"

"I think," Henry says in a clipped tone, "the less she knows, the better."

"Guess not," Corrine says, pouring what must be expired milk down the drain. "I'd fill you in, Faye—I'm leaning toward believing you don't know what's going on; you're not a very good actress, to be honest, smart of you to focus on the directing thing—but I really think it will be better coming from Henry."

"Do *you* know what's going on?" I say, hoping to provoke her. "Do you know what they did to Sarah?"

Corrine fills a glass with water. She comes over and places my flavorless prison meal in front of me. "Faye," she says with something approaching gentleness, "who do you think wrote the suicide note?"

The cereal is that brand that offers a diet plan on the back of the box. Replace two meals with this cereal, it says, and you could lose up to ten pounds in two weeks. I tried it once, and I am as lightheaded now as I was when I stepped on the scale after two weeks to discover that the back of the box wasn't lying.

Corrine groans at the dazed look on my face, like she expected more from me. "Faye, come *on*. You really thought that my dumbass husband, God rest his soul, turned to your dumbass boyfriend—take the hit, Hen—and said, 'Hey you know what? Sarah can't seem to get pregnant and seems a little devastated about that. She can hardly get out of bed. She can hardly face the world. She can hardly stand to look at anyone who could be so glib about having children, and we might be able to use that to throw everyone off the scent. We have a key to their place. PT is out of town. We could sneak in there. We could write something short but real-sounding. I mean, no, we've never experienced anything like this, but we have hearts and minds, so we can use those to at least imagine what someone going through what Sarah was going through might feel. What do we come up with? How about—*It's too much.* Because that's what it is even though it doesn't make sense. It's nothing when you should have something, and it's nothing over and over again, and it's simply too much nothing. Then, after we've gone outside and pushed her scull into the lake, we have to go in the bathroom to throw up, because again, hearts and minds, we have those, and this is all just so awful and sad, but it's also the way it has to be because this was an accident and at least one of us has been accepted into the investment trading program at J.P. Morgan, and God *forbid* we jeopardize that. And while we have our heads in the toilet, we happen to notice a negative pregnancy test in the trash can, and we're just like, holy shit. Holy *shit.* And so we fish that out and we leave it next to the laptop before we go.' Truly, Faye, think for one fucking second." Corrine jams her index finger into the side of her head forcefully. *Think*, you fucking idiot. *Think.*

"I don't think like you do," I say to her.

Corrine screws up her face to make a mockery of my face, my voice. "You're so cool, Faye, because you don't want kids."

I shake my head. *No. You misunderstand.* "PT meant something to me that someone like you does not have the capacity to understand."

Corrine's body jerks, like she's woken from one of those falling nightmares in the moment before she hits the ground. It's that word, *capacity.* Something about it shames her. The tips of her ears turn a virulent red. "Campbell meant something to me, and when he called me in a blind fucking panic, I agreed to help him because

I loved him and I didn't want this to ruin his life. And then"—Corrine erupts with hideous laughter—"I got what was coming to me." She takes the sweatshirt that's thrown over her shoulders like a cardigan, and she wraps the arms tighter around herself with a shudder. "I had to use an egg donor with Tookie, did you know that? I did seven rounds of IVF. Seven. I'm definitely getting cancer from that, and in the end I still had to turn to a binder full of women who are so flush with fertility they have eggs to go around. I did my best to choose someone who looked like me, who was built like me, but nature has a pretty sick sense of humor. So sick that six months ago I missed my period for the first time since I was thirteen, despite having what the doctors call *very low ovarian reserve.* I made it all the way to the twenty-week ultrasound. That's a significant milestone, in case you don't know. It's when you find out the sex. I was having a boy. I had decided on a name. I got shit monogrammed. I was showing, and I continued to show even after I walked in on Campbell fucking my little brother's girlfriend and no longer needed the embroidered crib sheet. Anything after twenty-four weeks is not considered a miscarriage but a stillbirth. He *looked* like a baby." Corrine's cheeks are hot and streaked with tears, real tears, and she turns away from me to wipe them off with the sleeves of her sweatshirt. I want to tell her that she doesn't need a menthol stick to pull off the grieving widow act. She just needs to relive the agony of this experience and she will be fine.

"I am sorry," I tell her.

"You don't mean that."

"I do."

"No," Corrine spits, her eyes red and wild, "you might think you mean it, but ultimately, you are the one who is incapable. Until you have someone in your life you love so much that you would take a bullet for them, even on the days you wish they were never born, there are limits to what you can feel."

"I'll just have to take your word for it," I say, and I make sure to direct this straight at Henry. He is staring at me with his hard eyes, and I suddenly understand that expression in the literal sense. If our eyes fell out of our heads at the same time and hit the floor, mine would squish and seep. Henry's would dent the wood.

"You need to eat something," Henry says to me, but his concern is only a practical one. "It's not close, and we're going on foot."

I stare at my cereal bowl. "I'm not going anywhere with you."

Corrine comes over and presses the pistol into my temple. Fear drop-kicks my stomach. I've held a gun before, but I've never felt the metal of a muzzle against my skin. This one is rough and scratchy, revealing its age. It is obviously an antique; Corrine wouldn't hold anything as base as a Glock. I bet it belonged to someone's grandfather, passed down like a Patek, and it keeps knocking against the bone in my temple because Corrine is trembling with the restraint of not blowing my brains onto the kitchen table. "Eat your fucking Wheaties, Faye."

I look to Henry for something. *Something.* And for a

moment I think he will save me not because I am more of a liability dead than alive but because it is me.

"Eat, Faye," Henry says, almost kindly. "This is the last thing you have to do. And then we can all go home. We never have to see each other again."

# Chapter 29

The trail on the south side of the lake is wide and welcoming, glowing from within at golden hour. Skinny white pines and sparsely needled evergreens replicate in a destabilizing pattern of sameness. Some kind of bird beeps with the insistence of a morning alarm clock. Underfoot the trail is soft and springy, weirdly waterbed-like. We fan out, walk three across, bouncing like we are in a good mood. I have no idea where we are going, but Henry is carrying the same shovel PT must have carried when he set out to find Sarah, and I am too smart to play dumb.

I go over everything I've told Henry about my life the last few days, the deranged and devoted things we've said to each other, the stupefaction on his face when he put his hand between my legs for the first time in a dozen years, and it feels like there is a foreign object lodged in my lungs. It was real, it had to be, but stumbling alongside him, sweating from my scalp, I am forced to admit that it was not enough. That the whole time, this other, more sinister plot was unfolding, one I am still trying to track. Hard as it is to imagine Henry playing a part in PT's death, I can at least understand the why of it—PT found out what they did to Sarah, and he had threatened to go to the police. But at what point did Henry link up with Corrine to decide that Campbell had to go too? What happened to make him turn against his oldest friend?

I turn over various scenarios as we walk and walk and walk. We cross a brook that babbles all year long, not just the odd February, "springtime" on the dusty hiking trails in Southern California. We hopscotch its moss-furred stones. We twist through gorges and karate chop wild grass through an open field, descend onto soggy ground where the trees crowd, wet and musky smelling, and the temperature drops precipitously. I must shiver, because from his hiker's backpack Henry tosses me a fleece he grabbed from the coatrack by PT's back door. I put it on and jam my fists into the pockets. My fingers graze something worn and soft, and I remove my hand to find I am holding a receipt from Walmart for rechargeable marine batteries and a pack of Pall Malls, dated ten days ago, around the time PT would have learned the truth about Sarah's death. I feel like someone has touched an ice cube to the back of my neck. I know he had finally, properly quit a few years ago, which means he wore this fleece on his drive up here, stopped for supplies, saw the cigarettes behind the counter, thought if ever there was a time to give in to temptation . . . I curl my fingers around the feathery slip of paper, hold his secret close. I knew I'd bump into him again.

The woods have dimmed by the time we venture off trail, evade the evergreens' spiny branches, and stop at a pair of split trees that share roots, red and waxy as overgrown radishes. Dorothy Parker's hand remains. "*Scratch a lover*" etched with a steel tool into the first of the twin trees. "*Find a foe*" on its conjoined trunk, where Henry goes over to stand now and block the inscription with his back. He walks toe to heel, heel to toe, arms held out like he's on a tightwire stretched between the Chrysler and Empire State buildings. He stops just shy of two recent excavations. PT was so close to finding all of her. Henry rakes back browning pine needles with the tip of his shovel, and then he and Corrine start to dig.

I sit on the trunk of a fallen tree, with the wet wood soaking through my pants, dragging a stick through the forest's black goo like I am dipping a quill pen into an inkwell. I don't need to see myself to know my face is pale and moist. An old injury in my shoulder flares, not an injury actually, but tissue damage from carrying an overstuffed tote bag all those years I played a twentysomething with her nose to the corporate grindstone. Wardrobe stuffed it with actual books and a laptop and a spare pair of shoes and makeup, and by the end of the show's run, I was walking around with one shoulder hitched higher than the other. With my fingertips I trace the ache to my jaw, tapping, massaging. I must hit the operational center of the pain, because a sudden bright spot blasts my vision, and when the spots fade, I'm thinking about that doomed trip I took with my husband to Hawaii three years ago, the vacation that fell the week PT brought the film students to Los Angeles for a set visit.

An unseasonable cold front had moved through the

Pacific Islands region that week, and a cloud cover clung stubbornly to the resort. We holed up in our hotel room, drinking Miami Vices, dozing, watching movies. We did spa treatments one day, and after our massages as we soaked naked in the private Jacuzzi, I put my hand on my husband's soft cock underwater. He had laughed, uncomfortably, then pushed my hand away. We had an outdoor shower attached to our villa that we used separately. My husband and I have never showered together.

On the last morning of the last day, he reached for me in bed. I had gotten high the night before and eaten two dinners—one at the restaurant and another at midnight from room service. All week I had ordered fish and smiled benevolently at the waiter when he asked if I had left room for dessert. *Just a peppermint tea, please.* I was holding out hope that back in our hotel room my husband would look at my flat stomach in my delicate lingerie and smell my peppermint breath and have to have me. Every day that passed and this did not happen, I slumped deeper into despair, and by the last night I was desperate for some form of carnal pleasure. I ate pasta and cheesecake in the hotel's formal dining room. Back in our room, chicken tenders and a warm brownie with vanilla ice cream off the children's menu. In the morning, I was sluggish and gassy, and when he reached for me, I initially patted his hand good-naturedly and murmured something about having to get ready to go, but on my way into the bathroom I'd stopped, turned around, and taken in my husband in the bed. He was returning emails with a smile on his face; I could hear the swoop of the messages. My husband claims to hate work, to find it unrewarding and stressful, but the way his face gets whenever he clocks in begs to differ. He'd had a good vacation, and now he was ready to get back to what made him smile. The words flew out of me raw. No sanitized *I feel like* statements so that the other person does not get their back up against the wall. I had lost all hope, all will, for resolution.

"You knew we didn't have enough time."

My husband had turned his head on the pillow, blinking at me innocently. "Enough time for what?"

"To fuck." I let that hang there; I knew he hated the word. He hated all words related to sex as far as I could tell. His shoulders tensed, and he would get a queasy expression on his face, like he was being forced to watch a woman give birth. "You initiated, just now, because you knew I'd say we have to get ready to go. That way you get to leave here and say, 'Hey, I tried. She was the one who turned me down.' "

"Um," my husband said, setting his phone down on the bed, preciously, like it was a valuable made of crystal. He pulled himself into a seated position and stacked two pillows behind him so he could sit up comfortably while we had this conversation. God forbid the man ever be without neck support. I waited for him to say something, but he just stared at me patiently, waiting for me to explain why I was ruining the last five minutes of our vacation.

"We've been locked in this room together all week. Why didn't you want to fuck me the first night? Or the first morning? Or the second or the third or the fourth?"

"Jesus Christ, Faye." My husband ran his hands down

his face and then back through his dark hair, making it stand up on end. His hazel eyes were wide with exasperation. "We don't have to. It's fine. Just please. Stop yelling at me."

"I'm upset, okay? I'm upset and I'm trying to talk to you."

"I didn't *do* anything!" my husband cried, and I tensed. This was always where our fights led. To my husband proclaiming his innocence in a shrill voice, and that day he even crossed his arms over his bare chest like women do when someone accidentally walks in on them changing. I could not believe I was standing here fighting to fuck this man.

"You are acting like you're the one who wants to do it," I said, mustering every ounce of patience I had, "and I'm the one who doesn't, and that's not what's happening here. I don't want to do it like this, okay? When I feel like shit and the clock is counting down. I wanted to do it the first night, wearing what I was wearing when I came out of the bathroom." It was a little Kiki set that I had ordered online and that my assistant accidentally unboxed. When she handed it to me, she said, *Have fun on vacation,* while wriggling her eyebrows, and my heart felt heavier than a human head.

"Faye, you looked great. It's just . . ."

I waited him out a moment. "What? It's just *what*—"

"You. You! It's like your stress, just . . . like . . . radiates off you. It's, like, a thing on your to-do list. That's what it feels like."

All bets were off then. "Fucking *is* a thing on my to-do

list at this point. Do you think I actually want to have sex with you anymore?"

"Right back at you," my husband snipped.

"Yes, I'm aware you don't want to have sex with me. It's not the slap in the face you think it is. You have never wanted to have sex with me, and I've tried to talk to you about it, and you insist that you do want to have sex with me, and then when I tell you that's literally the definition of gaslighting, you tell me to stop saying the word *gaslighting* because it's an annoying word. So thank you, for stepping into reality with me for once, and admitting that you have never cared about fucking me."

"That's not true," my husband insisted, and I threw up my hands and started to protest, but he spoke over me. "Hold on. *Hold on* a second. Let me talk." He waited to be sure the floor was his. "I did want to fuck you in the beginning, especially when . . ." My husband shook his head and muttered something under his breath. He thumped his hands on the bed. "Forget it. We have to pack. We can't miss this flight. It's the only one off the island today, and you have to be on set tomorrow."

"No. Finish what you were going to say. Especially when what?"

My husband sat there unmoving, his hands flopped up to the ceiling like I had asked him which way to turn in a maze and his guess was as good as mine. "I don't really know. You were just different in the beginning."

"Younger? Newer? Hotter?" Standing there, with my high ass and bouncy little boobs, I was thirty years old.

"You looked up to me."

I gasped. Took a step away from him. I could not believe he had just said that. "I cannot believe you just said that."

My husband looked a bit stunned too. We were in the business of paying lip service to inequalities and representation and making space at the table, and so he knew how that sounded. But then he seemed to think about it a little more, and he laughed darkly. "I mean, Faye. That's a little rich, coming from you. You asked me to hit you at one point. To, like, pin you down and pretend like ... whatever. You wanted to trade sexual favors for expensive dinners like you were an actual hooker. *That* isn't too indelicate for you, but me saying I miss when you needed me a little bit more is?" He shrugged. "I just thought it was kind of a turn-on when you, like, asked me for help with Excel. Or you fucked up Jonathan's lunch order and you'd come to me, wringing your hands with tears in your big brown eyes. And honestly, Faye?" He is staring out the window, spellbound by the rough rhythm of the ocean and whatever cognizance has finally paid him a visit. "It didn't feel like something on your to-do list then. It felt like you really wanted me too. It was like you got off on being helpless."

"That's it," Corrine says now.

I stretch my neck long, tilt my head this way and that, trying to see. Something profoundly grotesque appears to claw at the fungus floor of the forest. I lean forward, make out the curvature of a rib, bring the back of my arm to my mouth. I turn away, but still I hear them collect the pieces of her and deposit them into a large drawstring knapsack, the kind the dry cleaners give you for all your silk blouses and trousers.

We come upon a wide stretch of trail I recognize, dead and downed trees dappled with exceedingly green growth. It is a magical panorama, lush and Tolkien, and two people are taking in every last inch of it, walking the trail hand in hand with matching, wonderous expressions on their faces.

"Fuck, fuck, shit, fuck," Corrine says.

"Give Faye your hat," Henry says out of the side of his mouth, and then Corrine caps me lopsidedly. I'm adjusting the brim as the couple picks up their pace to approach us. The man has a long gray beard and spiffy round eyeglasses. His wife has her hair tied back in a silk scarf, bright lipstick.

"Oh my gosh are we happy to see you," the man says. "There was a bear."

"We didn't run," the woman assures us.

"Yes," Corrine agrees. "Never run."

They nod. Yes. Yes. Never. Their cheeks are flushed, their eyes bright. This is a tale of survival they will tell again and again and we are their first audience.

"This is private property," Henry says.

The man frowns. Looks around as though there might be some sign posted that will say otherwise. "Since when?"

"1878," Henry says flatly.

The wife laughs initially. Her teeth are large and uniform, not quite white. Veneers. The plague has spread outside of Los Angeles. "Oh, you're serious?" she says.

Her carefully painted lips turn down. "We're so sorry. We thought this was Heaven Hills."

"Do you have a map?" Henry is speaking with a mechanical kind of patience.

The husband pats down his pockets, produces a friendly looking cartoon of the Southern Adirondacks, unfolds it to reveal glossy ads for local inns and restaurants and maple sugar factories. Henry places his fingertip on a thin red line. "This is where you are." He follows the trail with his finger until it intersects with a yellow loop. "This is Heaven Hills."

"Whose property is this, then?"

Henry refolds the map and returns it to the owner. "It's mine."

# Chapter 30

It is dark by the time we return to the cabin, and my limbs are throbbing dully with exhaustion. I all but collapse on the sofa in the brick-red Santa Fe pattern and lie there for a long time while Corrine and Henry stand too close to each other in the kitchen area behind me and exchange words in heated whispers.

"She doesn't have a choice!" Corrine explodes, and then I hear her heavy jock-girl footsteps come nearer to me. She half circles the coffee table and stands there, appraising me. I'm in the fetal position with my knees tucked into my chest.

"You need to shower."

I stare up at her with undisguised contempt. Her thin blond hair is shellacked to her skull with sweat. A bald alien, beamed into my bedroom to abduct me for the purposes of their strange science. "That's your concern at the moment?"

"Yes, because you look like a hostage." She stares into the kitchen, where I assume Henry still stands. "Both of you do."

"I am a hostage."

"Get up, Faye."

"Fuck you, Corrine."

Corrine's eyes bulge in her big bald-looking head. I wonder if anyone had ever said that to her before or if I have the honor of being the first. "Get the fuck up," she growls, "before I shoot you in the face."

I do not move. I've had it with her telling me what to do. "You can't shoot me," I tell her with a heady rush of fearlessness. "I can say anything I want to you, and you can't shoot me. I can call you a dead-eyed fish. I can tell you that your son is a sweet kid who stands no chance, because he has a mother who displays such obvious disdain for him. And you have to take it because unlike you, I am a valuable, contributing member of society who has not murdered anyone for money." I raise my eyebrows at her tauntingly while Corrine chews up the insides of her mouth and undoubtedly fantasizes about pecking my eyes out of my head, but in the end, she takes it, and this emboldens me. I am too important to kill. I do have a hand, and now is the time to play it.

I sit up on my own time and adjust my position so that I am longways on the couch and can turn my head between Henry in the kitchen and Corrine fuming on the other side of the coffee table. "Since when did this property pass to you, Henry?"

"Technically," Henry answers, "it's not mine yet."

"Why not?"

"Because PT left it to Henry *and* Campbell," Corrine says on the other side of me, "and no one knows Campbell is dead yet."

I turn back to Corrine, see her licking her lips with abject pleasure that she is privy to all the gory details that I am not. "Private property within a public park has always been a tricky issue," she explains. "So these guys have their little club to protect their little island and prevent the big, bad government from swooping in and taking what is rightfully theirs. There's this language they've had formalized—willing seller, willing buyer. Sadly"—she sighs, decidedly not sad—"Camps was unwilling."

I swivel my head, slowly, to look at Henry, understanding beginning to dawn. "You're selling?"

Henry bows his head. It's a yes.

"But . . . why?"

"Faye." Corrine laughs. "Why does anyone do anything? For money. Retire before thirty-five, buy a third house, hire a third nanny, never have to share a California king with a scummy finance bro again *money*."

"This is the largest piece of privately owned land in all of the Adirondacks," Henry contributes in a much more decent tone. "The Forest Preserve will buy us out and then some."

"But then the lake won't be private anymore."

"Boo-hoo," Corrine says. "We'll just have to cry into our golden pillows."

Henry rubs his shoulder, like it is sore from carrying Sarah, though how much could a skeleton weigh? It occurs to me, then, why we had to do what we did today. "If the lands are public, obviously you can't keep a body buried here."

"Do you feel better now?" Corrine says. "Nancy fucking Drew. You figured it out."

"I'd like to know how you're going to explain Campbell's death. I'd like to know what you expect me to say and not say when you let me go. I'm not going to do any of it, but for shits and giggles, tell me."

Corrine throws her head back on her neck, closes her eyes, and probably counts to ten in her head. "You need to shower," she says after about four seconds. "We're already off schedule here."

"I'm not cooperating until you tell me."

Corrine groans and opens her eyes. "I am going to sound the alarm tonight, okay?"

"Tonight?" I repeat, incredulously. Outside, the sun has left the clouds smudged like charcoal. It *is* tonight.

Corrine continues in a put-upon tone, like I am a parent who has asked their teenager to elaborate on their plans for the evening before I will agree to give them the keys to the family vehicle. "Campbell was supposed to be here a few days to summerize the cabin. I've been getting messages and phone calls from him, but two days ago they stopped. I got worried. Drove up here to check on him. His car wasn't in the parking lot, which was strange, but the boat's there, so I took it to our cabin and poked around. Okay, clearly he's been here. The bed is slept in. There's food in the kitchen. But he's not *here*. I search the woods, in case he's out there, injured or ripped to shreds by a bear. God, wouldn't that have been convenient? Anyway. I'm truly baffled as to where he might be, and it's getting dark, and so I decide to take the boat to the clubhouse to try and catch a signal and call someone. And there, I come upon a devastating scene." Corrine says no more. She does not need to. It is my handiwork she will discover. Henry never even moved the body. My stomach roils, picturing Campbell lying there with one eye open and one eye shut while Henry and I carried on the way we did these last few days.

"Meanwhile," Corrine continues, "back at the colleges, a secondary tragedy is unfolding. Twenty-two-year-old Emma King has overdosed and left a suicide note, confessing to her crime of passion. Campbell tried to break up with her at the lake and she lost it. She didn't mean to hurt him. One second that ceremonial rock was on the ground and the next it was in her hands and she does not know how to live with herself after what she's done. She threw it in the lake, thinking she would try to cover up her crime—those are your prints taken care of, Faye—but then she couldn't figure out what to do with the body, and she just went back to the cabin and sort of disassociated for the next twelve hours." Corrine clucks tragically. "The police will find Campbell's car at the train station, CCTV footage will show that Emma was the one to park it there within twelve hours of Campbell's time of death, that she purchased a ticket for the R-10 local, exiting at the Geneva station and taking an Uber back to the colleges, where she bought some real bad shit to put up her nose with the intent to lay her head down and never wake up."

"Your second staged suicide," I remark. "You should start charging for your services."

"I basically have," Corrine agrees with a laugh. "And my brother will be handsomely compensated, of course."

I stare at her. "Your brother?"

Corrine gazes out the window, at the sky bruised with dusk. "Right about now, my brother is on his way over there with the merchandise and some sad-sack story about missing her and begging her to give him another chance and an offer to get fucked up on his dime. You met my brother, so you will understand when I say that I have all the faith in the world that he will pull this off."

What was his name again? Loafers without socks. Wet douche hair. *Win*. Yes. I too have faith. "And you think I'm going along with this?"

Corrine's laugh is a harsh one syllable. "That's what Henry keeps promising. You have too much to lose to be snarled in scandal, so you'll just keep your head down and make your movie and go on with your life. But I am not convinced. You two seem pretty cozy. I mean, you're wearing his wife's jewelry for fuck's sake, and it is so not your style."

My hand flies to the heart at my chest, covering it reflexively.

"What I am saying," Corrine continues, "is that I feel that we are still lacking . . . collateral . . . from you."

"And my career-suicide post is not collateral enough?"

"While you're here, yeah. But once you're off this island, you'll log in and change your password and we'll lose the upper hand. And in this day and age, women can pretty much make a case of anything. You're just gonna say you were abducted, you're just gonna say you were *traumatized* and acting in self-defense."

I was gonna say that, if it came to it. "What is it you think you're going to make me do?"

Corrine sweeps an arm in Henry's direction, rather grandly. "Hen? I think it will be far more poetic coming from you."

I turn back to Henry to find him looking at me with those cold blue eyes, sorry and not sorry, remorseless and full of remorse. "It needs to look like you came here willingly," he says. There is tension at the corners of his mouth. Not a smile, but an acknowledgment of the absurdity of the situation, that this is how it would end for us. "It needs to look like you love me."

# Chapter 31

The three of us pile into the runabout and chug back to Henry's side of the lake. Between the fallen tree that looks like a Revolutionary War cannon and the one that rears out of the water like a mutant shrimp, Corrine puts the engine in neutral and upturns the knapsack over the side of the boat, hailing the surface of the lake with Sarah's vertebrae and ribs. The sound is utterly heinous, and I tip my face upward to override my sense of hearing with sight. Darkness has fallen, and the night sky is strung loosely with stars, some brighter and stronger than others, like a wire of Christmas-tree lights plugged in for the first time after a cold year in storage. Corrine puts the engine in gear and turns the wheel toward Henry's shore.

I step out of the boat before anyone can tell me what to do, brushing past Henry tying up the bowline. Corrine marshals me down the dock with the pistol at my back. "No," she barks from behind. I turn and see her flick the pistol away from the main house. "Cabin." I veer left on the stone path.

I go inside and stand stoically by the edge of the bed with my arms folded across my chest. It is dark as a movie theater in here, and the picture outside the windows shows Henry's incredible Viking form skulking down the dock. He disappears from sight, and I hear his boots crunch close, then farther away, close and far. When he appears in the doorframe, he is carrying an armful of kindling. He steps around Corrine and kneels before the fireplace. We wait wordlessly while he crosshatches a base, then strikes the long wooden match that startles his profile in an abrupt burst of flame. He returns the screen and stands. Corrine holds out her hand like Henry owes her money, and he drops the key to the cabin into her palm. She curls her fingers into a fist with an evil landlord's smile.

"Well," Corrine says cheerfully, "I'm going to make my way to the clubhouse so I can give my brother a call and see where we're at with things. You kids have fun."

She walks out, careful not to give us her back, and locks us inside. We face each other, avoiding eye contact, and listen to her clomp down the dock and start the engine to the boat. When the chug-chug-chugging fades, Henry takes a small inhalation, the kind you take before you say something big, and I pull my shoulders back and ready myself.

"Faye," Henry starts. He looks at me with haunted eyes, his body silhouetted orange by the fire. "All of that, back there, was to protect you."

I laugh in disbelief. Not what I was expecting him to say. I'll give him that.

"I know how it sounds, but Corrine is convinced we are plotting against her and she hates you and she has a gun."

"This has all been about protecting me, right?"

Henry is quiet a moment. "No," he admits. "I need this money."

I smirk. "Points for honesty," I say. "But if you even think about touching me right now, I will really, properly, fight you. You will be raping me for real." We are supposed to use Henry's phone to film ourselves *making love*. A lot of women my age are repulsed by that expression, but when I hear it, all I feel is a terrible two-year-old's rage.

A sex tape, a *making love* tape, is the ultimate form of collateral. I will not be able to use any of the excuses Corrine enumerated earlier. That I was brought here against my will, traumatized and acting in self-defense. It will look like I killed Campbell because he discovered I was having an affair. Fuck worrying about casting my movie; I'll be bleeding dry my bank account to afford hot power-lady lawyers to defend me in a murder trial that *House in Habitat* will cover in a vicious series for all her hippie, tin-fedora-wearing followers.

Henry lowers himself onto the edge of the bed, halving his hugeness in response to that. "I need to tell you something. Can you just hear me out?"

"Do I have a choice?"

"Yes." Henry glances up at me sharply. "You always have a choice with me."

"I will throw up."

Henry exhales hard through his nostrils. Roughs up the back of his hair. "You are exactly the same, you know."

I stare down at him. "It takes extraordinary nerve to say that to me right now."

"When it comes to how you are, when things get serious, when things get soft—"

"Please, I beg of you—"

"You are impenetrable."

I shake my head tightly. Everything Henry is saying is an echo of everything my husband says of everything Henry said to me before that. I screw my eyes shut, waver uneasily on my feet. I can feel this thing, the answer to this question—what are we *really* doing here?—filling out, solidifying, but I cannot yet get my arms around its shape. "Why didn't you tell me you were planning on killing Campbell? Why didn't you tell me Corrine has been involved since the start? Why give me half the story?"

"Because if I told you everything, the question you would be left with was why. Why sell?"

I open my eyes. Yes. The answer to that question is the shape of it. The Henry I knew valued the family history of this land and the responsibility he inherited to protect and preserve it. The Henry I knew would not siphon it off for money. The Henry I knew did not *need* money. But sitting on the bed before me, his head lowered in shame, is not the Henry I knew.

This Henry begins to tell me the truth.

His wife is sick. Not dying sick, but chemically unwell. Bipolar is what the family doctor suspects, but she refuses to submit to an evaluation or seek treatment, so he can only speculate. She suffers from episodes of mania that culminate in obscene spending sprees. Henry goes to bed with two cars in the driveway and wakes up to three. She enrolled their children in a kindergarten that cost as much as the colleges. She books Emirates flights to the Maldives that she misses, and she makes risky investments. Once, Henry went up to summerize the cabin and when he came back a week later, she had installed painted Toto toilets in all the bathrooms, seven thousand dollars a pop.

"Henry," I say, as aghast as he was to learn my husband and I do not fuck. "How have you allowed this to go on?"

Henry's shoulder blades expand and expand wider with long, deep breaths, the kind your doctor tells you to take at your annual checkup to make sure there's nothing rattling around where it shouldn't be. He tells me that it started small. Little things, like hiring a night nanny for the first six months of his daughter's life when most people do three months, or one, or none at all, and definitely not for twenty-four hours a day. But his wife would assure him that someone in her family was paying for it. Some rich childless aunt who doted on her like she was her own. But when the bill arrived in the mail, suddenly the aunt was reneging on the offer. When Henry tracked her spending, when he pointed out that they didn't need a third car or a fourth or toilets with a gold maple-leaf motif on them, he was told he was being controlling. He was reminded that this was an issue for him. He was reminded of what he did to me.

*You said your control issues got in the way of your last relationship*, Henry's wife would say. *You said to tell you if history started to repeat itself, because you did not want to lose me too.*

"After a while," Henry says, "I was just . . . unable to discern if I was the problem or if she was. And then it didn't matter anymore, because we were falling behind on our mortgage payments, and I thought it would be a wake-up call for her. She promised it would be. And for a while I thought we were through it. She cut back on her spending, and a part of me knew it was too good to be true, and of course, it was." Henry pauses. Takes a deep inhale. "She had opened a credit card, in my dead grandmother's name. And so we were on the hook for all of that, plus paying for a lawyer to keep her out of jail for identity theft, and eventually the house was foreclosed upon and we were evicted."

*Evicted.* It's such a dirty, lowbrow word. The sort of word that does not belong to Henry's world, that would have made more sense in mine, at least back when we knew each other. I feel my innards twist and revolt, imagining Henry destitute, *vulnerable.* I don't want to think of him like that. I don't want to fuck someone like that.

"That finally snapped me out of it," Henry says. "I asked for a divorce. She moved in with her parents, and I came here. I had a lot of time on my hands. Quiet hours, to think. To step back and see things for what they were. I could make out my marriage for what it was. I could make out what happened with us, here." He pauses, looks around the room like he's watching the two of us deteriorate the past. "I was scared of losing you, and I treated you horribly, but also, in treating you so badly, I made it easy for you to leave." His gaze lands on the wispy flames of the fire, the occasional flashes of blue. "I could have supported you to the ends of the earth, Faye, but the problem was that I loved you, and that was intolerable for you."

It's like there is a second set of eyes inside of my head, blinking twice for help, warning me off. *Intolerable.* I can only tolerate seeing so much.

"Obviously," Henry says with a miserable laugh, "I still love you. So I kept up the facade that you like, that you need, to be able to tolerate me. That I have money. Stature. Influence over you. That I can still push you around." He looks down at his hands on his lap, anguished. "I wish you could just love me too, but I will take whatever I can get from you."

I look around the room, mystified. The truth has exploded between us, and there should be bloody brain matter on the rough rug and the log walls, fragments of my skull. My mind has been *blown* out. The truth is a bomb site, severed electrical lines at your feet, the long and daunting labor ahead of rebuilding, rewiring. Henry is so far from the first person to suggest I have an issue with intimacy, but until now it has always seemed to be an abstract and numberless problem. How can I say what it all adds up to when the figures have been concealed from me?

When I am the one doing the concealing?

I come around the corner of the bed so I am facing

Henry, though I keep my distance from him. I am shaking, surging with adrenaline and knowledge that feels new but is actually very, very old. Henry looks up at me, his face warm with fire and cool with moonlight. Both things. He is both things. "I have to tell you something," I say.

The thing that happened at the daycare. The thing we laughed about while watching my show projected onto the wall of PT's cabin. That's not it. That's part of *it*, but it's not the root that needs to be yanked so the weed stops growing back.

When I was about nine or ten years old, I told my parents. I don't remember what possessed me to confide in them, what must have presented as the proper segue to someone who still preferred her Velveteen Rabbit with the silk-lined ears to a pillow, but I remember they were furious, which is what I was afraid they might be, only to my complete shock, their anger was not directed at me. They were stomping around, talking about making calls to lawyers and congresspeople and other parents. But first they wanted to know, they needed to understand, why I did not tell them what was happening while it was happening. I had paused, not because I needed time to think about my answer but because the answer seemed so obvious I could not understand why they needed to ask at all.

I was being punished because I had misbehaved, I managed to convey to them in my nine-year-old's way, and I was afraid of being punished a second time at home. Why would I tell them that someone was hurting me when I deserved to be hurt?

*But*, they had said, as befuddled as I was, *we are the ones to decide what you deserve*. We are your parents, and so we are the ones to slap your soft cheeks when you leave your wet towels on the carpet, to give you the silent treatment when you get a bad grade, to berate you and call you selfish and ungrateful when you fail to recognize all that we have done for you, to wash your mouth out with soap when you sass us and when we march you to the bathroom only to discover that the Irish Spring bar is too big to fit in your small mouth, we are the ones who get to tell you to take a bite of it, to chew and swallow instead. We get to do all this to you because we love you.

Henry's face is still but for small flickers of movement in his jawline. There is an angry, sensual energy coming off him, and it has rearranged the molecules in the air, sparked a brushfire of goose bumps along the backs of my arms, the tops of my thighs. Whatever is about to happen, whatever Henry is about to say, it will be new for us.

"Hearing that," Henry says in a husky voice, like he has been startled awake by the garbage trucks too early in the morning, looked down, realized his cock was swollen against his leg, reached over to wake me too, "makes me fucking crazy."

Blood booms from my heart.

"Crazy, Faye. It makes me crazy."

I stare at him, feeling like there is a button at my throat that needs undoing. Illuminated by the wrath of the fire, Henry has never looked more terrifying.

"I'll kill them," he continues in a soft and maniacal voice. "When we get out of here, I'm killing them. Anyone who put their hands on little you. I don't care if you tell me not to. I don't care if you tell me no." He is watching me as he says this, observing me, breathing hard through his mouth. I say nothing. I do nothing. But I signal him anyhow. He gets up slow, unfurling himself inch by exhilarating inch, and then he begins to approach me in his graceful, wolfish way. I am frozen to the spot. When Henry has set eyes on you, it is too late to run.

"Do you hear me?" he says, coming nearer.

I nod. Behind me, a piece of burning wood splits and steams.

"Do you understand?"

Again I nod.

"Full sentences, sweetheart."

"I understand."

Henry stops before me, above me. His hair is wild from the boat ride over here. Little devil horns, all over his head. His lips are an unbelievable bright cherry red, and when he puts them on mine, he tastes like a blast of cinnamon. I grind my pelvis into his, filled with strange, tender aggression, and Henry's groan rumbles the walls of my throat. He kisses the bridge of my nose, my eyelids, he bites the divot in my upper lip, telling me that only he gets to put his hands on me, and only because I ask, and because he will do anything I ask, until we are eighty years old and rocking in our rocking chairs on our front porch, watching our grandchildren shoot each other dead with water guns. If that's what I need, that's what I fucking need.

"Stop," I tell him, but he doesn't. "Henry, stop." I twist my face away; I push him off. He takes me by the wrists and begins to back me into the bed and he only stops when I tell him to give me his phone.

This is what Henry has always wanted from me. The rough stuff, the mean stuff, the exposure and the humiliation, that's my idea of submission. But this is his. My doe eyes. My pliability. The stuff that hives my skin but is knotting me up all hot and tight every time I glance at the windowsill to see Henry's phone turned on us. *I am being forced to do it like a sweet, normal girl*, I tell myself, *and yet it is also what I want.*

Henry and I are standing in the glow of the fire, swaying together like someone is sawing a violin off camera. He wedges a finger under my chin and lifts my face to his. His eyes are a metallic gray-blue, and my fingers are drawn to the swell of his pink lips. Henry gives me a discreet nod. *That's right. That's good, Faye.*

He slips his hand beneath my hair and kisses me, walking me until the backs of my knees bump the edge of the bed.

"Tell me you missed me," he says into my ear. He sits me down, kneels in front of me, waits.

I say it, staring at his mouth I have missed like home.

Henry kisses me, says with his lips on mine, "So sweet." A filthy noise comes out of me, one he does not need to ask for. He slides off my pants. He unbuttons my shirt and pushes it down my shoulders where it catches on my elbows and stays. He's sitting on his heels, between my legs, and he's toying absentmindedly with my pussy, watching as my jaw goes slack, as my cognitive abilities decline.

"I love when you spread your legs for me," he says, and then he puts his warm hands on my knees and pushes them flush against the edge of the bed. He lowers his head and in a slow and specific pattern, his tongue makes its way up my inner thigh, tracing his next instruction. An *M* at my knee, an *O* where a miniskirt stops, an *A* . . . I moan obediently at the place where he draws the last letter.

My fingers in his hair, one hand behind me for balance. I lift myself into him and release, the nanosecond beat between his lush mouth and the cool nothing air inducing an agonizing, ever more urgent rhythm. Pleasure stabs at my middle, and I let out a pained whimper that I have not gotten what I need yet, that I will too soon.

"Fuck," I say, clutching the hair at his scalp and smashing his mouth into my clit. "Fuck." Something is spilling inside of me, creeping into my every corner, filling me with a warm, impossible feeling. I slip a hand between us and pull myself farther apart, and with his tongue Henry pens my pussy a love letter. *Home,* he writes. My pussy is home. *Safe.* My pussy is safe with him. *Safe. Safe. Safe.* The word is an accelerant. I fuck his face. I am safe. I show him everything. I am safe. I thrust myself into his mouth, I give him everything, and I ride the release like a lucid dream. *Henry,* I am marveling while my body soars over the atmosphere. I soar and I soar and I soar and I land in the palm of his hand. Henry is covering me, holding me like you would an open, pulsing wound to limit its exposure to air. I curl over him, kiss myself on his mouth, reach down between us and undo his belt, unbutton his pants. Henry rises over me and crosses his arms over his torso, gripping the hem of his shirt and sliding it over his head, tossing his sandy hair this way and that. I put my hands on his lean torso. I look up at him in awe, tug down on his pants. He puts his tongue between his teeth and hisses as fabric snags on his cock. I hold his eye as I kiss the blood-warm head, blow cool, soothing air on him. A sharp, startled exclamation from Henry, and then he's picking me up, wrapping my legs around him, dampening himself on me and easing inside like someone trying to find the most comfortable position to sleep. He lays me down on my back in a single fluid movement, like he picks up Faye-shaped weights every day in his basement, like he's been training twelve years for this very moment. My necklace flips up, the heart lands in my mouth, and I bite down like I am in pain. Henry brushes the hair out of my eyes and mouth, unearthing me, revealing me, and he puts a thumb on my chin so that he can watch my face. He goes slow, his forehead creased with arousal and determination, and when he can no longer go slow, he buries his face in my neck. "Say you love me. Say you love me and this will all be over."

I press my lips together in defiance. I refuse to do it, so that when Henry reviews the tape, he will be forced to say it's not good enough. We will have to do it again, and again, until he believes Corrine will be pleased with the result. I lift my hips to meet him, I let him all the way inside even though it hurts, especially because it hurts. He comes with a vicious cry, his hand around my throat.

Punishment for daring to defy him, or maybe he doesn't really want me to say it either. Maybe he is also realizing that the moment I do what he says is the moment this ends.

I love him, and that's why I won't say it.

# Chapter 32

I make the fatal mistake of falling asleep on Henry's torso, arms and legs barnacled to him in sweaty, symbiotic attachment. I was only planning on closing my eyes for a few minutes. I wanted to be dressed when Corrine returned, to have the buttons of my shirt buttoned to my chin, held high. Instead I stumble headfirst into terrifying dreams of waking to find that Henry's form has been replaced by my suitcase. Inside are my linen clothes and gold jewelry and my forty-two-dollar shampoo. My laptop logged in to the many luxury e-commerce sites I surf when I have writer's block, fantasizing about the events future me will attend, the people who will admire me and give me the attention that I am starved for at home. These were once my essentials, and now they feel mocking and immaterial.

"Faye," Henry's voice is saying, impossibly, because he's left me alone in this bed. He has abandoned me. "Faye."

My eyes flutter open to find Henry standing over me, holding my shoulders and rocking me with gentle urgency.

"The police are here."

I stare at him, foggy and uncomprehending.

"You have to get dressed." He pulls me into a seated position, swings my legs around and places my feet on the floor, begins to dress me like I have just come out of surgery and my limbs are still anesthetized. Out the front windows, the lake is dusty and unattended to in the predawn dim. A patrol boat is docked at the pier. There are flashlights. Holsters. The crackle and quick death of a radio signal.

My knees knock together, my mind wakes up, and I start to help Henry but put the wrong buttons in the wrong buttonholes. "What are they doing here? How did they know? What do we say?"

"I don't know," Henry says, an answer to all of it. And then he sighs, the saddest sigh I have ever heard. With strong and steady hands, he rebuttons my shirt for me. I put my arms around his neck and hold him for the last time, maybe. He is warm and Henry-smelling, and he holds me back and I know he is thinking the same, that I am warm and Faye-smelling and this cannot be it, an ending where we don't make it. I pry myself away from him and go over to the door, and I remember that while I never won an award for my acting, I have for the words I wrote for my character, and that I must have said them convincingly enough for the voters to vote for them.

"Help! We are in here. Help! Please!" I rattle the doorknob. I sob with gusto. I hate this ending; I refuse it.

From the other side comes a calm and slightly

inconvenienced voice. "This is Officer Kline with the Saranac police. I need you to unlock the door."

"We can't!" I cry. "We are locked in here. Corrine Holland has the key. She went to the clubhouse, but she has a gun—"

"Corrine Holland is in our custody."

I turn back to Henry with rabid eyes. He's sitting on the bed with his hands steepled over his mouth. If they've found Corrine, they've found Campbell. I turn back to the door. I think faster than I ever have before.

"Thank God," I say, and I repeat it again with a wail. "She killed her husband. And then she locked us in here, and we have been so scared she was coming back to kill us. Did you get my message? Please tell me you did." Behind me, I can feel Henry staring at my back, bewildered.

"Two hikers found a note scrawled on a receipt in mud. It said, *Help*."

I close my eyes. Press my forehead against the door. "That was me. I wrote that. I dropped it on the trail for them to find. Thank God. Thank God they picked it up."

"Ma'am," the officer says. "Are you hurt?"

"No. No. We're okay."

"Does anyone in there have a weapon on them?"

"No! Of course not. We're so relieved you found us!"

"Okay, then," he says, and am I wrong, or does he sound more reassuring now, speaking to me the way you would the victim of a violent crime? "I'm going to radio someone at shore to see if they can get the key off her.

Hang tight for now. Can you please identify yourself and any other persons in there with you?"

"My name is Faye Heron," I say. "And I'm here with Henry Spalding. Please. Help us."

# Chapter 33

The Saranac police station is located in a former Army National Guard armory. It has to be at least twenty thousand square feet, and most of the building appears unused and pitch-black. The floors have recently been mopped in the lobby, and I stare at my small muddy footprints next to Henry's Bigfoot ones while a baby-faced administrator tells the officers that interrogation rooms two and three are open, and so are four and five, and so are—

"We got it," Officer Kline says, cutting him off. When we first arrived, he had explained that this was temporary housing for the force while their new headquarters are being constructed just outside of town. I asked him all kinds of questions about that and acted as invested as one can be about the challenges of moving vending machines containing opioid reversal spray bottles, because I want him to like me and I need him to believe every lie that comes out of my mouth.

"This way," he says to us with a tilt of his head. Before the administrator buzzes us through to the back, he says over his shoulder, "Talley, can you grab some waters and put them in two and three?"

Invisible bias had me convinced that all three officers outside the cabin door were men. But when someone finally got the key off Corrine and set us free, it was a woman in her mid-twenties named Officer Talley who escorted me down the dock with her purple fingernails at my back. She has not stopped staring at me since.

Henry and I follow Officer Kline a few steps into a corridor lined on one side with doors and on the other with a series of windows showing the armory's strip of muddy lawn and beyond it a homely stretch of state road. Officer Kline taps his hip to the keypad for room number two and tells me to go in and sit down and someone will be in to take my statement soon. Stepping away from Henry and into that room feels like a surgical separation. I am aware of every stroke of the bone saw as the door swings shut on Henry, standing solemnly in the melancholic morning light, looking at me like he needs a squeeze of morphine too.

The room has flat gray carpeting, mismatched dining room chairs around a small wooden table. Mounted black cameras train their beady red eyes on me. On the table is a Dixie cup with a collection of blue and black pens. I stare at those pens and I wonder if it is some kind of psychological test. If they already know that five days ago I incapacitated Campbell with a lowly BIC and then I murdered him with hardly any effort at all.

Officer Talley comes in with some water and a chewy bagel, cream cheese in a ketchup packet. She stares at me more while I eat. The only time she speaks is to ask me if I would like any coffee and when I say I am okay because I can only imagine what armory coffee tastes like, she teases that maybe later someone will make a Starbucks run. I can't tell if she hates me or if she's buttering me up to ask for an autograph.

Officer Kline comes back into the room with a crumb in his facial scrub. He asks me to move to a different chair, indicating the cameras, saying something about the angle, and we ring-around-the-rosy until he tells me to sit.

"Okay," he says, a little bit short of breath. He's a skinny man with a blond goatee and a small gut. "I'm going to read you your Miranda rights now. You're not under arrest, but you are being questioned in police custody, so that's why I have to do it. Do you understand the difference?"

I nod, thinking, *Now there's an authentic detail.*

"You need to verbalize your answer, ma'am."

And there is another. "Yes."

He goes through the whole thing, weird not to hear it in the *Law & Order* voice, punctuated with the *Law & Order* gavel bang, and I nod and I nod, even at the part where he talks about my right to have an attorney. I do not want to ask for counsel, because it will make me look guilty, and because I am guilty and any counsel in their right mind will advise me against moving ahead with this.

"Do you understand these rights as I have read them to you?" Officer Kline asks.

"I do."

He fixes me with a long look, no doubt waiting for me

to say that I'd like to place a call to a lawyer in some high-rise in some swanky part of some wicked city. Instead I ask him about Emma.

"Emma?"

"Emma King. The young woman I told you was in danger. Is she okay?"

"I don't have an update for you at the moment," Officer Kline says cryptically.

I stare at the pens on the table. They would not let me around the pens if they thought I was the bad guy, I think, and then we begin.

By the time I need my first bathroom break, we are not even halfway through my statement. They bring in lunch, more water. I keep talking, take another bathroom break. Then I am left alone for a long time with the pens. A plain-clothes officer comes into the room, holding a Starbucks cup, and identifies himself as a homicide detective from Albany, and the other officers bow their heads and leave the room as though the pope has arrived. I tell the story again to the pope. Then he leaves, and I'm left alone for some time, and when the door opens again, it's Officer Talley asking me if I'd like to make any phone calls. My husband, I tell her somberly.

Next to the vending machine with the opioid reversal spray, Officer Talley feeds two quarters into the pay phone's coin slot, and I punch in my husband's cell. He does not answer, likely because he does not recognize the number, so I leave a message and tell him it's me, that I'm going to wait a few minutes and try him back, and he needs to pick up this time because it is an emergency. "I'm not hurt," I add before I hang up.

When I call him back, he answers on the first ring. I tell him an abbreviated version of the story I've been telling all day. When I finish, my husband doesn't say anything for a long time. Then, "Do you need a lawyer?"

"No," I say. "I haven't done anything wrong."

"Fuck you, Faye." He hangs up.

# Chapter 34

It is dawn again when I am released from police custody. Officer Kline pushes open the door, and I step out onto the landing, feeling wobbly and disoriented, like no time has passed and also like I'm losing my grip on reality, unable to recall even the most recent of events. What did I have for dinner last night? Where did I sleep? Wait. Did I sleep?

It does nothing to ground me that standing on the shoulder of the state road are two figures who do not belong on this plane of reality, and when they see me, they raise their long lenses to their faces like snipers posing to shoot. Officer Talley and her purple fingernails, texting her friends, her family: *You'll never guess who is here.* Her friends and family texting their friends and family and so on and so forth until someone at TMZ picked up in the game of telephone.

"Faye," they call out, trying to sidestep the officer who has been dispatched to keep them from crossing the road. "What happened, Faye? Faye, are you hurt? Faye, does your husband know you've been with your ex-boyfriend this week?" They keep saying my name until it has lost all meaning, until I forget the person whose masquerade mask I wore to attend my life all these years.

"Should I get you something to cover your face?" Officer Kline offers. He is still unsure about me, I can tell. He says there will be more questions. Follow-up. I am not allowed to fly back to California just yet. I'll need to get a hotel. Maybe for the month. They have more questions for me, but for now, I am free to go.

I shake my head. It's too late. In the parking lot, Henry is about to climb into the back of a Tahoe with vinyl police-department decals. But he notices me and turns, his hands in his pockets.

His hands are in his pockets.

He is not handcuffed and neither am I.

We had about half an hour, Henry and I, alone in the cabin, while one of the officers took the patrol boat back to the parking lot to ask Corrine to turn over the key. Time enough to get our stories straight.

We came here together. We did not know anyone else was here until we heard shouting coming from the direction of the clubhouse. We went to investigate and found Campbell deceased; Corrine had a gun. She forced us into the boat, drove us to the other side of the lake. She marched us into the woods with the intent to kill us, but by the grace of God we ran into those two hikers and I was able to slip them a message. She got spooked, forced us back onto the boat, and locked us in the cabin. We thought she would come back to kill us or maybe that she had left us to starve to death.

*At least we'd go together*, we thought.

The parking lot spans the length of the armory, a city block long. I walk briskly, the snitches across the street in lockstep with me. Their cameras flash and fire, shutters opening and closing with the stridency of insect wings. They capture me break into a run. They capture Henry turn toward me, the slight bend at his knees. I throw myself at him, and he catches me midair, spins me slowly, like we are taking first looks for our wedding photographer. He puts my feet on the ground. I raise my face to his. I tell him I love him and I won't ever stop.

"That's it," I say to the room of Hollywood executives for whom this tale is for. "That's the end."

# PART 4

# Chapter 35

I reach for my glass of lemon water and sip to a polite round of applause. I've pitched rooms where buyers have stared me down in furrowed-brow silence, where the head of drama originals at [redacted] once dozed off. I'll take a seated ovation any day of the week over that, but it is no guarantee an offer will follow.

"So many twists and turns, Faye."

"How do you even come up with something like that?"

"I blushed."

"Speaking of, is your vision for this full-frontal nudity?"

"Wow, Claire, diving right in."

"Ask me to dinner first," I say cornily, and everyone laughs. I let it die, tune my voice to the one I use when we get to the questions and comments portion of the pitch. I turn to Claire, who is the head of mid-budget indie development and wears the thick-framed reading glasses to prove it. "I'm not opposed to full-frontal, but I also don't want to get slapped with an NC-17 rating."

"It's the kiss of death," she agrees, and I know which film she is thinking about when she says this.

"I want this to be as erotic as it can be while remaining extremely commercial."

"What I love about female directors," someone says, "is that they're not afraid of that word."

*Then hire me*, I think. *Pay me a fraction of what you would pay a man. Save my career.*

"Can you tell us a little bit about where this idea came from?" someone else asks carefully.

I am sitting at the head of a sterile conference table in the villainous glass headquarters of a global streamer, facing six executives of various rank and file. Each one, in their own way, stops what they are doing to hear my answer to this question. Phones turned over on their faces, Stanley cups down. Outside, strong, dry winds yank the palm trees west. This morning, when I woke, I was prepared to hear from my agent that today's pitch would need to be rescheduled. But here I am, begging like a dog to write, direct, and star in my next film, red-flag warning be damned.

"Well," I say. "The answer to that is kind of a two-parter." I tell them that back in the spring, my beloved film professor passed away from a heart attack, and his nephew, a former classmate and friend of mine, asked if I would speak at his memorial.

"Campbell?"

I smile. "Yes. 'Campbell.'" It was the first time I had returned to campus since graduating twelve years ago. It was the first time I was going to see a lot of people I hadn't seen since before I won an Emmy for the episode of television I wrote about my ex-boyfriend.

"I gasped when Campbell showed up at the lake," says the content associate with the slicked-back ponytail.

"Don't worry," I assure her. "As we speak Campbell is safe in Connecticut, doing whatever it is annoyingly perfect husbands and fathers do there."

"What about 'Corrine'?"

"Ice-cold bitch, but not a murderer as far as I know."

Some light laughter.

"But in regards to 'Henry,'" Claire says, all business. "What was real there? He was at the funeral, I assume?"

"With his wife and kids."

Claire doesn't take her eyes off me. "What happened?"

"Just like I said. We were briefly under the same roof. We saw each other in passing. Then one of his daughters had a tantrum during the slideshow. He left. We never even said hello."

"I see. So everything after that. That's where we leave reality."

"Reality," I repeat with a laugh. I gather myself to get into it. "Well. As you know. My husband and I have decided to end our marriage and dissolve our production company. Initially, people were shocked but generally supportive. They liked us as a couple, and we seemed so good together, what could have happened? Our goal was to separate amicably, but then we couldn't work out who got ownership of our biggest piece of IP, and that's when my husband hired a crisis PR team and the rumors began to circulate online. Obviously, I cannot prove who is behind them. But those are the verifiable facts." I take a beat. Sip my water. "There's no use sitting here pretending like it hasn't affected me, both from a bottom-line perspective and on a deeply personal level. It hurts to be lied about, to be misunderstood, and the story of Faye and Henry—'Henry'—and what happened at the lake is my response to that."

"Absolutely," someone agrees noncommittally.

"Let us have a chat, and we'll get back to you," says Claire, her poker face pleasant. I thank everyone for their time.

# Chapter 36

The sirens start on my drive home. Home is like "Henry." Like "reality." Another thing in quotation marks. My husband took the house at my bidding. I was the one to file, and I thought it was the one mercy I could show him. I wanted to keep things amicable in the hopes my brother-in-law might not feel the need to retaliate on behalf of his little brother, whom everyone always called the nice one. If I'd known how mean nice guys can get, I would have changed the locks while he was at the gym. The other day, I drove by and saw a construction crew in the process of building out a wooden stud wall, and I had to pull over to catch my breath. He had demolished the original fireplace with the crack in the facade, the one that predated PT and postdated him too, and it felt like a war crime, like bombing Notre-Dame, an act the UN should condemn.

I rented a storybook Tudor in the treetops of Kenter Canyon with original tile that looks great in pictures and grungy in real life. It is quiet and peaceful and exhilarating and heartbreaking. If not for my divorce lawyers, I could go days without using my voice. My friends and colleagues are familiar with the ghoulish tactics of crisis PR teams; it's not that they believe what's being put out there about me, it's that the public does. It's that I carry a stink. They will keep their distance until a pop star gets arrested for drunk driving or an Oscar winner fails to endorse the correct political candidate, until the tides begin to change online. *Hey. Is it fucked up we all collectively turned on this woman for the crime of ending her marriage?* Even if she cheated, even if she told him she wanted kids then reneged, even if she's kind of getting old, even if she only won an Emmy because she's white and passably pretty, though not nearly as pretty as everyone once believed, it's not like she's transphobic or anything. *You'll have your renaissance*, my former agent and best friend kept promising me, but then I realized she removed me from her close friends list on Instagram. Her stories used to appear with a green ring, and usually I would watch them and know exactly where she was, because I was invited to all the same parties. That was when I picked up the phone and called her rival.

Some of my neighbors are on the street, packing up their cars. I slow to speak to the older couple with the three rescue dogs who have no idea who I am. I roll down my window, and I can smell that it's bad.

"Are we under evacuation?" I ask the husband. I watch as a piece of ash floats into my car and lands on my lap.

"Ready, set, go," he says. "Did you sign up for the alerts?"

"I thought I did."

"Double-check to be sure. I did it through the LAFD site."

"Okay," I say. "Thanks."

"Stay safe," he says.

"You too," I say, and something about this exchange makes me want to cry.

I park in my short driveway and go into the house, turn the TV to KTLA. On-screen is a map, and I locate my new street in the yellow zone, only half a mile from the red. This means I need to pack my prescriptions and passport. The wedding album I'll leave to burn. I turn up the volume and go around the house, throwing what matters into a suitcase. I can't find my travel jewelry case, maybe I left it at home-home, and so I load myself up with all my gems and wheel my carry-on out to the car, looking like the Queen of Sheba. Then I go inside, sit on the couch, and wait to be told what to do.

The west side is burning and so is the east, and the evacuation line keeps inching closer. I nearly book a hotel on a sceney strip of Sunset in West Hollywood but impossibly, apocalyptically, a third fire breaks out in the middle of the urban grid. I need to get out-out, I realize, and so I get in my car and drive north toward the hotel in Montecito where Jackie Kennedy and JFK had their honeymoon. I did this drive with my husband so many times, the mountains on one side and the ocean on the other, more times than we had sex, if I had to guess. My display screen lights up with a call from my agent. My new one, Caroline, who is not my best friend and hopefully never will be.

"Faye," she says. "Where are you? Did you get evacuated?"

"Just a little bit ago," I say. The alert came as I drove under an ominous cloud of smoke that clogged the coast of Malibu. "But I'd already left."

"Good," Caroline says. "Okay. Good."

"Are you okay?"

Caroline lives in the flats of Beverly Hills, but even the flats are in trouble. "For now, yes. My in-laws are here. They live in the Palisades. We keep checking their Ring. People are saying their entire neighborhood is gone. Hundreds of houses."

I feel like someone stomped on my windpipe. I hate this kind of fear. "How is that possible?"

"I don't know," she says, sounding just as scared as I am. Agents are supposed to put a shiny spin on bad reviews, rejections, first-season cancellations. But the end of the world is a foreign market. "Hey," Caroline says, slightly more upbeat, "how do you think the pitch went today?"

"They clapped."

"That's good."

"An offer would be better."

"I'm trading with Claire. Hopefully I'll have more for you tomorrow. As long as Los Angeles is still standing."

"I guess we'll see," I say, depressed.

"Claire loves you. She's a huge fan."

Agents are always saying things like this, but huge fans

pass all the time. I ask her if she's heard anything from the other studios I've pitched, and she tells me no new developments but that, for now, no news is good news. "Passes come faster than offers," she reminds me. "And this pitch has generated so much interest. We're going to get an offer, maybe even more than one. Everyone wants erotic thrillers right now. Everyone."

"But not everyone has an ex with a hotshot brother as litigious as mine, do they?"

"Coming, sweetie!" my agent calls. "Faye, sorry, I have to go."

I tell Caroline to stay safe, that old Los Angeles fire-weather chestnut, and hang up.

# Chapter 37

My room is not yet ready at the hotel. They've had a sudden influx of guests, due to the living nightmare unfolding in Los Angeles, and as an FYI, they've waived their no-dogs-allowed policy for the time being. It's just me, I tell the receptionist, and she says I can go and grab something to eat at the bar if I'd like and that my room should be ready by the time I'm done.

The wood-walled tavern is as I've imagined the cabins at Lake Wanika. I've been there, of course, but memory is the original unreliable narrator. There are a few patrons scattered about, their suitcases by their sides, heads rounded over their phones, and in the corner by the garnish station, I see a face I recognize. I am planning on turning away, hiding out in my car until my room is ready, but then she lifts her face and looks directly at me, and we have no choice but to acknowledge each other. I roll my suitcase over with an apologetic smile.

"Fancy seeing you here," Claire says.

"I was going with *long time, no see*."

Claire offers a polite laugh. She's wearing the same

clothes that she was wearing in our pitch meeting today—black suit skirt that hits her at mid-calf, Nikes, and an oversized gray sweater, which she uses now to wipe a smudge from the lens of her nerd-girl glasses.

"Where do you live?" I ask.

"I'm south of Sunset on Swarthmore." She finishes her glass of wine. "In the Pacific Palisades."

"Oh no," I say gravely.

Claire signals the bartender for another round. "Yeah."

"Have you heard anything?"

"Just a bunch of unsubstantiated rumors on Nextdoor that everything is gone."

"I mean, it's Nextdoor."

"That's what I keep telling myself," she says, but she does not sound optimistic.

"I'll give you your space," I tell her, but Claire shakes her head.

"Have a drink with me. Keep me from doomscrolling, please."

"What are you having?"

"Some thirty-dollar glass of Pinot Noir that is dangerously drinkable."

"I'll do the same," I say to the bartender.

"Would you like to just get a bottle?" he suggests, and Claire and I look at each other, say in unison, "Sure."

I shimmy my tote bag off my shoulder and go to hook it under the bar but find that Claire has taken them all. I don't want to ask her to remove any of her things, so I sit down with my large tote in my lap. I make a tremendous amount of noise doing this, all my rings and bracelets and charms clinking and clanking together. Claire looks me over with a laugh.

"You're like that episode of *Friends*."

"Which one?"

"The one where Joey puts on all Chandler's clothes. Except, it's jewelry."

"I can't find my travel case anywhere."

"I use this one from Amazon that I got the last time I was evacuated, because I was like you. Wearing everything. I'll send you the link. Super cheap. Apparently it's what all the jewelers in the diamond district use."

"God bless a good Amazon find."

"So," Claire says as the bartender pours her a half-inch taste of the wine. "Your pitch today." She swills her glass, knocks it back. "Great," she tells him, then turns to me. "I need to know something."

My heart bangs in my ears. We should not be having this conversation, Claire and I. She knows it too. But her mouth is stained purple, our city is burning to the ground, and there is the sense that we can say anything to each other without consequence.

"Is it true?" she wants to know.

I clear my throat, itchy with my toxin-tour through the westside of Los Angeles. "What part?"

"That your husband didn't fuck you."

My smile is rueful. That's the part I would want to know, if I were on the other side of the conference room table. "My agent would tell me to tell you that I took inspiration from my marriage, but that the events and characters themselves are fabricated."

"And would that be true?"

I stare at the bartender's modest pour. That's how you know it's a nice bottle of wine and not just an expensive one. Carefully meted-out splashes that ensure you're always sipping, savoring, but never drinking.

"No," I say.

Claire blows all the air out of her lungs. "Wow."

I wince. "Caroline is going to kill me for telling you that."

We sit. We sip. We savor.

"Actually," Claire says, "I think this is good."

"Good?"

She turns to me, her eyes magnified and determined behind her glasses. "I want to make this film with you, Faye. I think it's nasty, and real, and extremely fucking hot. I mean. We know that women have rape fantasies, right? *Fifty Shades* was page after page of chicken scratch and still it was a phenomenon, even among smart women. But how do you do an elevated version of that in today's climate? It's a delicate line to walk and no one is even trying. The industry operates from a place of fear and anxiety and you don't need me to tell you that it shows in the flaccid final cut."

Claire pauses so that the bartender can top her off, waits for him to move away and attend to someone else. "The talk around town is that everyone loves this pitch but that they're too scared to touch it because they don't want to be sued into oblivion, but if you think about it, he only has grounds to do that if what you are claiming about him is true, and what man in his right mind is going to come out and admit to having the sex drive of a doorknob?"

I stare at her, my chest ballooning, my heart rising. "I want to make this movie with you too."

"You need a hit."

I look down at my hands. All the rings on my fingers and not a single wedding band. "I can't believe I thought I needed one before."

"My ex is a punk too. You'll get through it. Speaking of—" She lifts her phone. "I should give him a call. He had the kids when we got the evacuation notice. They went to my in-laws' in Newport." She takes one last sip of her wine. Tells the bartender to put the bottle on her room. She hoists herself off the stool and reaches for her bag hanging underneath the bar, finally clearing space for mine. I remove my big tote bag from my lap and hang it up, and now that I have some breathing room, I take off my coat too, the long suede one some stylist convinced me to buy but was so expensive I'm too afraid to wear it. I fold that in my lap and smile at Claire, who, standing, is about eye level with my collarbone. "Oh," she says, startled. "Just like from the story."

I touch my chin to my chest to see the silver charm snagged in the button of my shirt. I shake out my collar, straighten the chain.

"So you took it when you two broke up?" Claire cocks her head, studies me with X-ray eyes.

I laugh off the concern on her face. "I promise I wasn't held against my will for a week in the Adirondacks, Claire. It's just a fantasy."

Claire raises her eyebrows and presses her lips together, emitting a dubious vibration. She turns and rolls her matching hard-shell suitcases behind her. Unwatched, I slip the pendant under my shirt and lay my hand over its familiar shape. There are times I think the metal organ beats with blood, warm as my own. Times too, that I think we did change the ending.

# Acknowledgments

I wrote the first sixty pages of this novel on a writing retreat to my alma mater, Hobart and William Smith Colleges. It had been years since I had been back to campus and at the time I was living across the country in Los Angeles. There was no easy way to get there, but something called to me to return. It was March and a heat wave had blasted the campus. My writing professor, Grant Holly, had passed away suddenly while showing a movie to his screenwriting class, the same class I had taken nearly twenty years before. He simply put his head down on his desk and did not wake up. He was the longest-serving member of the faculty and a fit and handsome man who wore black T-shirts exclusively—it is not possible that he is gone.

Grant Holly helped me get my first job in the industry—first, as a summer intern in the Los Angeles offices of a talent and literary agency, and then again as an assistant in the New York offices. It was there I met another recent college graduate, Alyssa Reuben, who would go on to become my book agent in another six years and continues to be my most trusted confidante in the industry. Another writing professor, the talented and immensely kind Deborah Tall, selected me for the writing scholarship that made it financially feasible for me to attend the colleges to begin with. She passed away from cancer only a few months after I graduated. She had a lovely, gentle voice and wrote beautiful poetry, and the life I have now started with her.

The older I get, the more grateful I am for the opportunities I had at a young age. What an extraordinary privilege to attend college on a writing scholarship that all but required me to focus on the only thing I cared about, the only thing I was good at; to have professors who championed me and helped me find my footing in the real world.

There is a chapel on campus, built in 1866, and in the 1960s construction began on a tower that would unite the library with the place of worship. The president at the time, the Reverend Dr. Louis Melbourne Hirshson, reportedly said that he wanted to connect the brain of the colleges with the heart, and though I do not consider myself religious, indeed I felt that divine connection every time I sat in the upstairs tower to read, study, or write with the winter sunlight streaming through the stained glass windows. I cherished returning to this place to work on this novel, and I am deeply grateful to the hospitality of the colleges and in particular to President Mark Gearan for hosting me so generously.

Marysue Rucci, editor extraordinaire—thank you for shaping this thing with me, for pushing me, for telling me when it wasn't there and helping me get to a place where it finally was. Anne Speyer, thank you for the read at the eleventh hour and the note that helped it click into place.

Thank you to Clare Mauer and Brianna Yamashita for getting this novel out into the world, and to the new UK team—Charlotte Osment, Phoebe Morgan, Justine Gold, Jade Unwin, Madeline Allan, and Sabah Khan. Thank you to my agents at CAA, Michelle Weiner and Joe Mann, who help my books find life after publication.

To my husband, Greg, I love you and I love being a parent with you.

To my daughter, Sydney, I love you and I love being your mom more than anything in the world.

# About the Author

Jessica Knoll is the *New York Times* bestselling author of *Bright Young Women*, *Luckiest Girl Alive* and *The Favourite Sister.* She adapted and executive produced *Luckiest Girl Alive* for the screen, starring Mila Kunis, released on Netflix in 2022. She lives in New York City with her family.

# More from Jessica Knoll

**‘A great story that you can’t put down!’**
**Reese Witherspoon**

Her perfect life is a perfect lie. Ani FaNelli is the woman who has it all: the glamorous job, the designer wardrobe, the handsome and rich fiancé. But behind her sharp edges and meticulously crafted façade lies the darkest of pasts …

OUT NOW

# More from Jessica Knoll

**'Jessica Knoll is one of my favourite authors. Every new book is a treasure to be hoarded'**
**Louise Candlish**

*The Favourite Sister* follows a pair of competitive and uber-successful sisters whose secrets and lies result in murder. Perfect for fans of Liane Moriarty's *Nine Perfect Strangers* and Caroline Kepnes's *You*.

OUT NOW

## More from Jessica Knoll

**'Knoll sets about dismantling every last Bundy myth with a controlled but palpable rage'**
**Catherine Ryan Howard**

*Bright Young Women* is an unflinching thriller based on Ted Bundy's heinous crimes, as two women search for justice in the wake of his brutal murders.

OUT NOW

**Bringing a book from manuscript to what you are reading is a team effort, and Simon & Schuster UK would like to thank everyone who helped to publish *Helpless*.**

**Editorial**
Charlotte Osment
Phoebe Morgan
John Sugar
Gail Hallett

**Proofreader**
Moira Eagling

**Marketing & Publicity**
Lily Searstone
Justine Gold
Sabah Khan

**Sales**
Olivia Allen
Jade Unwin
Heather Hogan
Sorcha Mulligan
Katie Sormaz
Madeline Allan
Jonny Kennedy
Richard Hawton & the rep team

**Audio**
Alice Twomey

**Design**
Sian Wilson

**Production & Operations**
Isabelle Gray
Mike Messam

**Finance & Contracts**
Luke Shaller
Maria Mamouna
Isabel Ireland
Keely Day
Meshach Yeboah